Dreamin' Dreams

A Book of Short Irish Stories

Brendan Gerad O'Brien

Dreamin' Dreams

Contents

Dreamin' Dreams

Dreamin' Dreams

I Dreamed another Dream

The priest's face was pale and solemn as he shook the earth in his hand for a moment before scattering it into the open grave where it pattered down onto the coffin.

'Ashes to ashes, dust to dust.' His voice was heavy with melancholy and when a thin wisp of his hair fluttered in the breeze he touched it instinctively.

I glanced across at Zoë. She was standing with her father who was trying to shelter her from the rain with a big black umbrella. The soft drizzle mingled with the tears that lined her face. She leant her head against his shoulder.

'In the name of the Father, and of the Son, and ...'

The crowd muttered *Amen* and began to drift away, anxious to get out of the cold as quickly as they could without looking indecent.

Over twenty people had attended the funeral and afterwards most of them came back to Zoë's house where food and drinks were laid out on crisp white tablecloths.

We helped ourselves and wandered about in little groups, talking softly and commenting on how sad it was that Zoë's husband Kieran had died so suddenly - and in such strange circumstances, too.

'Tell me, Liam,' Zoë's father put his hand on my shoulder. 'What do you make of it all? I mean, what do you *really* think happened to your brother? Was the coroner right when he decided on an open verdict?'

'I honestly don't know, Paul.' I glanced across at Zoë as I picked up a glass of wine and took a sip. 'But what else could he say? No one will ever know what happened that day. There will always be that awful question - was it just a terrible accident, or was it …'

'Suicide?' His eyes had a hurt look in them and he shook his head.

'Paul,' I patted him on the arm. 'We've been down this road a hundred times already. The coroner looked at all the facts and the only conclusion he could possibly come to was an *open* verdict. It was the only choice he had.'

'Ah shur, I know that!' Paul bit into a sandwich and wiped the crumbs from his mouth. 'But I still can't figure out why my son-in-law would deliberately go out and kill himself. What would possess him to do that, for God's sake? He was only twenty-five years old. And it wasn't as if he was in any sort of trouble or anything. Or that he was unhappy, even. You saw him the night before he … the accident. You said yourself he was in great form. Didn't you?'

'Look, Paul, I'm really, really sorry. But I'm just as upset as you are. I mean, he was my brother, after all. But still, you have to admit it was all a bit strange - you know - how he died.'

Zoë came over and kissed me gently on the cheek. Paul gave her a hug.

'Well, I still think they're wrong,' Paul muttered to himself. 'I don't care what they say, it was definitely an accident.'

I rubbed my eyes and gave a long sigh. Paul was right, of course. None of it made any sense. Kieran drove a battered old Ford Escort and no one knows why he decided to turn right at the railway crossing in Farranfore and drive back along the tracks towards Tralee. He should have been going to work in Killarney. The Cork Express hit him at ninety miles an hour.

Dreamin' Dreams

Forensic tests showed the car was still in gear. The speedometer was stuck on thirty miles an hour and the clock had stopped at eight forty six exactly. There was absolutely no trace of drugs or alcohol in Kieran's body. Not even aspirin. My brother was in fine physical health at the moment of impact.

'And another thing,' Paul said loudly, the wine starting to take its toll on an already emotional father-in-law. 'Zoë said the last entry in his diary was; 'I dreamed another dream!' What the hell was that all about?'

I shook my head. What could I say? I know it sounds crazy, but the whole thing had *started* with a dream.

We were hunched over our pints in Maguire's pub one hot Friday night last year. Pat Foley was making a terrible row on the piano as he competed with the noise and laughter that came in waves from the usual crowd crammed into the public bar.

Up on the shelf behind the bar the television was showing news footage of the atrocities in war torn Yugoslavia. People who'd lived together for generations were now tearing each other apart and the images showed tanks and soldiers fighting their way through burning towns and shattered villages.

One shot lingered on a bullet riddled sign with the name of the town almost obliterated from it.

Suddenly Kieran sat up straight and grabbed my arm. 'Did you see that?'

'See what?'

'That *sign*. The name on that *sign*.'

After numerous pints of Ireland's finest stout I had trouble seeing the TV set, never mind the picture on it.

'What about it?'

'I've seen that sign before.' He pointed at the TV

with a quivering finger and his face was creased in an unusually serious expression. 'I've definitely seen that sign before.'

'Of course you've seen that sign before,' Eamon Maguire butted in. 'Shur hasn't it been on the bloody news every night for the past few months? Aren't we sick and tired of seeing it, day after day - Bosnia, Yugoslavia? And I wouldn't mind but we don't even know what they're fighting about.'

'We don't even know who they *are*, never mind what they're fighting about,' Michael Quinn blurted.

'No!' Kieran was clearly irritated. 'I'm not talking about the fighting. I'm talking about the sign. The name on the sign! I've seen that name before. I think I've been there.'

'What?' I exploded with laughter. 'Shur the farthest you've ever been from Tralee was the time we played football in Fermoy. And we were still in school then.'

More laughter. Pat Foley's voice got louder as he screeched completely out of tune with the piano. The regulars got louder too as they tried to talk above it.

Kieran had a little blemish on his forehead, a small patch of dry skin just above his left eyebrow. Whenever he got flustered he would start poking at it with his finger and within seconds it would be red raw. Now he was furiously rubbing at it and already it looked like a small squashed strawberry. He slammed his fist on the bar.

'I'm serious!' he shouted.

It was no good. Maguire's on a Friday night was no place to be serious. The laughter and the music drowned him out.

Later on we went back to Kieran's house and as we

sat drinking coffee and eating chips he was still muttering on about the sign outside the village on the television. Eventually he wore us down and Zoë made more coffee as we promised to be serious and listen to him.

He told us he'd had a dream and it was so vivid that when he woke up the next morning every detail of it was still crystal clear in his mind.

In the dream he was a young man. The day was bright and very warm. He was walking through a village. The street was wide and dusty and all the buildings around him were wooden structures. Some of them were two stories high. They reminded him of the American Wild West. But he knew he wasn't in America. He sensed that he was somewhere in Europe. Somewhere near the Mediterranean. He felt comfortable. This was his home.

Then something caught his eye and his heart skipped a beat. Coming over the hill and down the track to the village was a group of horsemen. In his mind Kieran recognized them immediately - the way they were dressed, the way their bows were strapped across their backs, the way they carried their spears.

They were part of the dreaded horde of Mongolian pony soldiers that was sweeping across the whole of the known world at that time in history.

As the soldiers spurred their ponies into a canter Kieran was already running across the street and into one of the buildings. He was calling to someone. He couldn't see who it was but he was climbing the rickety stairs two at a time to find them.

He'd just reached the landing when the first pony galloped through the door below and came clattering up the stairs behind him. He threw himself over the window ledge and dropped to the ground. Now he was staggering away in terror.

He sensed a pony behind him. As he turned he could see a soldier couched down in the saddle, his spear pointing straight at the back of a young girl running behind her mother.

As the soldier drew level with him, Kieran threw himself forward and slapped the spear into the ground. The impact catapulted the soldier into the air and in the blink of an eye Kieran had mounted the pony with the animal hardly breaking speed. And as he galloped out through the other side of the village he passed a large wooden sign with a name burnt into it. It was the same name as the one on the news bulletin.

When he saw two more riders coming down on his right and cutting him off he turned sharply and headed towards a long wooden fence.

With a mighty burst of speed the pony cleared the fence. But it hit the ground awkwardly on the other side and staggered before sagging onto its knees. Kieran flew over the pony's head and crashed heavily onto his back.

The last thing he saw was the two pony soldiers clearing the fence behind him and two spears coming down on him at incredible speed.

Zoë and I listened patiently as he stressed again and again how vivid the dream had been - the fear, the panic, the rush of adrenaline. And surely the name of the place told us something! He had been there before - he was convinced of it. He had lived there. He had died there. And the blemish on his forehead was red raw from his finger rubbing at it.

After that I went home to bed.

Dreamin' Dreams

A couple of months later Kieran came charging in through my back door. 'I'm after dreamin' another dream!' he gasped.

This time, apparently, he was in American uniform and somewhere in Europe. He knew it was shortly after World War Two. He was a Major in the Diplomatic Corps and for some reason he was in a Russian Army camp having a conversation with a Russian general.

There were hundreds of tents all around him. A mob of Russian soldiers was watching him very closely. The atmosphere was exceptionally tense. Through the wire that surrounded the camp Kieran could see a wide expanse of open ground. And he knew instinctively it was no-man's land. On the other side, he was sure, was West Germany.

As the Soviet General escorted him through the camp he was asking about some secret concessions - something to do with access to the Western side of the border. Kieran felt very uncomfortable.

A train appeared belching huge plumes of white steam and it began to slow down as it approached the tiny landing stage near the camp. But instead of coming to a halt it jolted forward and crashed through the feeble barrier that was lowered across the track.

Then all hell broke loose. The train appeared to be filled with people, their terrified faces staring out in disbelief. The guards opened fire and as the bullets slapped into the framework around them the faces dropped out of sight. Windows were disintegrating in clouds of flying glass and splintered wood.

Soldiers raced after the train and they were quickly overtaken by a cluster of motorcycles that bucked and wobbled across the uneven wasteland. Then a jeep came sweeping around the outside and raced to head off the train that was still being peppered by hundreds of shots.

The cannon on the jeep spat a string of tracers that raked along the ground in front of the engine. And when they tore a groove along the entire side of the machine it seemed to quiver for a moment before erupting in a huge yellow ball. The carriages piled up behind the wrecked engine. Terrified survivors clambered out of every opening only to be attacked and clubbed by the soldiers who reached them first.

In this dream, Kieran turned to face the Soviet General only to see the soldiers bearing down on him with their bayonets flashing and their eyes screaming for blood. The General had a gun in his hand.

'So, Major.' His face was a sneer. 'This was all part of an evil American plan. Distract my men and have a train full of convicts escape to the West.'

Kieran didn't have time to answer before the General fired a single shot.

This time he'd seen no names, no signs. But Kieran was adamant he knew the approximate time and place.

My wife Angela beckoned me with her head. I followed her into the kitchen.

'Look, Liam, your brother's clearly not dealing with a full deck of cards here,' she growled in a strained stage-whisper. 'So can I suggest you take him home and get Zoë to have him looked at?'

'Ah, come on now,' I laughed. 'Just because he had an odd dream or two doesn't mean he's got a screw loose.'

'*What*?' Angela's eyes flashed. 'He's got a whole *head* full of loose screws! Your brother's away with the fairies and you think that's all right, do you? Well, I do not, I'm afraid. Can't you see he's frightening the cat? Get him out of my house right now and tell his wife to have him certified.'

'How can you say a thing like that? You don't like my brother, do you? You never have.'

'Of *course* I like your brother,' she lied, hesitating as she tried to elaborate. 'Well, maybe not a lot, I admit. But I like him. I'd say I like him as much as I like … well … migraine. But that's not the point. Get him out of my house. He is not acting like a rational human being. Heaven knows what he'll do next!'

What he did next was spend two whole days in the library going through every book relating to Europe immediately after World War Two. He found nothing, so he took a week off work and went to Cork City. When he came home he had a smile on his face as wide as a new moon.

'I'm only after finding it.' He had a delighted glint in his eye.

He had a copy of a Daily Mail article dated June 1947. It was only a couple of paragraphs saying that one hundred and seventy two people died when a passenger train went out of control and fell down an embankment near the Polish-German border. The dreadful accident also claimed the lives of an American Major and a Sergeant who happened to be visiting the crossing as part of a Soviet-American cultural visit.

That was probably the moment we realized Kieran's dreams had become an obsession. He had a car full of books when he came back from Cork and Zoë said he was constantly looking for programs on the TV about the paranormal. He visited clairvoyants and mediums, and he drove everyone completely mad.

Dreamin' Dreams

His final dream was the last straw.

This time he was in some huge building in the Middle East. He was in combat gear and he knew he was part of an elite Special Forces team. They were on a rescue mission. He was on a balcony and he was holding a rope. He knew he had to swing across a courtyard to a balcony on the other side. It was an easy manoeuvre. It took very little effort and he landed lightly on the other side. But as he rose to his feet he realized to his horror that he'd fallen into a deadly trap. Before he could recover he felt a pistol being pressed against the back of his head. Then a blinding flash.

'Now *that* one's going to be hard to rationalize,' I told him.

'It will. But I think I've figured it out. You see, I was born in June 1969. This dream, well I'm sure it was during the troubles in the Middle East at that time. And I'm also sure I was with the Argyle and Southern Highlanders regiment.'

'What? But that was a very short dream. Where did you get *that* idea from?'

'I just know.' He smiled strangely. 'So I'm going to write to the Royal Scots Headquarters and ask them if any incidents like this took place on the day I was born. I believe that, at the moment I died in my dream, I was born into this life.'

The letter that came back from the Royal Scots was amazing. The Lieutenant in charge of their museum was just as mad a Kieran himself. And just as excited about the theory of reincarnation. And it so happened there *was* an incident recorded in their annals of a daring rescue that took place on that very date.

Apparently a team of British diplomats was sent into

an isolated village to meet with the leaders of the rival factions. Two of the diplomats were murdered and the rest taken hostage.

The Government had no choice. A successful operation was mounted and the diplomats were released unharmed. Two of the soldiers were awarded the highest honours for gallantry, one of them posthumously. That soldier, a Lance Corporal, died at approximately six minutes past three in the morning. The exact time Kieran was born.

Sadly Kieran's obsession had become an irritation now. He was like a wild preacher desperate to tell his story to anyone within ear shot, friend and foe alike. Those who weren't quick enough to get out of his way were latched onto like a limpet mine. They could do nothing except sip their beer and nod politely.

It came to a head one night last week when the beer was flowing freely. Kieran got the impression no one was taking him seriously. His emotions got the better of him. He staggered to his feet.

'I'll prove it to you.' There was a strange quiver in his voice. 'When I'm gone over to the other side I'm going to make contact with you. I'll show you all right! I'm going to prove it to you once and for all.'

He pointed straight at me and tears filled his eyes. 'I'll be back.'

'As what, though?' someone asked in a tone that was completely devoid of respect.

'What do you mean *as what*?' Kieran's face was red with indignation.

'Well, don't the Indians believe you come back too? But not necessarily as a human being. Look how they treat their cows - Sacred! My mother-in-law would have a great time over there.'

'You could even come back as a pigeon,' someone else called out above the ever increasing sniggering. 'You could sit on top of the Church steeple and do your business on all the people you don't like down below.'

'Or you could be a seagull, squawking all day long out in the town dump and scavenging to your heart's content with not a care in the world.'

The blotch on Kieran's forehead was rubbed raw again.

'Enough!' he cried, and he shot out the door.

And that was the last time I saw him alive.

I picked up another glass of wine, nodded politely to some of the mourners and sat down beside Angela on the sofa.

'Poor Zoë.' Angela squeezed my hand. 'She looks dreadful. I only wish there was something I could do to help. I don't even know what to say without it sounding ridiculous.'

Behind us a baby started bleating and everyone glanced around at the pretty girl with the long ginger hair. She cooed at the bundle in her arms as she looked over at Zoë. 'Is it all right if I make up his feed?'

'Of course it is.' Zoë jumped up and took the bundle then helped the mother out of the armchair. 'Come on through to the kitchen.'

Angela got up too and followed them.

'Do you want me to do anything?' I called after her.

'You could put the kettle on, get some hot water to heat the bottle,' Zoë said as we all traipsed into the kitchen behind her.

I filled the kettle and plugged it in.

'Sam, you know Kieran's brother Liam, don't you?'

Angela said to the girl.

'I do of course.' A wave of ginger hair fell around her shoulders as she turned to me and held out her hand. 'I'm so very sorry for your loss, Liam. I just couldn't believe it when John came back over to the hospital to tell me about it. He'd only just gone home to have a shower and a change of clothes. He'd been over in the Maternity with me all night, waiting for little Calum here to make up his mind if he was coming or not. Anyway, he was just putting the key in the front door when Jerry Sweeney the postman told him about the crash. Of course they both knew Kieran - they were all at school together. John was so shocked he came straight back over to tell me.'

Steam from the kettle made the net curtain on the window flutter and I rushed over to switch it off. The baby had stopped crying now and the girls all fussed over him.

'How heavy was he?'

'Oh, he was a strapping nine pounds six ounces.'

'Were you on time?'

'Right on the day,' Sam cooed. 'He decided to make his appearance at exactly eight forty six in the morning. He didn't want to keep his poor mammy waiting any longer.'

I was about to pour the boiling water into the jug when something made me stop. What did she just say? I turned around slowly when the baby gave a deep gurgle. Actually, it was more like a cough. For a fleeting moment it almost sounded like he'd called my name.

A funny tingle crept up my back. Angela had the baby now and was rocking him gently.

'Will you hurry up with that hot water, Liam,' she

called over her shoulder. Then she made some soothing noises at the bundle. 'Is that a beauty spot on his little forehead?'

'I don't know what it is,' Sam said. 'It's nothing serious, though - just a funny bit of dry skin. The doctor thinks it'll clear up soon.'

I moved closer and peered down at the bundle. At that very moment the baby's eyes opened wide, deep dark blue, and they looked straight at me.

An ominous smile flickered briefly on the corners of his mouth! OK, it could have been wind. But it looked measured - a bit *too* deliberate.

The eyes didn't deviate from mine as a tiny finger reached up and rubbed the patch of dry skin on his forehead. Which immediately became red, almost like a tiny squashed strawberry.

Dreamin' Dreams

A Very Peculiar Christmas Holiday

'Well? Did you get that stupid car fixed?'

'*What?* I'm only just after finishing work,' was all I managed to croak. And that came out as a feeble yelp. 'When did I have the time to get the car fixed?'

I didn't even have the key out of the front door yet. The cold December evening was blowing in behind me and making the curtains dance.

'I don't *care*!' Jayne shrieked as she scooped the baby off the floor and strutted angrily into the living room. She flopped down onto the sofa. 'Have you any idea what it's like having to catch a bus into town with the baby under one arm and the pushchair under the other and ten bags of shopping and no seat for you to sit down on?'

She wagged a bottle of milk at me before popping it into the baby's mouth and continuing without drawing breath.

'You have to go rummaging in your purse for the exact money while the people behind you are tutting in your ear and then the stupid bus takes off before you're ready so you end up galloping down the full length of the aisle and landing in a heap at the other end. I'm fed up with it! Do you hear me? *I'm fed up with it!* So you'd better get that stupid car fixed right now or you can do your own bloody shopping from now on!'

I sagged into the armchair, deflated and disappointed. Well, I'd rushed all the way home from work with the perfect gift for her - tickets for the holiday of a lifetime! In San Francisco! For Christmas!

It was *supposed* to take her breath away.

All right, so I'd forgotten about the stupid car. Which

is hard to believe considering it was going to cost me a week's wages for a new clutch. But in my defence I could only say I got caught up in the madness of the moment.

And what a moment! Talk about being in the right place at the right time!

And I *really* thought Jayne would be well up for it. Especially when she saw how cheaply I got the tickets in the first place.

It had been just another ordinary day when I spotted Mickey Dunn coming out of the factory gates at the end of our shift, shuffling along with his hands deep in his pockets.

'What's the matter with you?' I rushed to catch up with him. 'You've got a face on you like a robber's dog!'

He gave a snort and shook his head. And the bunch of curls on his forehead swayed with the movement. But he didn't answer.

'Well?' I asked again after an awkward silence.

'Ah, tis nothing.' His voice was deep and gloomy. 'Nothing at all.'

'But aren't you going on holiday in two weeks? To San Francisco, no less. And with the beautiful Eileen Grey. You should be over the moon, a man in your position.' I gave him a poke with my elbow. 'Imagine getting away from this gloomy auld place for two whole weeks, eh? I'd nearly give my right arm for a holiday like that.'

Mickey's face changed shape, shrinking into itself in a mask of gloom. 'I won't be going, though.'

'You won't be going? Why ever not?'

'Well, tis Eileen.' More gloom. 'She's after dumping

me.'

I studied him carefully. Mickey Dunn was the kind of guy who if he told you what day it was you'd still check with a calendar. You never knew if he was winding you up or not. He had more neck than the average giraffe. He could steal the eye out of your head and come back later for the eyelashes.

But, somehow, you could never take offence at him. A loveable rogue, that's how they described him.

But right now he *did* look seriously dejected. It was very rare to see Mickey Dunn with a face so long his chin was dragging on the ground.

'I'm sorry,' was all I could say. 'When did this happen?'

'Ah, sure, it's been on the cards for a long time now.' He glanced sideways but I couldn't read his expression. 'I've had my suspicions for a while, of course. Then I phoned her from work the other morning to ask if she'd got the passports sorted out, and before I could get a word in she's purring down the phone and calling me *Wayne.* Her voice was weird, all husky and soft. Really slushy stuff, it was! Maybe I should have said nothing and just let her carry on. But instead I told her it was me! Well, didn't she nearly bite my head off? She called me all sorts of names and told me never to call her out of the blue like that again. Especially when I'm supposed to be in work. She made out I was spying on her, that I didn't trust her and all that kind of rubbish.'

He gulped and his Adam's apple rippled up and down his neck like a yo-yo behind a rough dishcloth.

'And I know what you're thinking.' He put out his hand and stopped me in the middle of the road. 'You're thinking I should have ended it right there and then. But

21

me being the big eejit that I am - and madly in love with her too - I just swallowed my little bit of pride and hoped it would all just go away.'

Our bus came along and rattled to a stop, swamping us in a cloud of evil smelling smoke. We shuffled on board and sat at the back.

'As luck would have it, though, I still have the tickets,' Mickey sniggered from behind his hand. 'Right here in my pocket. But it was a close thing, I have to tell you. Very close indeed! I was actually taking them over to her house. Well, you know what she's like - she has to be in control. Otherwise she's not enjoying herself. She gets it from her mother, you know. Well, you've seen her mother, sitting in the garden polishing her jackboots for the Gestapo reunion. And what about that big bullwhip hanging above her mantelpiece, eh?'

He gave a feeble cough and wiped his eyes. Good grief, I thought, don't start crying. Not on a bus full of hairy factory workers. The bus hit a bump and we all wobbled.

'Anyway,' he flicked something off his top lip, 'when I got to her house I noticed the washing on the line at the back of the house. And a dreadful sense of foreboding swept over me. My good lord, you should have seen the size of her mother's things! That bra with the two enormous humps on it would have excited any red blooded camel, I can tell you. And as for the, you know, unmentionables, *well*! Billy Smart's Circus could have moved in there, and that's a fact.'

His eyes were like saucers now.

'Unfortunately, at that very moment Eileen came out of the front door and assumed the look of horror on my face was some kind of uncontrollable lust and she let rip at me. Suddenly I'm a pervert in need of locking up! Unbelievable as it seems, she thought I had the hots for her mother. *Well, if that's the kind of thing you're looking for, there's no way on God's earth I'm going to America with you. I'd never know what you'd be up to when my back's turned.'*

I chuckled at that. Micky didn't. His voice was dripping distress.

'She was screeching so loudly the neighbour's windows shattered. I had no choice but to walk away. But that's not the worst bit. As I'm scurrying off down the road running for my life I see this shiny red sports car cruising up to her house. It stops outside the gate. And there's Eileen with a silly grin on her face fawning all over the driver. If I had been closer I'd have, well ... I'd have pulled off his wing mirrors.'

Another bump and another wobble.

'One thousand euros I'm after paying for that holiday,' Mickey sighed. 'One thousand euros! I must have been mad.'

'So what are you going to do now?'

'I don't know.' He gave a weary shrug. 'It didn't crossed my mind to take out insurance. Well, I thought wild horses wouldn't stop Eileen from going to San Francisco. But there you are! *I* didn't want to go there in the first place, you know - I can't stand the thought of flying all that way - but at the time I was blinded by a strange passion for the woman.'

'No insurance? So you can't even take them back to the travel agent?'

'Well, it doesn't matter now, anyway.' He gave a throaty sigh. 'I haven't the heart left in me to worry about it. On the one hand I miss her terribly, but on the other hand I wake up at night in a dreadful sweat and I feel so relieved that I've managed to escape her clutches. Imagine ten years down the road when she's turned into her mother and you can't take her out in daylight in case she frightens the neighbour's cat? What a nightmare that would be.'

'Why don't you just sell them, so? Put them on e-Bay.'

'Ah, I can't be bothered with all that right now.'

'They cost you a thousand euros and you can't be bothered?' I laughed out loud.

'Well, there's only two weeks left to go.' His nose twitched. 'Where am I going to find someone to buy them at this short notice, even if I give them away at half the price? Or even a third of the price.'

'A third of the price?' I gasped. 'You'd sell them for three hundred euros?'

'Four hundred.'

I thought I caught a twinkle in his eye but he quickly looked out of the window. I scratched my head.

'Three into one thousand ...'

'Ah, tis too late now, anyway. Who could get two weeks off over Christmas at such short notice, like I said?'

'But *our* factory is shut for the Christmas. *I* have the two weeks off myself.'

And that was that. With a sudden rush of blood to the head and without as much as a nod towards the consequences, I bought the tickets from Micky Dunn.

Well, you'd have to be mad not to grab an opportunity like that!

Wouldn't you?

Of course I had to borrow the money from Jayne's

Christmas fund, the one she'd been saving towards since last January. My mother kept it in an old cocoa tin under the kitchen sink. She wouldn't notice that I'd crept in and borrowed it. And I *was* going to mention it to Jayne - as soon as we were on our way. She'd be *so* proud.

But right now, as I wilted under the glare of my beloved Jayne, I didn't think this was a good time to bring it up.

'So, what's for tea?' I flashed my most penitent smile.

'We've had ours. *Yours* is in the dog.'

My heart sank. I hated these sulks. Sometimes Jayne could sulk for a whole week. I needed space to consider my options. I grabbed my coat and retreated to Maguire's pub where I plonked down on a hard stool and propped myself up on the bar, avoiding the puddles of spilt beer.

What the hell possessed me to act so impulsively? I must have had a short circuit in my one working brain cell! My stomach heaved when I thought about it. If I didn't get the car fixed Jayne was going to give me some serious grief. But it would be nothing compared to what she'd do to me when she found out I'd spent all her Christmas savings too.

I threw a handful of coins on the counter, enough for a pint of stout and a packet of salted peanuts.

'Will you be buying a ticket for Saturday's raffle, Michael?' Mrs Maguire's peroxide blond hair glowed like a halo around her head in the light from the solitary bulb. 'They're only a Euro each.'

'What's the prize, Mrs Maguire?'

'A digital radio,' she beamed. ''Tis one of them remote control ones.'

'I've got one of them already.'

'Now don't be so mean,' she pouted. 'Tis for charity, you know.'

'Don't talk to me about charity. I'm a very poor man myself, as you well know. I'm so poor people break into our house and leave us things.'

'Ah, go away, you big eejit.' She gave me a thump on the arm. 'Sure isn't it just a bit of fun on a Saturday night? Tis a bit of a laugh, helps to get us into the Christmas spirit. The money we raise will go to the St John's Gregorian Boys Choir to encourage them to continue with the Christmas Nativity.'

She rattled the tin under my nose.

'You won't be making enough out of a raffle to encourage a budgie to sing, let alone a whole choir,' I mocked.

She gave an almighty laugh that blew the froth off the top of my pint, and the slap on the back nearly cracked a rib.

'Oh, won't we now? Well, I'll have you know we made over nine hundred euros for the nuns last week.' She gave me a wicked wink. 'The old man says tis just a dirty habit with them nuns, but I says we'll have 'nun' of that kind of talk in here!'

'Nine hundred euros?'

'Oh, yes - easily. And we made more than that the week before. It all depends on what the prize is.'

My head buzzed with the makings of an idea. 'So who organises these raffles?'

'Derek usually organises them. You know my son Derek, don't you?'

She nodded towards the bar. My blood ran cold.

'Oh, Derek's out - er - come home, has he?'

'He has!' Mrs Maguire had a proud look on her face. 'So just go over there and ask him. He'll be glad to give you all the details.'

I glanced over at Derek Maguire, a six-foot ex-boxer and all round barbarian who was thrown out of the French Foreign Legion for being too aggressive.

'Well, I ...'

'So what were you thinking about anyway, Michael? Was it for a charity or something like that?'

'Ah, well, I was just thinking about a friend of mine.' I knew I was stuttering. I was never able to think on my feet. 'Well, he's a cousin actually. You know, a distant cousin. On my mother's side. You wouldn't know him yourself. Anyway, he's been very sick recently. They said he should get away for a while. To help him recover, if you know what I mean?'

'Oh, that's very thoughtful of you, Michael Galvin. I didn't know you were so kind, you being you and all that?'

'What do you mean?' I put on my most indignant expression.

She chuckled and patted me on the arm. 'A chancer, that's how I'd put it. A chancer.'

'That's a terrible thing to say, Mrs Maguire. And you after knowing me all my life.'

She nodded gravely. 'A chancer. But never mind about that right now. What were you proposing to put up as the prize? That's if you were serious about a raffle at all.'

'I am!' Again the indignant face. 'And I would like to put up a holiday for two in San Francisco, so there!'

Her eyes popped. Then they narrowed.

'A holiday for two in San Francisco? What's the

catch?'

'Oh well, it has to be taken in two weeks' time. That's the only snag. But it will be for two whole weeks in the sun, away from all this cold and rain. Just imagine, Christmas in San Francisco!'

Her eyes narrowed even more so I took out the black envelope with *Lucy's Luxury Holidays* in gold letters across it.

'Now feast your eyes on that, Mrs Maguire.'

She held the envelope like it was red hot and scrutinised every word on the tickets. She was frowning when she handed it back.

'Lucy's Luxury Holidays? Where on earth is that?'

'It's in Killarney.' I slipped the tickets back into my pocket. 'On the main street. I asked my mother. She thinks it's over a Chinese Chip Shop.'

'It sounds very posh,' Mrs Maguire conceded. 'But isn't San Francisco a nice warm place? So why doesn't that cousin of yours just go there himself?'

Gaaadddd … stop with the questions, Mrs Maguire!

'He's terrified - that's it. The poor sod is terrified of flying, so he is. Absolutely terrified. Well, not of the actual *flying*, you understand. Tis the crashing that worries him, if you see what I mean? Even the thought of getting onto a plane gives him palpitations. E nd hasn't he got enough of them already? But, of course I had no idea he felt like that when I bought him a holiday in the sun. It mean, how was I to know? A kind heart, that's me all over. Impetuous, with no thought about the consequences.'

'Take them back to where you got them, so!' Now she had an even smugger look about her.

'Ah, now I can't do that. I forgot to take out

insurance. Well, I didn't think I was going to need it, did I? I mean, why on earth should I take out insurance? Didn't I think he would be delighted to go to America? Who in heaven's name would turn down a chance to go to San Francisco? Especially if it's free? Well, I ask you!'

'What about yourself, then? Take Jayne and go.'

'I wish I could.' I tried a sad face. 'But tis way too late for all that. We wouldn't have enough money to take with us. And it would be a nightmare trying to get someone to have the baby and all that. You know how it is!'

Mrs Maguire nodded again. 'A chancer!' she muttered.

'But what about the raffle, though?'

It was as simple as that. Before I could change my mind, Derek advertised it as the main Christmas Draw. It would pull in the crowds on Saturday night - you could tell by the look on his face.

And it did. You could hardly get in the door, and when you did the punters were four deep at the bar, pushing and shoving and bellowing out their orders.

The Maguires were loving it, flying up and down the length of the bar passing pints over the customer's heads and happily short-changing them. No one questioned them because they were anxious to get their drinks out of the way of flying elbows and back to their seats.

And there was a wonderful atmosphere that night, full of the festive spirit. And a lot of stout too. I couldn't even get a place to stand properly, never mind a seat.

And by eleven o'clock all the tickets were sold. At the final count we'd taken over one thousand Euros. And it was mine - all mine! Well, less 20% that went to the

Maguires, of course, for their commission. That's how it is under the Charity's rules, they told me.

When Derek gave the brass bell a long shake the silence dropped like a curtain. All eyes turned towards Mrs Maguire and her paper bag full of raffle tickets. Through the thick haze of cigarette smoke we watched her stick a huge fist into it and rummage frantically. She held up her selection.

'Tis a pink ticket. Number seven!'

All the heads bowed together in a huge wave as everyone looked down.

Now I'm not saying it was a fix or anything, but no one actually saw Derek buy a ticket. So when he threw his enormous body up in the air and whooped in delight the whole bar looked up in disbelief.

'Tis mine!' he roared. 'I've got the number seven.'

And before anyone could utter a word a hand the size of a small shovel plucked the black envelope from behind the bar, and Derek lurched off up the stairs at the back of the pub.

I was as surprised as everyone else. Of course I was. But what could I do? It was imposed upon me to accept the donation on behalf of my very sick cousin. And with the seasonal wishes ringing in my ears I made an indecently quick exit through the side door.

Then a strange thing happened. The shaft of light from the open door fell across a car parked on the other side of the road. For a second the inside was lit up.

And I swear I saw Mickey Dunn and the lovely Eileen Grey enveloped in a passionate embrace on the back seat.

Naw! I shrugged it off. Would he make up a story like that?

Anyway, I danced all the way home, my mind racing with a concoction of plans. I wouldn't say anything to Jayne just yet. I'd replace her Christmas fund first thing in the morning and then I'd get the car fixed. I'd drive it home on Monday afternoon and watch the surprised look on her face.

Yes, Jayne would wonder. And I'd let her wonder - until she admitted that sometimes even I can get it right. Not very often, I admit. But when I *do*!

She was in the kitchen when I bounced in.

'I was just going to make some coffee.' She appeared to have calmed down. Things were looking good. 'Do you want some?'

'Yes, please.'

'Oh, by the way, your mother called in on her way home tonight.' Jayne put her head around the door. 'She said you were asking about Lucy's Luxury Holidays?'

'Yeah?'

'Well, she said to tell you not to bother with them. They went bust last week. Apparently hundreds of people lost all their holiday money …'

Dreamin' Dreams

Bunny Dundee

The donkey was mad. We all knew that. You only had to look at the cut of him. He had a lump missing from one of his ears and all his bones were poking through his motley skin. If you wandered too close to him he'd snort and discharge a cloud of malicious vapour. And the dark sinister eyes would challenge *you* to challenge *him*.

With his skinny bow legs and volatile temper he was the stuff of nightmares. Mothers would use the scary stories about him to terrify their children into behaving.

So for years he was the source of great amusement around the little market town deep in the heart of County Kerry.

It stood to reason, of course, that an animal like that would have an owner every bit as odd. And there was no one odder than Bunny Dundee.

Bunny was a Professor of Thermometry. Apparently the first job they gave him was to study some rocks in the middle of Australia. They didn't tell him it was the hottest place on God's earth and he should stay out of the sun in the middle of the day.

Bunny didn't. The sun boiled his brain. So when he landed back at the family farm near Duagh he was speaking gibberish. And using extremely long and complicated words too.

And he went everywhere in a rush. As if everything in his life had a desperate urgency about it. He wouldn't even sit still long enough for someone to cut his hair. Now it was almost down to his waist.

They called him Bunny because of his passion for rabbits. He spent most days hunting them. But the sad pile of skins he brought to market made you wonder where he found them. Bunny's skins looked like they came off rabbits that were very old. Or already dead.

Anyway, every market day Bunny and the lunatic donkey could be seen tearing around the town square scattering the cattle and the sheep and leaping between the trucks and the tractors. And the rabbit skins flapping in the breeze would draw random bursts of laughter from some brave soul. Then the donkey would snort and the lads would run.

The first time I set eyes on Bunny Dundee was during the long lazy summer of '62. I was sitting on the counter of my uncle Moss's Harnessmaker's shop when Bunny shot in the door in a high state of agitation.

Moss turned around on his stool and looked over the top of his glasses. 'Well, well, tis Bunny himself. And how're you this lovely fine day?'

Little beads of sweat glistened on Bunny's face as he leant his elbow on the counter, took out his pipe and stuck it in his mouth. Then he lit a match and gave a long drag.

'Well, tis like this,' he finally said from behind a cloud of smoke. 'I'm after having a communication this very morning that provoked a level of distress in myself that instilled in me an awareness of ...'

Moss looked sideways at his nephew Mick who was busy stuffing a donkey saddle with lumps of coarse horsehair, and he tried not to smile. 'Bunny, what does that mean, exactly?'

'This!' Bunny pulled a letter from inside his jacket. Moss took it from him and read it himself. That way he saved a lot of time.

And as Moss scanned the official looking piece of paper the only sound you could hear was Bunny sucking on his pipe.

'Well, how about that?' Moss gave the letter a little shake in the air as he turned back to Mick. 'Brendan Galvin is staying in America after all. You know he owns the farm where Bunny lives? Well, he's offered it to Bunny for a fraction of the going price.'

'Well, that's wonderful news,' Mick answered.

The noise that came from Bunny was more like a sob than a suck. 'Then tell me,' he boomed. 'Where am I going to get the finances for such an enterprise?'

'There is that, I suppose,' Mick conceded and stuck a huge needle into the belly of the saddle and stitched away quietly.

Bunny's erratic movements stirred up a mild breeze and it fanned the aromatic scent of leather in little waves all around the shop.

'Anyway,' Bunny continued. 'After giving it considerable consideration and a lot of deliberation, the final outcome could bode rather unfortunate for a relatively close companion of mine.'

We all turned to look at him. He took a long dramatic drag on the pipe. 'I'm going to have to sell the auld donkey.'

This time we all looked at each other. 'What? Sell the auld donkey?'

'I know.' Bunny waved the pipe like a grieving shepherd would wave his crook. 'But isn't the auld donkey the only asset I have to my name? Tis the only way I'll raise the funds.'

There was no going back now. He'd made his decision. So Bunny tugged importantly on the lapels of his jacket and ground his teeth on the stem of the pipe.

'Right.' His chest rose with purpose and smoke

belched from the corner of his mouth. 'I'll bid you all good day, so.'

With that he gave a jaunty flick of his flowing locks and tore off to untie the donkey from the No Parking sign out in the street.

Unfortunately he collided with the Widow Maria and sent her sprawling backwards into the street, scattering her basket of groceries all over the road.

Bunny gave a growl and he and the donkey shot off around the corner leaving the Widow Maria to scramble to her feet all by herself. She staggered in the door of the shop, gasping and wheezing and cursing like an old Royal Navy stoker.

'Did you see the cut of that big eejit?' she bellowed at no one in particular. 'Charging out of here like a lunatic with his hair flying in the air and knocking me clean off my feet into the gutter and not a notion of an apology out of him. What's the likes of him doing walking the streets anyway frightening decent people like me and causing chaos wherever he goes? And you're encouraging him by letting him come in here talking the rubbish and drinking the tea and not a care in the world while the likes of me are mortally afraid in case he bowels us over. You shouldn't be encouraging him, you know. You should be sending him away home for himself and give the likes of us some peace at our age for the love of God 'cos we're not getting any younger, any of us.'

When she stopped for breath Moss gave her a sympathetic smile. She pulled a face, spun around and she waddled off up the town.

'Frustrated,' Moss nodded to himself.

'*Oh?*'

Dreamin' Dreams

'Well,' he continued for my benefit. 'That woman used to be one of the greatest ballroom dancers of her time, so she was. She won medals all over the world. Even America, she was that good. She and her husband were the World Champion Ballroom dancers for years and years. No one could touch them.'

He waited for a reaction. We nodded.

'Then one day the husband goes and dies on her. No warning or nothing. So from then on she's been a bit peculiar. You know? Frustrated for the want of a good dancing partner. The trouble is there's no one around these parts that's good enough to take her on.'

Anyway, word spread about Bunny Dundee's famous donkey. Now it wasn't just the *skins* on the donkey that were for sale now - it was the donkey himself. Bunny put a For Sale sigh on a piece of string around the donkey's neck and all day long they were either ignored or avoided.

And that's how it was for the next few months.

Gradually Bunny got more and more despondent until in the end it wore him down. In a fit of hopelessness he tied the donkey to the Church gate and went in to have a word with The Almighty.

The sight of Bunny crumpled on the back seat of the Church touched the heart of Father O'Dee. He rushed over to give him comfort, expecting maybe to hear a confession as well. What he didn't expect was the life story of a donkey.

Now Father O'Dee was a kindly man blessed with a wonderful gift of patience. But after half an hour of listening to the ramblings of Bunny Dundee a wicked thirst came upon him. So they retired to his office - the lounge bar of the town hotel.

And after a few small whiskeys the Divine inspiration came upon Father O'Dee.

'A dance.' He gave his thigh a resounding slap. 'Shur that's it! We'll have a dance - one shilling a ticket.'

'What?' Bunny's pipe was in mid-air, half way to his mouth. 'Have a dance for an auld donkey? Are you after losing your marbles?'

He suddenly realised who he was talking to. 'Sorry, Father.' He crossed himself and scattered ash down the front of his shirt.

'Ah sure, tis a grand idea.' Father O'Dee was rubbing his hands in excitement. 'And I know the very band that'll play for us, too. They're marvellous with the music and the jigging and the hopping. They'll set the town on fire, so they will. We could even have a competition. Cash prizes and all that. It'll be grand all together. I'll see to it immediately.'

And off he shot, leaving Bunny flicking bits of hot ash from his lap.

Father O'Dee decided to schedule the dance for the end of the month. This was to give him enough time to prepare. It would also coincide with The Races, which was the busiest week of the year.

Thousands of people were expected to converge on the town so he very cleverly mentioned the dance - and the competition - in his Sunday sermon and again on the late Mass on Tuesday.

Posters were drawn up and stuck all over town, in shop windows, on every blank wall, even on the electricity poles that stretched for miles along the straight road to Ballybunion. One even appeared on the dustbin outside the Protestant Church in the middle of the Square.

Race Week brought the Carnival and it filled the town with colour and noise. Piped bands marched around the streets and the porter flowed freely. Music poured out of every pub all day long and late into the night. And every conversation turned to the dance in aid of a lunatic with a donkey that was organised by a priest. The tickets were bought more as a dare than anything else.

And, surprisingly, it was a huge success.

The big night came and so did the crowds. And as the spotlights flooded the stage Father O'Dee, with all the pomp and ceremony he could muster, rose himself up to his full five feet in height. And with his little round face a picture of pious dignity he announced the mysterious band.

The Lower Rock Street Quartet! Only there was eight of them on account of they needed someone to play the drums as well. And an accordion because what good was an Irish band without an accordion? And a flute. And a tin whistle.

They started the evening by asking for requests. And the dancing was wild and furious. The noise was deafening and it went on into the early hours of the morning.

It was the talk of the town for weeks afterwards. But, strange as it may seem, no one noticed that Bunny Dundee and his donkey had disappeared. No one had clapped eyes on them since before the dance.

Then a few months later a tall smartly dressed man appeared in the doorway of Moss Scanlon's Harnessmaker's shop. His face had a wonderful glow about it as he spread his elbows all over the counter. Moss took a slurp from his mug of tea and manoeuvred himself around on his stool.

'How can I help you?' he beamed at the man.

The man produced a pipe and made a great show of lighting it. When he was satisfied with himself he waved the pipe in the air.

Moss looked at the man's neatly trimmed beard and tidy haircut and his eyes lit up.

'Well, my good God,' he gasped. 'Bunny Dundee! And where have you been, stranger?'

Bunny chuckled. 'How're you, Moss?'

'I'm fine. But what about you?' Moss looked him up and down again. 'By the looks of you, the dance worked out all right.'

'It did indeed.'

'Well, you certainly look good.' Mick glanced up then carried on stitching a greyhound muzzle. 'Does this mean you've bought the farm?'

'Well, not exactly.' Bunny stabbed the air with the pipe again. 'I mean, Father O'Dee is a real saint and all that, so he is - God bless the man. D'you know, after he extracted his expenses - and a little bit for the collection plate, of course - he give me enough money to purchase not only my own humble abode, but also a big lump of land as well? And there was even a bit left over for a drop of the hard stuff. By way of celebration, you understand. Now, isn't that phenomenal?'

'Well, that *is* great,' Moss agreed. 'But tell me this, why haven't you bought the farm?'

Bunny took a long drag on the pipe. 'Well now, that's a very delicate situation. Cos there's good news, and there's not so good news.'

Moss gave the top of his shiny head a rub with the edge of a ruler. 'What's the bad news first?'

'Well, to tell you the truth, it was the day Father O'Dee had the notion about the dance.' Bunny shook his head sadly. 'I was so excited didn't I tear all the way home at the gallop? It was only when I got to my own front gate that I realised the poor auld donkey wasn't capable of such exertion anymore. Anyway, I think I was getting a bit too heavy for him as well, the poor auld thing.'

Moss blinked a few times and pushed his glasses back on his nose so he could see the situation more clearly.

'You're not telling us the donkey is ...?'

'Ah, sure he is, the poor auld thing. Stiff as a board he was the next morning. And after all the years I spent looking after him, too. T'was very sad. Very sad indeed.'

'What's the good news?'

'Well, I was so upset about the auld donkey that I was in desperate need of a bit of company. So I decided to take myself off to this famous dance. Anyway, I met Hetty Hurley there and we were having a great time flying around the floor when I gets a tap on the shoulder. And there's the Widow Maria.

How can it be that you can dance like that? she bellows in my ear. *You can't even walk down the street in a straight line without knocking decent people into the gutter with your two left feet?*

I've been a dancer all my life, I tell her. All Ireland Champion four times, and Munster Champion for seven years running. And I have the medals to prove it, if you would care to look.

I don't believe you, she says, grabbing me by the shirt and dragging me onto the dance floor. *Show me what you're made of, so!*'

'Oh!' was all Moss could say as we gawped at Bunny and waited for more.

'Anyway.' Bunny took another drag on the pipe. 'The fact is, I don't want to spend the money just yet because of the way things are developing between myself and the Widow Maria. Just in case I have to give it back to Father O'Dee, you know?'

'Oh!' Moss said again.

Just then a shadow loomed in the doorway.

'Bunny,' the Widow Maria purred. 'I thought I'd find you in here with all your friends. Hello boys.'

'Hello, Maria.'

'Sorry we have to rush off like this.' She continued to purr as she slipped her arm into Bunny's. 'But we're off to Limerick for the finals of the Munster Ballroom Dancing event. We're the favourites, don't you know?'

Moss blinked a few times behind his glasses. 'Things are looking good all around, then.' He winked at Bunny.

'Well, tis early days yet.' Bunny's eyes had a wicked sparkle in them. 'Early days. But, yes, they certainly are looking good.'

Dapper Danny's Amazing Welsh Cousin

Dapper Danny was everything people said he was - a dapper little man. Standing five feet tall in his socks, he was always immaculately dressed in a crisp, starched shirt and dark trousers with a crease in them you could cut yourself on.

Of course everyone said it was all right for him because, being so little, he could buy his clothes in the boy's department of Dunn's Stores. But that wasn't the point. Dapper groomed himself religiously and he was fiercely proud of it.

Now Dapper Danny had a wife, Mary. She stood five feet tall as well - only all the way round. When you saw her coming towards you in the street it was more like a roll than a walk.

Dapper, on the other hand, had a walk on him like a ferret. Just crossing the road involved at least eight manoeuvres. He'd dart in front of Mary then slip sideways, slide in behind her then back in front again. And all the time his head would be twisting and turning this way and that to see who was looking at them.

Because Dapper Danny had a desperate need to be seen. He was terrified that if he wasn't seen around the village he'd quickly be forgotten. And he had an irrational fear of being forgotten.

He couldn't put his finger on it, exactly. But he thought it stemmed from an innocent remark his Grandad made when Dapper was just a child.

Dapper worshipped his Grandad. He used to spend every summer with him on the farm. It was the highlight of Dapper's year. When school broke up he caught the bus to Listowel. Grandad would be waiting for him with the pony and trap tied up outside the church in the square. And they'd walk across to Kelly's pub where Granddad would have his pint of stout and Dapper would have a bottle of lemonade.

One day Grandad brought a fishing rod with him. When he finished his pint they strolled down to the river. And they spent a wonderful afternoon in tranquil splendour, sitting on the bank watching the gentle brown water go lolloping by.

They took a short cut back through the cemetery. Grandad stopped by an old headstone and took off his cap. He put his hand on the mottled stone and gave it a gentle rub.

'There lies my best pal, Jimbo Lynch,' he said with a sad sigh. 'Me and Jimbo, we grew up together. He lived on the farm next to ours and we started school at the same time, way before you were born. Actually, it was way before your mammy was born, too. And we were as thick as thieves, the two of us and our gang. We went everywhere together, did everything together. Especially the fishing. We loved the fishing. That very spot on the river where we were today was our special place. Me and Jimbo and our gang. We spent half our lives there.'

Grandad gave another long sigh. 'Would you believe I'm the last of the gang still alive? So when I go to that great farm in the sky, that's when Jimbo finally dies.' His voice was a croaky whisper.

Dapper looked from the headstone to Grandad then back to the headstone again. 'But, Grandad, it says on the gravestone that he's after dying in 1960.'

'Ah shur, it does.' Grandad nodded slowly. 'But isn't there an old proverb which says you live for as long as the last person that remembers you?'

Dapper blinked several times. Things like that went way over the head of a ten-year-old.

It was many years before the statement made any sense to Dapper. He was quietly sipping his pint in an almost empty pub on wet and windy evening. An elderly man was hunched over his porter at the end of the bar. Old Mac was wiping a glass behind the counter.

'Did you hear about Mossie Fitz?' Old Mac asked the man.

After a long pause the man scratched his nose. 'Who?'

Old Mac put down the glass, picked up another one and continued to wipe it. 'Mossie Fitz. You know Mossie Fitz!'

Another pause. 'I do not.'

'Ah, you do, shur. Wasn't he in our class at school?'

This time there was a longer pause. 'No. I don't know him.'

Old Mac put the glass on the shelf, picked up another one and idly wiped that too. 'He had a funny nose with a big knob on it.'

The man at the bar took a long, slow drink of his porter. 'Did he have a sister called Jennie?'

Old Mac thought a moment. 'No.'

'Ah, well, I don't know him, so.'

'But he did have a brother named Eamon.'

The man took another slurp of the porter. You could almost hear him thinking. 'Ah, sure, that's right. I remember him now, all right.' Another sip of the porter. 'So how is he?'

'He's dead,' Old Mac said as he put the glass on the shelf.

For some strange reason Dapper Danny was deeply

disturbed by the notion that the poor old sod was already forgotten even *before* he was dead. From that moment on Dapper made a point of going into the village every single day of the year, come rain or shine.

One day as Dapper and Mary were doing the rounds of the village Mrs O'Connor approached and gave them her best smile.

'Hello Danny. Hello Mary,' she purred. 'I was wondering if I could have a word with you. My son Seamus is looking for some advice.'

'Hello Mrs O'Connor. Of course you can have a word. Come over to the house tomorrow morning.'

'Saturday?'

''Tis my day off,' Dapper nodded.

'Oh, I see.' Mrs O'Connor frowned. 'But I thought you weren't working these days. I thought you did nothing all week.'

'That's true,' Mary agreed. 'But on Saturday he does nothing at all.'

The next morning Mrs O'Connor arrived with Seamus, a gangly youth with horrendous acne and crooked teeth. His baseball cap was on back to front. Four rings decorated in his ear and one glistened his nose. He nodded a sullen hello.

'The thing is,' gushed Mrs O'Connor. 'Seamus is thinking of going to England. And since you went there once he wanted to ask you about it.'

Dapper Danny blanched. How did she know that? His trip over the Irish Sea happened many years ago. He'd buried it deep in the attic of his mind. It was *never* to be resurrected! It was the stuff of nightmares. It left him emotionally scarred. He hoped that by never referring to it again it would be erased from history.

Now it was back, hitting him with a tsunami of emotions.

He'd only gone there in the first place because his beautiful cousin Helen had asked him to. She lived in a village called Pontllanfraith, just north of Cardiff in South Wales.

Helen had appeared out of the blue one day many years before. She was sitting in the kitchen when Danny sauntered in from school. Apparently Helen's mother was a third cousin of Dapper's father on his mother's side - or was it his mother on his father's side. Anyway, they'd come to Ireland for a short visit to catch up with all their relatives.

And Dapper had never seen a more beautiful girl in his whole life. Her flowing blond hair framed a perfect face. And her enormous blue eyes had a perpetual smile in them. Dapper Danny was totally and instantly besotted.

He was also fascinated by her amazing Welsh accent. And she was so polite and pleasant all the time. Just being with her made him dizzy.

The trouble was, Dapper had a problem. Whenever he spoke to Helen he got very excited. And when Dapper got excited his voice got higher and higher and faster and faster until even he couldn't understand what he was saying.

He could never figure out if the looks Helen gave him were of pity or just plain fright. And she didn't seemed comfortable when she was alone with him, either.

But in spite of that he spent every minute trying to impress her. He showed her off to all his friends in the street and he was very attentive to her every need.

Then one day she was gone again.

Dreamin' Dreams

'She had a great time,' he heard his mother telling the neighbours. 'She loved it here. The only thing she seemed bothered about was Danny, for some strange reason. I think it was because she couldn't understand a word he was saying.'

Still, Dapper Danny missed her terribly - at least till dinnertime when Pat Quilley turned up with a new bag of marbles.

Then years later, completely out of the blue, Dapper got a letter from Helen asking him to come and visit her during the first week in September.

It completely threw him. Half of him was excited about seeing her again. But the other half was wracked with apprehension. Would she be able to understand what he was saying? His voice was deeper, but still with a life of its own. And what would she think of him, now he was older but not much bigger? A man is very conscious of his height, in spite of the reassuring things his mother said to him.

'Beautiful things come in little packets,' she would tell him as he tried hanging upside down from the chicken shed with a sack of spuds in his arms.

'So does poison,' sniggered Mrs Lamb, the teacher.

Dapper Danny was romancing Mary at the time. They had so much in common. Well, she was the only one he could actually see eye to eye with. And Mary understood him. Maybe she would go with him.

'But what about my voice?' Danny implored her.

'Why don't you go and talk to Mrs Lamb?' Mary suggested. 'Doesn't she teach English up at that posh school? And isn't she also the drama coach? You've heard her telling people how to project their voice - how to speak properly.'

'A great idea!' Dapper cried, and he shot off up the hill to see the dreaded Mrs Lamb.

Mrs Lamb relished the challenge. It was a long hard task, of course, and it cost Dapper Danny a lot of his hard earned money. But in the end Mrs Lamb was exceedingly pleased with his progress.

So Dapper wrote to Helen and told her to expect himself and Mary during the first week in September, if that was all right by her. Then they went out and bought the tickets for the Rosslare to Fishguard ferry.

This all happened way back in 1973 when the fashion in England was very, very strange. People were going out in daylight with big hair and shirts so bright they could sizzle your eyeballs.

But the style in Dapper Danny's little corner of God's Earth was even stranger. Their only reference to what was happening in the world of fashion was The New Musical Express. And that was usually months out of date by the time it reached the village shop.

Still, Dapper studied it religiously - even if he didn't quiet grasp the finer points of colour co-ordination - and he managed to find an outrageously decorated shirt with a huge collar. And a tie that had a knot in it you could tie up an aircraft carrier with. Along with the flared yellow trousers and the shoes with three inch soles, he really though he was the bee's knees.

Of course what he *really* looked like was a garish Chinese kite that had crashed into a forest.

Anyway, the evening was bright and warm when they caught the ferry from Rosslare to Fishguard and they had a smooth crossing. They even managed to find an empty compartment on the train on the other side.

But they didn't have much time to relax because they

were deposited on Cardiff Station at the ungodly hour of five fifteen in the morning. Then the train went off in a cloud of smoke and noise and suddenly they were all alone in a strange station in a strange city. Nothing stirred. It was like a ghost town.

They didn't say a word as they dragged their huge suitcases all the way across to the bus station. Unfortunately the next bus to Pontllanfraith was not until nine thirty. So they sat on the cases and watched the antics of the pigeons that swooped and fluttered around them in the grey, empty dawn.

'I think we should look for somewhere to get a cup of tea,' Mary said after a while.

So off they staggered again, pulling the suitcases behind them.

'Oh, look.' Dapper spotted the name Mary Street on the corner of a building. 'They've named a street after you.'

'What?' Mary looked around expectantly. 'Oh, they have as well. Shur isn't that grand altogether?' Then she paused. 'But how did they know I was coming?'

Dapper scratched his head.

The whole city seemed to be deserted, enshrouded in an eerie kind of silence that was punctuated only by the clatter of Mary's stiletto heels on the pavement. And Dapper's heavy breathing.

Suddenly Dapper noticed a figure standing in a doorway. It was a real live British policeman, complete with the helmet and the enormous boots. Dapper was delighted. This was his first real opportunity to show off his expensive elocution lessons.

'I say, my good man.' Dapper's voice boomed like a gunshot in the quiet of the dawn.

The bobby jumped out of his skin. The cigarette butt shot out of his mouth and into the gutter and his hand went for the truncheon in his pocket.

'Could you direct us to a source whereby we might purchase a beverage?' Dapper was totally undaunted by the reaction. 'Perchance to retire our limbs to repose for a moment or two, thus enabling us to resuscitate?'

The bobby blinked several times. What Dapper hadn't realised was that Mrs Lamb was a *drama* coach, and the English she tutored him in leaned heavily towards her Shakespearean bias.

Hence the look on the bobby's face, which let you know exactly what he was thinking. *What on earth were these two lunatics doing out and about at this time of the morning? Surely they're not allowed out on their own*!

He was calculating the distance from the nearest care home in his head. It was at least twelve miles! *Surely they couldn't have walked all that way!* And certainly not with those huge suitcases. And why hadn't anyone noticed their escape? Maybe he'd better phone it through to the station.

On the other hand, though - looking at the cut of the man - he could well be a Social Worker. He was dressed like one, like he'd been in an explosion in a paint factory. And the way he *talked* - real gobbledegook!

So maybe he was just taking a client for a day out in the city.

'That's it,' the bobby gave a relieved nod, deciding it was too close to the end of his shift to get involved. 'You're on a day out, isn't it? A visit to the big city,'

Dapper blinked rapidly. The bobby took this as a yes and nodded again as he pointed a stubby finger towards the end of the street. 'Around the next corner there's a

little café that should do you nicely.'

Then he strolled off, still red in the face.

And the café certainly *did* look friendly and inviting as Dapper and Mary clattered noisily in through the door that gave a little tinkle of a bell as they opened it. Dapper left Mary with the cases as he sauntered casually up to the counter where a tall Asian gentleman stared at him blankly.

'Right, my good fellow,' Dapper clapped his hands together in anticipation. 'We'd like to partake of your excellent breakfast, if you please. Eggs, sunny side up, bacon crisp, and of course, black pudding. Toast would be nice, and a pot of your finest tea. For two.'

He flashed a smile. The Asian man's expression hardly changed, except to suppress the flicker of a smile that danced around the corners of his mouth. Then his eyes gave a slow, lazy blink.

'I beg your pardon?'

Dapper Danny blinked back.

Suddenly it seemed as if a light flicked on in the Asian man's eyes.

'Oh, I am seeing, now.' He gave a courteous bow. 'You must be a stranger to our beautiful country. Forgive me, but you do not speak like what us Welsh do by here, isn't it. You must be a visitor from across the sea. Ireland, perhaps?'

Dapper was amazed. He looked around at Mary.

'That's incredible!' he gushed. 'But how did you know that?'

The Asian gentleman gave a gentle sweep of his hand. 'Because this is a newsagent shop, isn't it?'

They sat in silence all the way to Pontllanfraith, their throats dry and their stomachs rumbling for the want of a nice cup of tea. Dapper Danny was beginning to regret ever coming here. He felt such a fool. All that money he'd spent on elocution lessons and the best of fashion, and still he blew it. What must poor Mary be thinking? Would he ever live it down? He'd be the laughing stock of the village when they got home.

Then all of a sudden Dapper Danny forgot about all that. The bus slowed down and cruised to a stop outside Evans the Butchers. And there, standing by the shop door, was his cousin Helen.

His heart leapt in his chest. She was exactly as he'd remembered her. Tall and elegant and exceptionally beautiful. And he was totally besotted all over again.

He was bouncing down the steps of the bus before the doors had fully opened. And he watched the beaming smile on Helen's face slowly fade with each step down that he took until he stood there looking up at her.

'Helen,' he gasped, ''tis so good to see you again. How are you?'

Helen blinked several times. 'Danny?' She composed herself quickly and leant down to kiss the top of his head. 'You haven't gro ... er ... well you certainly haven't changed in all those years. How are you?'

She turned quickly to the young man standing beside her.

'Danny, I want you to meet Dylan.' She took the young man by the hand. 'Dylan, this is my cousin Danny.'

Dapper had a bad feeling about this. He took the outstretched hand and shook it loosely.

'Dylan is my fiancéc,' Helen gushed. Now Danny felt his stomach turn. He didn't want to hear this. Mary thumping him on the back snapped him out of it.

Dreamin' Dreams

'You almost left it too late,' Helen was telling Mary as they walked on ahead. 'The wedding's at two o'clock. I thought you were coming yesterday. Still, never mind. We've plenty of time to get ready.'

Danny spent the next few hours in a daze. It was lucky Mary couldn't see the turmoil that was crashing around inside his head. How could Helen do this to him? She never mentioned a wedding in her letter. At least he didn't think she did. Maybe he should have read the second page. But he was so excited about seeing her again he just assumed it was to renew an old friendship. What was he going to do now? Had she no idea of how he felt about her? She was the love of his life. It was impossible to feel like this about another human being ever again. And now she was giving herself to another man. And with Dapper himself as a witness, too.

When Dapper Danny eventually came out of the dark haze of despondency he found himself sitting in a beautiful chapel. Mary was holding his arm in a most romantic way. She had a strange gleam in her eyes as she beamed at him.

Standing in front of them was a trendy young Vicar with flowing blond hair. He had the strong resonant voice of a young Tom Jones and it rippled around the rafters as he welcomed the bride and the groom, the best man, the bridesmaids, the mother, the father, the other mother, the other father, the ...

Dapper Danny cringed. His first love was being taken from him right in front of his eyes. He was wandering back into the black haze. But he snapped out of it when he heard the vicar ask if anyone knew of a just reason why these two could not be joined in Holy Matrimony!

Dapper Danny could never really explain what

happened next - though he readily admits it was a mad, rash thing to do. But in the blink of an eye he was up on his feet and crying at the top of his voice.

Of course, in this sudden rush of blood to the head, gone were all traces of his elocution and the calm projection of the voice. Instead there came a garbled stream of words that got progressively higher until they almost reached soprano. And his arms flapped frantically and his face got redder and redder.

It was only the sharp slap on the back of the legs from Mary's imitation tiger-skin handbag that shocked him into an abrupt silence.

Everything froze. Even the irritating bluebottle that was pattering against the coloured window behind them was suddenly still.

And all Dapper could see was Helen's face shimmering in a ghostly white halo, staring back at him in sheer horror.

He swallowed loudly.

Then the vicar gave a slow handclap and came across to Dapper, beaming all over his face.

'That was absolutely beautiful, Brother,' he called loudly, waving a hand around the congregation. 'Wasn't that beautiful? And what a marvellous voice! Absolutely wonderful. Not a hymn I'm familiar with, I'm afraid. Latin, was it? But beautiful, never the less.'

He took Dapper's hand in a firm grip.

'Only, in Chapel we don't actually start singing until the end of the service, you see?' He smiled, all teeth and twinkling eyes. 'Not that it matters, isn't it? Just so you know. But it *was* beautiful.'

Mary still believes to this day that the looks Dapper got at the reception afterwards were of supressed admiration. No one spoke to them, though, except Helen's family. But that was because the Welsh are a shy race, Mary insisted.

Dapper knew better, though. They thought he was a big eejit, dressed up like a dog's dinner and talking strangely. He couldn't wait to go home.

His only consolation was that Helen gave him a lovely kiss before she left for the honeymoon. Her beautiful soft lips lingered for a second as they brushed against his. He would treasure that moment for the rest of his life, intoxicated as he was by both her perfume and copious amounts of sparkling wine.

'So, what do you think?'

'*What?*' Dapper Danny snapped out of his daze. 'Oh, Mrs O'Connor. Seamus. I'm sorry, what were you saying?'

'I was saying, should Seamus take the chance and go to England to find himself a job?'

Mrs O'Connor was drinking a cup of tea. Dapper Danny couldn't remember making one for her. He shook his head.

Then Dapper Danny had the weirdest thought. For as long as he could remember he had this morbid fear that if he wasn't seen on a regular basis around the village he would quickly be forgotten. Yet, at the same time, there was a whole country that he hoped would never, ever remember him! Or his visit. He couldn't prevent an ironic chuckle.

'Danny?'

'What does Seamus do, exactly?' Dapper asked quickly, coughing into his fist.

The youth stared back with a mixture of arrogance and blankness.

'What?'

Dapper Danny gave a deep sigh. After his experience in Wales he always insisted on dressing in sober, clean and pressed clothes every day of the week. And he spoke precisely and clearly. And he believed that it gained him enormous respect.

He looked at the callow youth before him and could see no hope. What the little thug really needed was a good slap.

Or maybe an experience like the one Dapper had when he ventured overseas!

Dapper Danny grinned.

'Go on,' he said. 'Go!'

Eavesdropping

'Waiter!'

The snap of the fingers made the other diners in the Brandon Restaurant turn around to look at the man in the expensive suit. The discreet overhead lights glistened off his mop of greasy hair. And as his fingers flicked over the menu his deep eyes scanned the room to check the response from those around him.

The eyes touched for a brief moment on a young woman sitting alone by the window. Her heart skipped a beat. She stared back at him through huge glasses that made her look like a timid little owl. For a moment she thought he was bound to recognize her.

But then she caught the contemptuous flicker of a smile on the corner of his lips. She dropped her eyes quickly to her hands that were clasped tightly on her lap.

Of course he wouldn't recognise her, even though they'd both at the same company for many years. Because he was a highflying sales executive and she was just one of the many clerks who worked in the office.

And to get noticed by him you'd have to be blond and beautiful with legs up to your neck.

Eileen Flynn wasn't what you'd call beautiful. She wasn't blond either. She pushed her glasses back on her nose and took a sip of water.

The waiter glided over to the man's table and his face was discreetly blank as the man tapped on his mobile phone before putting it to his ear.

'Michael,' he laughed loudly. 'Tony O'Riley here. Listen, can you hold on a minute?'

He held the phone in the air and glanced at the wine list.

'Yes,' he mused without looking at the waiter. 'I'll have a bottle of the Hotes de Saville '69. And I'm expecting a friend. When she ...'

He looked past the waiter and his face erupted in a huge smile that revealed a set of perfect white teeth.

'Michael, I'll have to call you back,' he shouted into the phone and dropped it noisily on the table, totally ignoring the waiter.

The tall lady standing by the door patted her fluffed-up peroxide hair before drawing the imitation tiger-skin stole around her shoulders. Seeing the man stand up, she gave a delighted shriek and waddled in her high heels across the polished floor towards him. Her skin-tight mini skirt pinned her legs together as she went.

'Tonyee ...'

'Claire, my darling!'

Eileen Flynn sat up straight. This was the *real* reason she'd come here - to see Tony's new floozy!

She looked around quickly. The other girls should have been here by now. They said eight o'clock. She hoped they hadn't changed their minds. After all, it was *their* idea.

They believed it was their duty to know what was going on in their place of work. Like who was doing what, and to whom, and how often. And their interest was aroused when Tony was heard boasting to his pals in the canteen about his latest bit of stuff.

Tony was *always* boasting about his women. Some people actually believed him. Of course the rest of them knew that no man was so special he could have a different woman every night of the week. Especially a man *his* age.

And Tony wasn't rich either - so it couldn't have

been the size of his wallet that attracted them. Anyway, he was always pleading poverty, saying his wife and three teenage kids were eating him out of house and home.

But *still* he played around. It was as if giving up the wine and the women was like giving up the ghost itself.

This time, though, he insisted it was serious. Apparently he met someone in a club in Killarney who took his breath away and left him totally besotted. He'd been inflicted with a severe case of love at first sight. He was absolutely mesmerised.

So when the girls discovered that Tony was supposed to meet her in the Brandon Hotel tonight - apparently to ask her something very, very important - they just *had* to know! Who could she *be*, this angel from Heaven, that he was willing to sacrifice everything for her - his wife and kids, his house, his car, the cat, his collection of Dinky cars, his limited editions of The Beano?

They were determined to see for themselves.

And there she was - loud and brash and all over Tony like a spray-on tan.

Eileen Flynn sat up straight, her eyes like laser beams as they scanned the floozy from her head to her toes and back to the head again.

It took less than a heartbeat for what Eileen was looking at to register. And when it did it came at her like a slap from a wet jellyfish and made her gasp out loud.

She looked around frantically for her friends. Only now she was hoping they *wouldn't* be here. Not now!

This was dreadful! She couldn't believe what she was seeing.

The waiter had moved silently to a young couple at the table by the door. And he smiled sweetly at the way their heads almost touched as they moved their chairs closer together.

He gave a staged cough and they both snapped up straight.

'Would Sir like a menu?'

'I would.' The young man glanced at his girl and blushed. 'I mean we would. Thank you. Yes. Please. Thank you very much.'

The girl took the menu and their heads bowed together again.

By this time Tony was shuffling the chair under the ample seat of the lady in the tight skirt and he was flapping around her like an excited bee.

'So, Claire, my darling, what would you like to drink?' He glanced around with an exaggerated flick of his head. 'Waiter!'

The fingers snapped again. The waiter's response was to totally disregard it. Instead he leant towards the young man and pointed out the recommended choice for starters.

Tony made a great show of scraping his chair and clattering his elbows impatiently on the table, causing the highly polished cutlery to rattle like chimes.

Eileen Flynn adjusted her glasses and swallowed hard. Then she clutched her purse against her chest and stood up. With her heart thumping loudly she moved towards Tony's table. And when he fired an angry look at her she hesitated.

But only for a split second.

This was far too serious for her to be put off now. Her face was flushed with anger and embarrassment as she put her hand on the blond lady's shoulder.

'Her name's not Claire.' She was surprised by how

hoarse and dry her throat had become.

The lady jumped and spun around. 'Oh, my God!'

'Her real name is Mary. Mary Mills.' Eileen spoke quickly. 'And right now her husband thinks she's working shifts at that grotty factory on the other side of town.'

Tony blinked and big red blotches appeared on his cheeks. His wine glass went to his mouth then back to the table with a crash. The cutlery tinkled again.

'Who the hell are you?' He was completely flustered.

Eileen looked down at the woman whose face had turned as white as the tablecloth, and she sighed loudly.

'Well go on, Mammy.' Eileen poked her on the shoulder. 'Tell him who I am!'

The Last Confession of Father Stone

Jennifer Marshall stormed up the steps at the back of St John's Church and pushed the ancient oak door open with a mighty crash. Her high heel boots echoed on the terracotta tiles as she charged through the tiny lobby and marched aggressively down the corridor towards the main hall.

She was furious. It was Friday afternoon and she had to traipse all the way across town to find her mother just so she could get into the house when she got home from school.

And all because her parents were too old fashioned and boring to give her a key of her own.

Well, actually, it was because she once brought some friends home after school. OK, they were boys, but it was totally innocent. She *was* fourteen, after all. And it certainly wasn't *her* fault if her mother came home early and completely misread the situation.

They'd been sitting on the sofa quietly watching a soap on TV when Liam leant over to get some crisps from the dish on the coffee table. As Jennifer moved out of his way she knocked Paul's can of coke out of his hand. Paul grabbed at the can, Jennifer fell on top of him, and Liam lost his balance and fell on top of the both of them.

All Jennifer's mother saw was her precious daughter in a tangle of arms and legs with two young thugs.

Nothing would convince her otherwise. Jennifer could never be trusted again. She was grounded for a whole month. And from that moment on her mother was waiting by the front door to make sure that she came home *alone* from school, every day of the week.

Except on Fridays, of course. Friday was her mother's afternoon for doing the flowers in the church. However, Jennifer's father finished work early on Friday so he was usually home to meet her instead.

For some strange reason, though, her father wasn't there today. Jennifer waited for ages. Eventually she decided enough was enough. She was hungry and she was tired and she was going to miss her programmes. So she decided to go down to the church and have words with her mother. Things had to be said. And now she was mad enough to say them!

She pushed open the door to the hall and charged in. But there was no one there.

Her angry groan echoed back at her. Where was everyone? She stamped her foot and turned to go when she caught sight of herself in the long mirror behind the door. She gave a wide, satisfied smile.

At least her parents couldn't stop her wearing makeup. They *did* have a problem with her strange haircut, but the boys loved it. And they loved her deep red lipstick that contrasted nicely with her naturally long dark eyelashes.

The girls thought she was just a tart, of course. But she was hard and they wouldn't say anything to her face anyway. So it didn't matter, did it?

Jennifer had a sudden thought - her mother was probably over at the school. She'd been summoned yet again by Mother Superior to explain why her daughter was coming to school in a skirt that was no wider than a belt.

Jennifer chuckled out loud. So what? She had the legs for it. She gave a wiggle in the mirror and brushed her hair with her hand.

'Yes!' She gave a satisfied pout and strutted back out into the corridor just as the elderly priest came shuffling past. He looked her up and down and raised a quizzical eyebrow.

'Jennifer?' He gave a gentle smile. 'What are you doing here?'

'Hi, Father Stone. I'm looking for my mother. She's supposed to be here today. It's her flower day but there's nobody in the hall.'

He looked over her shoulder to see for himself.

'Well?' Jennifer glared at him.

'What?'

'My mother! Have you seen her? Is she here?'

'Well, I don't ... I think ...'

Jennifer inhaled sharply. She *hated* this. All she wanted was the stupid door key. She wanted to go home, have a bath, something to eat, and flop down in front of the television. She didn't want to hear the ramblings of a doddery old man.

'Oh, never mind.' She pushed past him and headed for the door.

'Jennifer.' His voice was soft and gentle. 'Where are you going?'

'What's it got to with you?' Jennifer's voice was *not* soft and gentle. It reeked of annoyance. 'Are you my mother?'

But as soon as she'd said it she was sorry. She buried her face in her hands and wished she could suck it all back.

This had become a habit now, being rude to people. She did it for the shock effect. It gave her a tremendous buzz to see the stupid look on their faces whenever she spat out her tirade of insults. She'd sneer as their brains tumbled into neutral and they struggled to find a response.

They never could, though. They'd just stand there and splutter, their eyes exploding with distress as she laughed back at them before strutting away off down the street. It was awesome!

But she never meant to be rude to Father Stone. She was very fond of the gentle old priest. She'd known him all her life. He'd baptised her, he'd conducted her First Communion, and he was there for her Confirmation.

She liked his kind face and the soft eyes that looked at the world with a wise understanding. He had a wonderful way of making her feel special, too. He made her feel like a person in her own right and not just another face in the sea of children that passed his way every day of the week.

Even when the flack was coming at her from all directions, when everyone tutted and said how she used to be such a pretty little girl and how could she have turned into such an obnoxious thug, Father Stone would smile at her with the same soft smile. He seemed to understand the turmoil that was raging in her head.

So when Jennifer Marshall looked up at him now she gave a meek shrug. 'I'm sorry, Father'.

He looked back at her with vague eyes and Jennifer felt a strange twang of sadness. Of course she knew what people were saying about him lately. He didn't look at all well, they'd mumble as he passed by. He was getting very old and very tired. And he seemed to be in a daze most of the time. They kept finding him in the garden talking to the flowers. And they wouldn't let him say Mass anymore, either. Not since the day he sat on the top step of the altar with the bottle of Communion wine and called *cheers* to the congregation.

'Are those cigarettes I see in your hand?' The old priest pulled a face.

Jennifer looked sheepishly at the packet and went to say something.

'Well, now, you can't smoke in here, you know!' Father Stone wagged a bony finger as he shuffled towards her. 'So we'd better go outside. We'll go around the corner and I'll have one with you.' He flashed her one of his knowing smiles.

They sat on the low wall by the beautifully manicured lawn that sloped down to the small row of ancient headstones. The wall was rough and cold and Jennifer wished for once she was wearing a longer skirt.

She took a cigarette out with her teeth and handed the packet to Father Stone. He put one in his mouth and took a long, slow drag as Jennifer held the match to it. She lit her own and flicked the match into the wild roses that bordered the lawn.

'I'd kill for a can of lager right now.' Jennifer blew out a stream of smoke.

Father Stone gave a chuckle and shook his head.

'What?' Jennifer couldn't resist smiling too.

'You young people.' He was still chuckling. 'You're all the same, so you are. You think *you* invented this ... *wild child* thing.'

'What *wild child* thing?' Jennifer spat out a flake of tobacco. 'And what would you know about this *wild child* thing anyway, Father?'

'Well,' he squinted as he turned his face to the late summer sun. 'As they say these days, I've been there, done that, and got the T-shirt.'

Jennifer laughed out loud this time.

'You've been there, done that? But you ... you're a priest!'

'And what does that mean?' His reply was unusually curt. 'Do you think I was born with this dog collar around my neck? Do you think I was weaned on Holy Water?'

Jennifer frowned. The old eyes had taken on a strange intensity she'd never seen before.

'No,' she said quickly. 'It's not ... it's just that, well, you're just too nice. I can't imagine you ever being a *wild child*.'

He gave a long sigh. 'Oh, yes. Shur doesn't everyone on God's earth go through times like that? When we reach the puberty stage and the hormones are rampant and they go straight to the brain. They cause all sorts of confusion. Black moods, and all sorts of pain - real and imagined.'

He wiped a bit of ash from his sleeve.

'Everyone goes through it,' he continued. 'But for some strange reason we seem to forget about it, blank it from our memory. We erase it completely then we can't understand what's happening to our own children when *they're* going through it. So no one ever prepares you for it. No one warns you that when you're approaching that delicate stage you could suddenly come crashing off the rails and create all kinds of distress to those around you.'

Jennifer contemplated this as she took another drag on her cigarette. 'I know exactly what you mean,' she nodded eventually.

'Do you?' Father Stone studied her for a moment, his eyebrows arched. 'The thing is, Jennifer, at your age you're not aware that every single thing you do or say has some effect on those around you. You don't comprehend that if you drop a stone into someone's pond it actually causes a ripple that goes on and on and on. It can take an awfully long time for that ripple to die down. And the pond is never, ever the same again.'

Jennifer wrinkled up her nose and gave a sullen shrug behind a haze of smoke. 'So what? I couldn't care less about other peoples' ripples!'

'No,' Father Stone answered softly. 'Sure no one does when they're that age. I certainly didn't.'

It was a few moments before Jennifer realised what the old priest had said. 'What do you mean?' She was curious now. 'So whose pond did *you* throw stones into?'

'Well,' Father Stone sucked in a long, slow breath through his nose as if he was considering whether to elaborate or not. He straightened up as he breathed out.

'The thing is, all I ever wanted to do when I was a lad was carry on with the farming, like all my family did before me. We had a good spread out near Camp, you know, overlooking the bay. We were totally self-sufficient, cattle, sheep, our own hay, wheat, barley. We grew our own vegetables and fruit. We made our own bread, butter, even the jam. I really believed that's what life was all about.'

He took a deeper breath and Jennifer thought there was a shudder in it.

'Then one day,' his voice dropped to almost a whisper. 'I suppose I was not much older than you are now, I came into town with some of the lads. We went to the pictures. I can't remember what the film was called but for some reason it had a very peculiar effect on me. I must have been at a vulnerable stage in my life, an impressionable phase or something. Because it turned my whole world upside down.'

Father Stone flicked another bit of ash off his trousers.

'Anyway, the film was about some American teenagers. You know the type. Hair all combed back and wearing leather jackets and jeans. They were driving great big cars with a beautiful girl on the front seat. I'd never seen anyone like that before in my life - the way they spoke, the way they strutted around. They seemed to live in a different world from the one I was living in. And I was absolutely mesmerised by it all. Suddenly everything in my life seemed so dull, so empty and unexciting.'

He looked at Jennifer and she gave a hesitant smile.

'Suddenly I wanted to throw stones into everyone's pond.' He snapped his fingers. 'I just didn't care anymore. My life had changed. At least my *perception* of my life had changed. I was a different person now. And I wanted everyone to know it.'

Jennifer watched him with a deepening interest.

'Well, I couldn't afford the leather jacket, of course. Or the jeans either. But I greased up my hair and strutted around with my collar pulled up saying things like *cool, man!'*

Jennifer gave a loud laugh. '*Cool, man*?'

'Oh, yes! And worse than that. I started smoking. In class! Our school building was tiny. There was only the one room and the teacher, Mr Casey, was a real tyrant. He wouldn't tolerate any kind of indiscipline. We had to sit up straight with our hands on the desk in front of us. And we could only speak when we were spoken to. I used to admire that man. I respected him. Suddenly I hated him. And now I was having no more of it. I can't remember what I said exactly that day but it had something to do with shoving his homework where the sun didn't shine. And I strode as cool as you like to the front of the class, lit a fag, and walked out of the door.'

'Wicked.' Jennifer clapped her hands. 'What happened to you?'

'Sadly I mistook the looks I was getting from my neighbours as some kind of admiration. Hero worship, even. But, of course it was nothing of the sort. They just thought I was a right eejit. It was only because of the respect they had for my family that they tolerated me at all.'

Jennifer took another drag on the cigarette, unsure of how to respond.

'Of course,' Father Stone took a long drag on his cigarette too and he blew the smoke out through his nose. 'Like all clowns I surrounded myself with sorry people who laughed at my jokes and giggled at my antics. And I *really* believed I was something special.'

A chilly breeze blew around the corner and ruffled the leaves on the rose bushes. Jennifer shivered.

'Then one day it all went horribly wrong.' The priest's voice had a heavy despondency to it now. 'Every weekend there was dance at Galvin's place, the local dance hall. Well, it was more of a big shed really. But it was the highlight of our week. Everyone came from miles around, young and old alike.' He reflected for a moment. 'Anyway, there was this one couple in particular who went to all these events. Helen Crowley and Michael Lane. They were a lovely pair. Wonderful dancers too. And great fun. It seemed like they'd been together forever. Everyone loved them. They were so beautiful together, always at the centre of things. And always so full of life. Then I came along.'

He took another slow drag of the cigarette.

'That particular night a sort of devilment took hold of me and I made a point of dancing with Helen at every opportunity. That's how it was done in those days, you see. You butted in by giving the man a tap on the shoulder and saying *'excuse me'*. Courtesy demanded that the man stepped aside and let you dance with the lady. And I was in full swing, I can tell you. I flattered her, charmed her. I swept her right off of her feet. The thing is, Helen wasn't what you'd call sophisticated. Not by today's standards, anyway. All she'd ever known was the simple country way of life. The old, dependable Kerry way. Everything in her life was predictable, routine, safe, reliable. Now in me she was seeing something completely different. Something wild. Maybe even something dangerous.'

He took a long, last drag on the cigarette before flicking the butt onto the gravel where it erupt in a shower of sparks.

'Anyway,' he rubbed his eyes with his fingers, 'I persuaded her to come outside with me. Just for a bit of fresh air, you understand? And that's when Michael found us. In the hay.'

Jennifer stood up with a loud squeal. 'What? You dirty old ... I don't believe it! You weren't ...'

Father Stone nodded slowly, his mouth in a tight line. 'Well, to be really honest with you, that's exactly what I *wanted* to happen. It was all about the effect, you see? I mean, what was the point of seizing the ultimate prize if no one knew about it? I didn't want *Helen*. I just wanted the glory. I wanted the credit. I wanted the reaction.'

'Oh, my God!' Jennifer sat down again, her eyes

wide now and twinkling in a mixture of disbelief and fascination. And she also felt strangely uncomfortable, not sure if she really wanted to hear any more of this.

'Give us another fag, Father.' Her throat was tight and dry.

Father Stone took the packet from the wall beside him and handed it to her. When he passed her the matches she lit one and put the packet back on the wall.

'So, what happened then?' She decided she *was* interested after all.

'Well, the next day Michael was gone. His mother came over to our house, crying as if her heart was breaking. Michael had left a note saying that he was going to England and he was never coming back. The look in his mother's eyes when she saw me was pure hatred. He was the only child, you see. They were depending on him to carry on with the farm. They never thought it would be otherwise. She was so distressed, the poor woman. Almost grieving, in fact.'

Jennifer studied the old priest, waiting for him to go on. He glanced at her before taking a sharp breath.

'Then,' his voice faltered as if the memory was too sensitive and he swallowed hard. 'A couple of months later Helen turned up at our door demanding to see me. Well, you should have seen the cut of her. Her hair was a mess. Her face was dirty. And her clothes looked like she'd been sleeping in them for a week. I'm telling you, there was no way I could be seen with her looking like that! I had an image, you know! What would people *think*? So I told her to go away and have a good wash. Come back when she'd made an appointment.'

Suddenly the old eyes filled up and Father Stone gave a deep, heavy sigh.

'They found her body the next morning in the ditch at the bottom of Foley's meadow. She'd had a miscarriage. The woman who found her said it looked like she had just curled up into a ball and gone to sleep with the tiny bundle in her arms.'

Jennifer's eyes were wide and anxious now, and she chewed hard on her fingernail. 'God, that's awful. What did you do?'

'Well, I decided there and then that I would do my best to stop other young people from throwing rocks into people's ponds.' Father Stone touched his dog collar with his long, gnarled finger. 'And how better to do it than by becoming a priest?'

'What?' Jennifer gave a disbelieving smirk. 'Just like that?'

Father Stone's watery eyes held hers for a moment. Then he nodded. 'Oh, yes. Just like that.'

Jennifer spat out a bit of fingernail. 'I'm sorry, Father. I don't believe people can change just like that!'

Suddenly Father Stone shot out his hand and for a fleeting moment a butterfly touched on it. The magnificent colours of its wings cast a gentle hue on the pale fingers of the elderly priest. Then, in the blink of an eye, it fluttered away up into the bright blue sky.

'Then can you believe that - just a very short time ago - that beautiful butterfly was nothing more than an ugly little slug crawling all over your cabbage and eating everything in sight? But it *was*. It was earthbound, slow, obnoxious - and a total nuisance.'

They watched it fly away up past the rooftop.

'Then suddenly,' Father Stone snapped his fingers again. 'The magic of metamorphosis. And immediately it's free. As light as a feather. It shrugs off its earthbound skin and floats away. Beautiful. Serene. So pure, so delicate.'

He stood up and brushed the last bits of ash from the front of his tunic.

'We all have a choice, Jennifer.' He patted her lightly on her shoulder. 'We all know the difference, when the moment comes, between what is right and what is wrong. We can all change our ways if we really want to. Always remember that!'

Jennifer caught sight of the butterfly again as it fluttered erratically back down towards them. And as it hovered in front of the magnificent coloured window of the church she took a last drag of her cigarette and flicked it away. It landed in front of one of the headstones.

'Oops, sorry.' She jumped off the wall, tiptoed across the manicured grass and picked up the stub. And when she turned around Father Stone was gone.

'Father?'

She clattered up the steps to the side door and gave it a push. It was locked. She gave a giggle. The poor old sod had locked her out. Still, her mother should be home by now. She hoped.

Jennifer felt strangely at peace with herself as she sauntered home, glowing inwardly but not quiet knowing why. Her mind was full of Father Stone's story.

As she came bouncing out through the archway to the old marketplace she slammed into an elderly lady and sent her staggering backwards into the road.

'Oh, I'm sorry.' Jennifer ran to her and took her by the arm. 'Are you all right there?'

She went to brush the lady's coat but the lady pushed her away with an angry yelp.

'Don't you touch me, you hooligan. Tis bad enough you knocking me over like that without grabbing at me as well. The very cheek of you and you dressed up like a dog's dinner showing everything you've got for all the world to see. You should be ashamed of yourself, you tramp! Go home to your mother. A good slap is what you want. And if I was ten years younger that's what I'd be giving you right now, I can tell you, you little tart, with your face painted up like a ... like a clown. Go on! Get out of it!'

Jennifer was stunned. She staggered back and looked around to see who was watching her. And she groaned when she saw Liam and Paul standing across the street grinning all over their faces at the expectation of a fight.

Jennifer knew she was all red in the face and with the flood of embarrassment came her old attitude. And as it welled up inside her she rushed at the lady with a furious snarl.

'You stupid old cow! Why didn't you look where you were going in the first place? It's all your own stupid fault. And what are you doing out on your own anyway? They shouldn't allow eejits like you out alone ...'

Suddenly a breeze wafted through the arch behind them and as it brushed past Jennifer it seemed to whisper her name. She spun around, startled. There was no one there. All that moved was a pale white butterfly, dancing around a clump of dandelions near the bottom of the wall.

For a moment it was all Jennifer could see - a stark white butterfly! It filled her whole vision, a halo of shimmering light that sent a tingle right through her body. It took a moment to compose herself. She turned back to the old lady.

'Look, I'm very, very sorry.' She held out her hand. 'You are right. It *was* my fault. I wasn't looking where I was going.'

'Don't you ...' the lady slapped the hand away. 'Will you just bugger off and leave me alone.'

With that she scurried off up the street muttering loudly to herself. Jennifer closed her eyes again and let out another long exasperated groan.

'Father Stone,' she muttered under her breath. 'You and your bloody butterflies. Well, I'm not sure I believe you. But I'll give it a try. I'm not promising you anything, mind. But I give you my word. I *will* try.'

She sauntered across the road to Liam and Paul who were looking at her very strangely now.

'What's the matter with you two?'

They shook their heads in unison. 'Nothing,' Liam said. 'But your mammy is looking for you.'

'Well, *I'm* looking for *her*!'

Liam cringed. 'Well, if I was you I'd go straight home. Because she was looking *very* angry when we saw her. She says she can't believe you didn't go to the funeral.'

Jennifer hesitated. '*What* funeral?'

'For that auld priest.' Liam pointed back at the church. 'You know, the drunk fella. Father Brick.'

'Not *Brick*, you eejit.' Paul gave him a push. 'His name was *Stone*. Father Stone.'

'Stoned, more like,' Liam sniggered, and they sauntered off down the street.

Dreamin' Dreams

Can't Take You Home Again, Kathleen

A weak February sun glistened on the patches of frost that still lingered on the pavement as the blue Mini Cooper turned into Rodney Lane and pulled up outside number six.

A young woman got out and glanced up and down the street, two rows of red-brick houses staring at each other across a narrow road. She knocked once on the flaking green door and went straight in.

'Dad?' Her voice echoed in the bare hall. 'Tis me, Rose.'

Jack Cassidy was sitting at the table in the kitchen wearing his flat cap and his overcoat. He looked up and smiled.

'Ah, there you are.' Rose gave him a cheerfully pat on the arm. 'Now I've put all your bags and stuff in your new room. So have you got everything else you want to take with you?'

Jack Cassidy nodded but said nothing. Rose understood. You can't live in the same house for forty years and not feel something when you leave. She watched the old face crease as the sad eyes looked around the room for the last time. He gave a soft sigh.

'Come on, Dad.' She put her arm around his shoulder. 'I know how you're feeling. But you have to agree, you've been here on your own for far too long. Tis seven years since Mammy died and tis a cold auld place. Shur you deserve better than this at your age.'

The elderly gentleman bowed his head and for a second Rose thought his eyes grew wet.

'But this new place you're going to – well, tis really, really nice.' She knew she was rambling as she struggled to inject some enthusiasm into her voice. 'All the people I met so far are wonderful. And they've got a lovely community hall where you can all meet up for a chat or to play cards - or whatever. There's so many things to do. Lots of people for you to meet. You're going to love it there, I promise you. And best of all, you'll have your own flat with its own front door. So if you *don't* feel like socialising sometimes, then you don't have to.'

Jack Cassidy sniffed and rubbed his nose with the back of his hand. But again he didn't reply. Rose gave him another pat on the shoulder. 'Anyway, I think we should be on our way.'

Jack Cassidy straightened his cap and shuffled slowly to his feet, making the chair scrape on the wooden floor as he pushed it back with his legs. And as he picked up the last few bits and put them in the small cardboard box on the table, a photograph dropped out of it and fluttered to the floor.

Rose bent down and picked it up.

'Well, well.' She studied the faded black and white picture of a pretty young woman standing by a river. Her jacket was slung over her shoulder and her face alive with a beautiful smile. 'And who's this, then?'

'Oh, that's just someone I used to know.' Jack Cassidy took the photograph from her. And as he slipped it into his coat pocket Rose caught a fleeting sparkle in his eyes.

'So who is she?'

'She's ... she was a friend. Just a friend. Someone I knew a long time ago.'

'And where is she now?'

Jack Cassidy picked up the box and moved towards the door. 'It was a long time ago. And as you said, we should be going now. People are waiting for us.'

'I bet Mammy didn't know about her,' Rose muttered as she brushed past him.

As Rose walked on ahead, Jack Cassidy took the photo from his pocket and gave it one quick look before putting it carefully back in the box. Then he followed Rose out and pulled the front door shut behind him.

As Rose drove out of Rodney Lane for the very last time she felt a heavy knot of anxiety in the pit of her stomach. Her father sat quietly in the front seat. She braced herself, anticipating a rush of emotion from him. An outpouring of the sadness he must surely be feeling as a major part of his life closed behind him.

But when she took a quick glance at him, his face showed no emotion at all. In fact he seemed quiet relaxed. There was even the hint of a smile on his lips.

Rose was sad and relieved at the same time. It looked like his mind had wandered again. Perhaps it was just as well. It saved him from the trauma of moving house. Hopefully by the time he came back to reality he'd be settled into his nice new home.

Of course she couldn't know why Jack Cassidy was *really* smiling. Yes, his mind had wandered. But it had wandered all the way back to the bright carefree days of his youth. And the beautiful girl in the photograph.

Seeing the photo again had opened a gap in the fog that cluttered his mind these days. It was as if someone had pulled back the curtains in a dusty old library and let a dazzling splash of sunlight burst through the haze. A beautiful clarity came with it. He was savouring the memory of Kathleen Griffin.

The mist of time had blurred the finer details and he couldn't remember very much about how she'd come into his life. He knew she worked in the little stationary shop in the town square. He was a budding artist at the time, getting by on some small commissions. He bought his easels and paints there.

And he was smitten by her cheerful, warm smile and gentle sense of humour - he *did* remember that - and he found any old excuse to call into the shop whenever he was in town.

There were four girls working in that shop but she was the one who always served him. And it made him feel pleasantly warm inside. Not that there was anything in it, of course. He was older, for a start. She could only have been seventeen and he was twenty-four. But the way her intense dark eyes smiled back at him made him feel special.

Then one warm sunny afternoon he met her in the street. Her mop of golden hair bounced as she walked towards him and her yellow cotton dress lit up her face. His heart gave a strange flutter.

He stepped out in front of her.

'Hello there.'

For a moment she was startled and her hand went to her mouth.

'Oh! Ah … hello there yourself. You're after giving me an awful fright.'

'I'm sorry.' Jack flashed what he hoped was a penitent smile. 'It's just that I'm actually on my way to your shop.'

'But we're just after closing. It *is* half past five, you know?'

'Is it?' Jack took a watch from his pocket. 'Well, so it is. Now isn't that a pity. Ah well, I'll just have to wait till tomorrow so.'

'You will.' Her eyes twinkled and she smiled back at him.

A bus came down the street and stopped outside the Post Office and the little group of people waiting in the shop doorway started shuffling towards it.

'I … this is my bus.'

'Oh?' Jack looked around at the queue. 'Listen, I was just wondering, where do you go for lunch? I mean, do you have a lunch hour?'

'Oh, I do. I have lunch from one o'clock until two.'

'And where do you go, usually?'

'Well, I don't go anywhere usually. I bring a snack with me. A sandwich or something. We have tea in the shop. We have a little room at the back. It's very cosy in there.'

'Then how would you like to have lunch with me? Tomorrow, say.'

'Tomorrow?' she repeated. 'Well, I … where?'

'Anywhere you like.' He looked up and down the street then nodded towards the tiny café in the corner of the square. 'What about that little place over there?'

She hesitated. She wasn't sure. This was so unexpected. A part of her said no, what would people say? What would the girls at the shop think? She didn't even know him that well. He was practically a stranger.

Yet something inside her tingled with excitement.

'All right, so.'

The last person was boarding the bus and she moved towards the platform.

'That's great.' Jack beamed. 'I'll call for you at the shop - one o'clock sharp.'

She waved as the bus pulled away.

'My name is Jack, by the way,' he shouted after her.

'I know,' she answered. 'And I'm Kathleen.'

The next day, just as the clock chimed one, Mr Broderick beamed from behind the counter as Jack strolled in.

'Good day to you, Mr Cassidy. And how are you today?'

'I'm grand.' Jack nodded a greeting. 'Grand altogether, thank you very much.'

He walked straight across to Kathleen.

'Are you ready?'

Everyone turned to look and she blushed.

'I am.' She let him take her by the arm.

'Don't worry there, Mr Broderick,' Jack chirped as he walked her to the door. 'I'll bring her back in good time.'

It took a second for Mr Broderick to respond.

'Oh, right you are, Mr Cassidy.' He rushed to open the door for them, and he looked Kathleen up and down.

'Two o'clock, Miss Griffin,' he said.

'Two o'clock, Mr Broderick,' she answered.

Although the exact sequence of events was a bit confused now, Jack could still remember the day he took Kathleen home to meet his mother. She welcomed Kathleen with a tray of tea on the lawn and sat beside her on the garden bench.

'My son has spoken a great deal about you, my dear,' Mrs Cassidy said as the pleasant afternoon drew to a close. 'He seems quiet taken with you. And I can understand why. I must say you're far prettier than I expected. Far prettier, indeed. Such beautiful dark eyes. And you have such a becoming manner, too.'

Kathleen blushed and stifled a cough with the back of her hand.

'Now I hope you won't mind me saying this,' Mrs Cassidy continued. 'And I hope you don't think I'm being too blunt. But I'd go as far as to say I think my son is in love with you.'

'Mother ...' Jack spluttered and splashed tea down his shirt.

'Yes, my dear.' Mrs Cassidy reached out and touched Kathleen's hand. 'But the question is; how do you feel about him?'

'Ah, Mother!' Jack had the strangest flutter in his stomach. A surge of dread at what the answer was going to be? 'Can't you see you're embarrassing her? How can you ask her something like that?'

But he needn't have worried. He would never forget the look on Kathleen's face as her eyes met his. 'If you really want the truth,' she took the old lady's hands in hers and squeezed them. 'I love your son very much indeed.'

When they married a year later most of the guests were from Jack's side because Kathleen only had a stepmother and an uncle. And her friends from the shop. But it didn't matter. Everyone who came to the service in the tiny chapel fell in love with the beautiful bride in the flowing white dress.

Later, at the reception, Jack's mother announced where the lucky couple were going for their honeymoon. It had been a closely guarded secret, a gift from the family. She beamed as she handed them an envelope with two airline tickets.

They were going to France.

Jack's uncle Colm worked at the Irish Embassy in Paris. He had a cottage in the country near the town of Rouen on the River Seine. He knew Jack had a passion for France. It had always been his dream to go there one day. Now he could.

Colm spent most of his time in his apartment in town so they'd have the cottage all to themselves for two whole weeks.

'I can hardly believe it,' Jack said when Kathleen managed to get him alone in the garden. 'I've married the most beautiful girl in the world. And now I'm going to France for my honeymoon. I just can't believe it. Mother said it would be a surprise, but I never expected this. Two weeks in France! Isn't it fantastic? Aren't you excited?'

'Oh, Jack, of course I'm excited.' Kathleen moved away from him, afraid she wouldn't be able to hide her apprehension. Because this was the summer of 1940 and there was a dark and menacing cloud hovering over Europe. 'Who wouldn't be? I'm excited for you more than anything. You've got this wonderful opportunity to live your dream. It's just that ... well, you have to think about what's happening over there right now. All we hear on the news lately is what the Germans are getting up to.'

'But that's not happening in France, sweetheart.' Jack laughed as he swept her into his huge arms. 'Going to France will be as safe as going to Dublin. The Germans won't be anywhere near us. The Maginot Line is right there between Germany and France. It'll be impossible for the Germans to get through that, I can tell you. Then there's the French Army. And the British have a huge Expeditionary Force there as well. We know Hitler is mad but I don't think he's stupid. He'll leave the French well alone, I promise you. We'll be as safe as the little church mice in Limerick Cathedral.'

Dreamin' Dreams

Kathleen leant her head against his chest and closed her eyes. She was struggling to suppress the dread that still lurked in the pit of her stomach. But the thought of a holiday in France excited Jack so much it was contagious. And as she listened to the rhythm of his heart she knew she'd been infected too. Anyway, right then she would have followed him to the ends of the earth.

Uncle Colm's cottage was incredibly beautiful, very old and very cosy. Low-beamed ceilings and narrow corridors lead to rooms that had little windows in them. They let you look out over amazing countryside that rolled away into a hazy line where the sky met the mountains.

A gentle breeze fanned the warm air as Jack dashed from room to room. Out the back door and in the front door, exploring all the nooks and crannies. Inspecting things that interested him, picking them up and putting them down again as he spotted something else. Kathleen trotted along behind him, loving every minute of it. She was so happy for him.

They spent the whole of the first week just wandering around the local countryside, exploring the woods and sauntering over the fields. They strolled in the long warm evenings and watched the sun go down from the bank of the river.

It was a long and glorious week. And after all this time Jack's heart still fluttered just thinking about the rare and beautiful feeling he got when he reached out to touch her hand.

It was hard to describe happiness like that. The unbelievable pleasure he got from just sitting in a meadow with neither of them speaking, comfortable in the warmth of each other's company.

Or sitting on a rug in front of the fire having supper, quietly watching the light from the flames dance in her eyes and highlight her hair as it fell gently onto her shoulders.

It still made him breathless.

The second Sunday morning was slightly cooler. A persistent haze filtered the sun and kept the temperature down. It was expected it to disperse in the early afternoon. Until then they were just going to laze about and enjoy the sounds of the countryside, birds singing, bees humming as they flitted in sporadic hoops around the flowers.

They were sitting in the kitchen drinking coffee and flicking through some glossy magazines when Colm's limousine roared into the yard in a cloud of dust and slid to a halt right outside the door.

'Oh my God, you're not still here?' His voice shook as he leapt out of the car and ran into the kitchen.

They both jumped up and watched him in amazement as he scurried past them and disappeared down the hall.

'Uncle Colm?' Jack shouted after him. 'What's the matter?'

Moments later Colm came back dragging a suitcase.

'Haven't you heard?' He was sweating heavily now. 'I thought you'd have heard. I was hoping you'd be gone home already.'

'Heard what?' Jack yelped in exasperation. 'What the hell's going on?'

'I'm so, so sorry.' Colm dumped a bundle of papers into a battered old briefcase and snapped it shut. 'I tried to get here sooner but everything's in chaos. It seems the Germans have broken through the lines and they're headed this way.'

'Oh dear God!' Kathleen ran to Jack.

'Surely you can't be serious.' Jack gave a nervous laugh. 'How the hell could the Germans break through the Maginot Line? How could they possibly ... what about the British? What about the ...'

'Do I look like I'm bloody joking?' Colm flapped his hands and spun around in little circles. 'No one broke through the Maginot Line. They came around it, didn't they! They came down through Belgium and Holland and they caught everyone on the hop.'

A thump of fear hit Jack in the chest and he wrapped his arms around Kathleen. 'So what are we going to do?'

'Just get some things together and I'll take you to the railway station.' Colm waved in the general direction of the bedroom. 'I think I have enough petrol to get us that far. We'll catch the first train to the coast and then get a boat to England.'

'But will there be a train today?'

'I don't know. The Embassy said all the trains were still running normally. And the boats, too. But that was a few hours ago.'

'Oh, Jack!' Kathleen seemed to sag in his arms.

'Hey!' Jack held her tightly and kissed her on the forehead. 'Everything's going to be all right. You'll see. We'll go with Uncle Colm now and everything will be just fine.'

The tiny railway station was cold and strangely quiet. Kathleen sat on Colm's suitcase and leant back against Jack. He wrapped his arms around her to shield her from the breeze that swept the dust in little clouds around their feet.

Scattered knots of people were spread out along the

platform and when they spoke it was in nervous whispers.

The hours dragged by but no train came. The Station Master didn't know what was happening. Every half hour he'd come out of his office and pace up and down the platform trying to look official. Then he'd disappear back inside again.

By mid-afternoon the tension was starting to build so coffee was provided in the waiting room. Sandwiches were brought out too but nobody felt much like eating.

Then as the sky faded from sharp blue to soft indigo to a dark bruise the temperature dropped with it. More and more people tried to squeeze into the small waiting room. There was nowhere to sit and they became agitated and restless.

Every noise made them turn around, hope in their eyes that it might be a train. When they realised it wasn't their mouths drew into tight lines and they give long hopeless sighs.

Uncle Colm made numerous attempts to contact Paris from the public phone by the main door. But the line was always busy and when he came back he was more subdued.

'What's happening, do you think?' Jack was talking to no one in particular.

'I wish to God I could get some petrol.' Colm rubbed his weary eyes. 'Just enough to get us to the coast. I used all mine coming back from Paris. I asked that miserable sod of a Station Master if there was anywhere in town but he just looked at me like I had two heads. He said if the French people couldn't have any, why should foreigners! The Military need it more than us, he said. And there's precious little of it anyway. So that's that.'

'How much longer do you think we should wait here?' Kathleen glanced up at Jack

Colm shrugged and looked around at the dark platform. 'I just don't know. If only there was a way I could get in touch with our people in Paris, maybe they could ...'

An almighty thud sent a wave of noise through the tiny railway station. A split second later it was lit up by a sharp white flash. The silence that followed was intense, but it only lasted a moment before a woman screamed and broke the spell.

Kathleen jumped up and grabbed Jack's coat.

The next explosion shook the walls with a violence that threw out the windows in tiny fragments of flying, blinding glass. This time everyone leapt to their feet and ran, clutching frantically at each other and stumbling over themselves as they pulled their children out of the way. Faces were twisted by blind terror, mouths open in frantic screams as they lashed out blindly towards the narrow exits.

'For God's sake, stay together!' Colm yelled as Jack grabbed Kathleen. They let themselves be dragged along by the wild rush of people, squeezing out through the exit and into the street now flickering with the flames that poured out of shattered buildings.

They turned in different directions, unsure of where to run.

'Over there, quick!' Jack roared. 'There's a church.'

They crouched low as they ran across the square and in through the huge oak doors. Others poured in behind them until the church was as crammed as the railway station waiting room. Men wrapped their arms around their wives as the children held on tightly to their legs. A sea of ghostly faces moved their lips in prayer as they huddled against the walls.

The lights hanging from the roof cast weird shadows as they danced with each explosion, muffled by the thick walls but still near and still terrifying.

Jack managed to squeeze Kathleen into a corner and he held her tight and pressed his face against the top of her head.

Then just as suddenly as the explosions began, they stopped. An eerie silence fell over the town. Slowly the people in the church began to move around again, speaking in hesitant whispers.

Kathleen's hand felt for Jack's and she squeezed it tightly as she looked up at him. Her eyes were wet.

'Tis all right, now,' he told her. 'We're going to be all right.'

'But who's doing this, Uncle Colm? Who's bombing us?'

'It looks like the Germans got here sooner than expected,' Colm replied.

'But why are they *bombing* us?'

'I've no idea, Kathleen, love. I don't think there's anything important in this little town. They must be after making a mistake or something.'

'Jack, I'm so frightened.' Kathleen was trembling. 'We've had such a short time together. Such a very short time - and now we're going to die.'

'No!' Jack held her tighter. 'Don't talk like that. We're going to be all right. See, they've stopped bombing us. So we'll be all right now, I promise.'

She looked up and kissed him on the mouth and the tears flowed down her face.

'I'm sorry,' she whispered. 'I know you think I'm

being silly but I can't bear the thought of losing you now. Not now. Not so soon. I love you so much, Jack. If anything happened to you I wouldn't want to go on living.' She kissed him again. 'So if we're going to die, I want us to die together. Like this. Holding each other. In each other's arms.'

Jack frowned and went to say something but the words stuck in this throat and he swallowed them down.

The building next door erupted and a cloud of shattered stone burst through the huge plate glass window of the church with a lethal fury.

Kathleen was screaming as Jack threw her to the floor and pulled his coat over the two of them. Her hands grabbed at him and she buried her face in his arms.

'Jack, don't leave me. Please don't leave me. Promise me, Jack.'

'Kathleen, sweetheart, of course I won't leave you. I would *never* leave you. You know that.'

'*Promise me!*'

'I promise you.'

'For God's sake.' Colm scrambled to his feet. 'We can't stay here. We're going to get slaughtered. The next chance I get I'm going out to get the car. That little bit of petrol I've got should get us out of the town at least. Out of the range of those guns.'

'You can't go out there, you lunatic!' Jack grabbed his sleeve. 'It'll be suicide. You have to stay in here. At least we have a chance in here.'

'What chance? It'll be suicide to stay in here, you mean,' Colm pulled away from him. 'We're like sitting ducks.'

Another pause in the bombing and this time the silence lasted longer. Colm scurried across the floor to the huge door and prised it open. A thin shaft of light drew a zigzag on his face.

He looked back at Jack. 'Are you coming with me?'

'No!' Kathleen held onto his arm.

'Look, we have to go now,' Colm insisted. 'We might not get another chance.'

'Jack, don't go!'

'Jack, it'll only take me a minute to get to the car! It isn't that far away. I'll run out and get it. Then I'll come back here for the two of you.'

He stood up and pulled the door open wider. 'You'd better keep a look out for me now.' He slapped his hand against the door in emphasis. 'I might not be able to hang about.'

With that he slipped out into the darkness and the door clanged shut behind him.

The minutes crawled by with an agonizing slowness, wrapped tightly in a tense silence that buzzed in their ears. Then out in the street a horn tooted. Jack ran to the door and peered out.

'Thank God.' He reached back for Kathleen's hand. 'It's Uncle Colm. He's back with the car, come on.'

'Jack …'

'Come on!' He pulled her after him. 'We have to go now.'

They stepped over the rubble and out into the street that was suddenly cold after the stuffiness of the church. The car roared impatiently as they picked their way across the road towards it.

They were less than a yard from the car when the night came alive again, shrilling with blinding, violent flashes. Explosions stomped down the street towards them like enormous footsteps, bursting open everything in their path.

Kathleen gave a terrified yelp and slide to a halt. Her hand jerked out of Jack's so abruptly it spun him around. He staggered, lost his balance and fell backwards into the road.

As he struggled to his feet everything became veiled in a surreal slowness. Every action was tangled up in a web of sluggish movement as if he was wading through the thickness of a horrible dream. He could see Kathleen spinning away from him. Her arms were wide open in terror as she made a frantic grab for the safety of the church. He tried to reach out and catch her but his whole body was weighed down by a dreadful fear.

Then Kathleen seemed to speed up as if she'd suddenly been released from the weird suspension. She was running back towards the open door.

'Kathleen!' It came out as a pathetic croak.

With all the strength Jack could muster he forced himself back onto his feet and threw himself after her. His legs were like lead and unbelievably weak.

The next explosion came from inside the church itself and it was enormous. An avalanche of shattered stone, glass and lethal shards of wood came spewing out. It blew Jack back across the road and hurled him against a wall. And into the blackness of unconsciousness.

He couldn't have been knocked out for long, though. Because Colm's voice was screaming at him to get up. He groaned and shook the rubble from his hair as he tried to roll on to his knees. Then he screamed in agony from the pain that made his leg buckle under him.

Wriggling onto his back he grabbed at his leg. And he howled again. The shaft that was poking through the cloth was a sliver of bone.

Bombs were still falling farther down the street but he could no longer hear them. His mind was numbed by the appalling pain.

'Jack! For God's sake, come on!'

Jack forced himself up onto his good leg, biting through the sleeve of his coat to stop himself from screaming again. He hobbled across the road and started clawing at the red hot blocks of stone, looking for any sign of Kathleen.

But each stone he pulled away only exposed another twisted mass of rubble underneath. His sobs were loud and angry as he tore at them, throwing them away in frustration.

The bombs had stopped again, amplifying the roar of the flames that were leaping all around him.

'Jack, it's too late, son.' Colm's voice was yelling at him from somewhere in the blackness. 'We have to go. Get in the car now!'

Shadows were flicking through the smoke at the end of the street. Now they were spitting darts of yellow that tore grooves in the ground around Jack's feet.

Soldiers! German soldiers!

Jack fell back away from them and turned towards the car. But he hesitated and looked back at the church.

A bullet hit the wall beside his head and spattered him with tiny fragments of stone.

'Jack! For heaven's sake ...'

The car was revving furiously and starting to move away.

Kathleen's voice in Jack's head had the clarity of a chapel bell on a clear summer's day - *Don't leave me, Jack! Promise me ...'*

And he *had* promised her - just a few short minutes

ago. He said he'd never leave her. *Didn't he*? Dear God, were they just empty words? Was his promise so meaningless? Just something he'd said to keep her quiet?

'Kathleen,' he heard himself crying. 'I'm sorry. I'm so sorry!'

And with a ferocious burst of strength he was up and over the rubble, dragging his shattered leg behind him.

Colm ran to him and bundled him into the car. Then they roared away into the safety of the night.

The ship moved with a steady roll that made the beams creak and groan, and all the passengers swayed in rhythm with it.

People were crammed into every available space. Some were stretched out on the floor with their battered suitcases under their heads and their bags full of whatever they could carry held tightly beside them. Others sat shoulder to shoulder on the stairways and along the gangways. The air was a heavy fog of cigarette smoke and the reek of beer that splashed all over the floor as men tried to pick their way through the chaos and back to their places.

Colm and Jack propped themselves against the rough bulkhead near the toilets. Tired and dirty and very, very uncomfortable, they let their heads flop back against the hard metal and tried to get some sleep.

But sleep didn't come easy for Jack. The pain from his leg was intense in spite of the medication he'd been given by the ship's doctor. They'd put his leg in a splint and cleaned the wound. But he was just one more in a long line of casualties desperately seeking attention. There wasn't time for sympathy - they gave him painkillers and send him on his way.

Dreamin' Dreams

Now the combination of fatigue and medication numbed his mind. But it didn't ease the chaos that raged in his heart. His emotions flitted from pain to anger, from bitterness to self-pity, from fear to the naked shame of running away and leaving Kathleen behind.

He struggled to untangle the events of the day but couldn't focus on any one of them. He remembered being in a car racing down narrow roads to the railway station. Then complete madness. Screeching bombs and numbing fear. Unbelievable pain. Shadows drowning his mind as he fought to stay conscious. The car skidding away from the blazing church, bouncing over pavements and across rough grass to avoid the main roads. The splashes of mottled lights flicking on the windscreen as it rocked and wobbled through the maze of damaged streets. High stone walls crashing down around then. And lots of noise.

When Jack's shattered leg knocked against something hard it caused an explosion of pain that lifted him out of the seat and into a dark hole of semi-consciousness where he stayed for the rest of the journey.

He vaguely recalled being hauled out of the car and dragged up some steps onto a train. Then much later being maneuverer up the gangway of a ship. And the constant pain!

He was flipped onto a table and strong hands pinned him down while a medic wrapped a bandage around a splint on his leg. A handful of tablets shoved into his mouth, a gulp of water from a tin mug washing them down. Then being lifted off the table and dismissed.

Now after sitting on the hard floor for so long, numbness had spread across the lower half of his back and he desperately needed to change position. Very slowly and carefully he eased himself up. As he took a cautious peek at his watch he became aware of someone hovering over him. He looked up sharply.

The young woman looking back at him was holding a cigarette to her mouth.

'Mr Daly?' Her accent was French and her voice was soft, almost a whispered. She bent down and took a closer look. 'Is that Mr Daly? Colm Daly?'

Colm opened his eyes with a start. It took a few second to focus then recognition lit up his face and he scrambled to his feet.

'Chantelle? Good God! What in Heaven's name are you doing here?' He held her hand in both of his. 'I mean, what are you doing here on this ship? Is your father with you?'

She stepped back and for a moment she seemed lost for words. Her eyes glistened with the hint of tears and she wiped them quickly with the back of her hand.

'Papa is missing. Our house blew up. I had only just gone out of the door. It was terrible. I didn't know what to do so I just ran. I ran all the way to the Embassy, and they helped me to get a lift to the coast. So now I …'

Colm squeezed her hand tighter. 'Dear God. I'm so sorry. I can't believe ... your father?'

He took off his coat and folded it on the floor, and he helped her to sit down on it.

'Jack, may I introduce Chantelle? She's my secretary at the Embassy. Chantelle, this is my nephew, Jack.'

'Hello.' Jack held out his hand and she took it lightly. 'I'm sorry about your father.'

'Thank you.' She brushed some loose hair from her face.

Colm took out a lighter, stretched across and flicked

it. Chantelle looked at the cigarette and put it in her mouth. Then she took the smoke in deep, closed her eyes then let it out again in a long thin stream.

Jack's leg was pulsing badly now and he forced himself to speak to distract himself from the pain.

'So where are you heading, Chantelle?'

Chantelle looked away and took another drag on the cigarette as if she had to consider her answer carefully.

'I ... ah ... I will go to London,' she said eventually, picking a bit of tobacco from her lip.

'London?'

'Yes, London.' This time she sounded more positive. 'I have a friend in London.'

'What part?' Jack waved the smoke away. 'London's a big place.'

'I know that. I have an address. In here.' She patted the pocket of her coat. 'So I will be all right. But what about you? You have been hurt. Will you be going to hospital?'

'Well, that's where he *should* go,' Colm answered for him. 'He *has* been hurt. Very badly, in fact. And I don't mean just his leg.'

Chantelle frowned as she tried to understand what Colm meant. She went to speak again but Jack turned away and closed his eyes.

The boat docked in the early hours of the morning in a harbour that was bathed in a bleak, cold mist and the passengers shuffled off in an impatient wave. Jack had difficulty walking with the crutches they'd given him and Chantelle was separated from them in the throng that was channelled down the narrow gangway by the tired, irritated crew.

As they shuffled through Immigration in a line that

moved as slow as a snail, Jack had to sit down on whatever he could find. It seemed like hours before they eventually emerged into the feeble daylight that was struggling to break through the low blanket of cloud.

Jack pulled his collar tighter around his neck and headed for the row of taxis strung out along the side of the dock.

'Your man at the desk said if we catch the nine-forty from Paddington we'll be in Bristol in time to catch the connection to Fishguard,' Colm was saying as he trailed along behind, shifting his suitcase from one hand to the other. 'We should be in time for the three o'clock sailing to Rosslare and be home sometime tomorrow afternoon.'

As they passed through the main gate Jack spotted Chantelle standing by the wall on the other side of the street. She looked lost. But he turned away. He was too exhausted to care. He was in too much pain. He just wanted to get in a taxi and sit down.

But his conscience wouldn't let him just walk on by. He tapped Colm on the shoulder and nodded across at her.

'Chantelle!' Colm rushed across the street and when she saw him her eyes smiled with relief. 'Why are you standing out here in the rain? Are you waiting for someone?'

Her shoulders gave a small shrug. She seemed reluctant to answer.

'Look,' Colm steered her towards the taxis. 'We're going to Paddington. Can we give you a lift somewhere?'

'What do you mean?' She looked startled and pulled away from him.

Colm frowned. 'You *did* say you were going to

London. Didn't you?'

'I … no, I said … I have friends …'

'Forgive me,' Colm said softly, resting his hand on her shoulder. 'But you don't seem very sure.'

Suddenly her eyes were wet and she bowed her head.

'What's wrong, Chantelle?'

'I have lied to you.' It came out as a sob. 'I have no friends in London. I have no address in London.'

'Oh dear!'

'In fact I don't know a single person in the whole of England.' She spat the words out in an edgy display of bitterness. 'France is all I know. My mother is dead a long time. And now my father too, probably. So I have no one. You know that, Mr Daly. You know all I had was my father. You knew that when I worked for you.'

'Hey, hey, hey!' Colm opened his arms and let her sag into them. ''Tis all right, now. Everything is all right.'

A car tooted behind them and they moved out of the way.

Colm sat her on a low wall and handed her his handkerchief. 'I'm so sorry. I didn't mean to upset you like this. It's just that I was worried.…'

'You should not worry about me, Mr Daly. I have some money. I will be all right. I will find some place.'

Colm ran his fingers through his hair. 'Are you sure?'

She nodded again and tried to smile but more tears came. The sobs were muffled by the handkerchief she'd pressed against her mouth. She tried to suck them back but they were too strong so she let them come.

Colm could only stand and watch as her shoulders trembled. He looked across at Jack and shrugged.

Eventually Chantelle took a deep breath, looked up

and dabbed her eyes with the handkerchief. 'I'm sorry, Mr Daly. I am not usually like this. You know I do not often cry like a child. But I am so frightened - standing here in this cold wet place. I am all alone now. No one left for me. No one.'

Colm looked across at Jack again and frowned. And Jack knew what he was thinking. When Jack gave a resigned shrug, Colm nodded thank you, took Chantelle by the hand and lifted her to her feet.

'Then there's only one thing for it. You'll have to come to Ireland with us. You can stay at Jack's house. My sister won't mind, not for a few days, anyway.'

Chantelle's stepped back and her hand went to her mouth again. 'Do you mean it? I … but I can't ... it would not be fair on you.'

'You don't have a choice,' Colm insisted. 'You can stay with us until we sort something out. We'll go to the Embassy in Dublin and see what they can do for you. After all, you're still employed by the Irish Foreign Office. Technically, that is.'

Jack's mother took the news about Kathleen very badly. When the taxi brought them home Colm had to sit her down in the kitchen and break it to her as gently as he could.

And she cried as if Kathleen had been her own child.

About Chantelle, though, she made no comment. But the look in her eyes said there was something vaguely indecent about it all. Kathleen was dead somewhere in France and already there was another girl in the house. It wasn't right!

But she said nothing. She showed Chantelle to the spare bedroom, just for a few days.

Jack moved back into his own room. But now

everything was so different. A cold and painful emptiness inhabited the space. Every corner and nook had a haunting sadness about it.

Colm drove him to the local hospital the next day to have his damaged leg re-set and put in a proper cast. And the cold clinical young doctor told him in a cold clinical manner that he'd probably have a limp for the rest of his life.

But in Jack's fragile mind that was unbelievably trivial. In fact it was so far down his list of problems it was almost invisible and he dismissed it out of hand.

Desperate to stop him from sliding any deeper into the pool of despondency he was already thrashing around in, his mother bought him some new oils, canvases, brushes. Anything to encourage him to take up painting again. Help ease the journey back to some sort of normal life.

It took time, on course. But gradually he started to wander back to the old familiar places Kathleen was fond of. As his confidence grew he took his knapsack with him. Finding a patch of safe ground he'd prop up his easel, spread out his paints and make a brave attempt at recapturing a moment from another time. Tender strokes in familiar colours were applied to the blank square of canvas. Green and grey for the Brandon Mountains as seen from the strand at Derrimore. Plain white for the windmill standing on the edge of Blennerville.

It helped to ease the pain of the day.

But not the pain of the night.

When the darkness closed in on him the nightmares came with it. He'd sit in the armchair in his bedroom with his eyes squeezed tight and a pillow over his ears, as if that was a magic buffer to block out the torment.

It never worked. The terrors still came. Little wisps of dark, brooding misery slithered in through every little gap in his defences and straight into his tortured mind. The pleading, terrified look in Kathleen's eyes as she begged him to stay with her. The scream of the bombs. The shattering, blinding flash of light. The horrific, final thud that took her from him in the blink of an eye.

Dear God, why hadn't he stayed with her? At least they'd be together now.

But he'd run away. Torrents of remorse flooded his mind night after night to constantly remind him. They smothering his senses in a fog of frustration and he ached with rage and prayed for the morning to come.

Colm went back to work in the Embassy in Dublin a few days later. He promising to get in touch as soon as he could arrange something for Chantelle. And Chantelle's visit stretched from a few days to a week, and then to a month.

Jack didn't mind. Despite her fragile grip on the English language, he found her easy to talk to. And he needed to talk.

As the nights drew in and the air turned cold she'd fold herself into the corner of the sofa and let him purge his demons. The flames of the log fire flickered in her bright blue eyes as she listened to him without comment or criticism.

She responded to his ramblings about his brief time with Kathleen with a rare and tender understanding.

And it was certainly doing him good. Chantelle succeeded in stalling the ugly bouts of depression that would otherwise have consumed him. With sympathy and tolerance she eventually enabled him to defeat the nightmares that waited for him every time the sun went down.

After a while she joined him on his long walks, even when the wind threw sporadic sheets of rain at them across the open fields. And when they got back to the house Jack's mother made tea and they sat around the large kitchen table.

As time went on a lighter mood began to creep back into their lives.

One day Jack came home from town and found Chantelle sitting alone in the garden. And he sensed something edgy in her manner. She seemed unusually tense. He sat on the bench beside her.

The smile she gave him was forced and she looked down at her hands.

'What's wrong?' He took a deep anxious breath.

She glanced up at him but didn't look in his eyes.

'I have received a letter.' She showed him the envelope.

'Oh?' was all he could say. A heavy knot fluttered in his stomach.

'It is from your Uncle Colm.'

'Uncle Colm? How is he?'

'He has a job for me.' Her eyes searched his face for a reaction.

'Oh. But that's great news. What kind of job?'

'It is with the Foreign Office.' Chantelle flicked the envelope with her thumb. 'I will be a translator.'

'Excellent. You'll be great at it, I'm sure.'

'I will.' There was the hint of a smile. 'But the bad news is I will have to go to Dublin. Colm has already arranged accommodation for me there. An apartment goes with the job'

'I see.' Jack choked back a sigh and tried a smile instead. 'And when do you have to start?'

'Monday.' She folded the envelope and put it in her pocket. 'Colm will meet me at the railway station on Sunday afternoon and take me to the apartment. Then he will show me around, explain what I will be doing.'

'As soon as that?'

'I am sorry.' She gave a resigned shrug and took his hand in hers. 'Colm said they need me to start immediately. With the situation in Europe they need someone with my experience.'

Jack closed his eyes and rested his head against her shoulder. He couldn't ignore the heavy lump in his heart. But he took a deep breath and shook himself out of the surge of disappointment. He looked up at her with a playful smile.

'You know something,' he teased. 'I think I might miss you.'

'You *might* miss me?' She pushed him away as she tried to read his expression. When she realised he was playing she slapped him on the leg. 'You had *better* miss me,' she laughed.

Later that night after Jack's mother went to bed they sat together on the sofa in the warm glow of the log fire. Rain pattered against the window behind them - light fingers tapping a beat on the glass. Jack watched Chantelle's face, partly shadowed by her flowing hair.

Her eyes had a distant, sad look in them. And the sadness spread to her mouth. She held her lips in a pout, pinching the bottom one with her fingers.

Jack had a sudden mad impulse to kiss those lips. He reached out and took her hand, and he gave it a gentle squeeze.

She squinted at him and a smile played on her lips. There was a brief hesitation as he drew her to him. But she didn't resist as he reached in to kiss her on the forehead, then on the cheek. Then his lips brushed against hers.

'Jack …'

'I don't think I can let you go,' he whispered.

'But I …'

He kissed her softly on the mouth again. 'I mean it, Chantelle. I don't want you to go.'

'But I have no choice.' Her breath was warm against his cheek. 'It is better that I go. I have been here for too long now. It is not fair on your mother.'

'Not fair on my mother?' Jack sat up straight. 'But my mother loves you, Chantelle. You know she does. She loves your being here. She loves your company. She's delighted to have another woman about the house. Especially in these troubled times?'

'Thank you for saying that, Jack. But you know it isn't true. I have been here for longer than we promised. It is time for me to move on. I will take this job and leave you to get back to your own life.'

'But I love you.'

It came out in a flurry of words he had no control over. It shocked him and he had to close his eyes.

He felt Chantelle stiffen beside him and he braced himself for her reaction. What he got was a soft, resigned sigh.

'I know you do.' Her hand squeezed his again. He opened his eyes and smiled at the way she was looking at him. 'But I must be in Dublin by Monday or I will lose this job. I need this job very much, you know? I have no money of my own. I cannot spend my life depending on your mother's good nature.'

'But we love having you live with us. We'll always take care of you.'

'No! It is no use trying to talk me out of. I will leave on Sunday. I will go to Dublin. My mind is made up.'

'Suppose I don't let you go?' Jack teased, taking hold of her arm.

'What will you do?' She slapped his hand away. 'Will you lock me up in my room forever like a prisoner? I would escape in the night and disappear. I'm good at escaping from mad men.'

'Are you now?' Jack took her arm again. 'And I'm good at finding people. I'll follow you and I'll stand outside your flat. I'll rattle on your window with a big stick until you let me in. Like the big bad wolf and the house of straw, I'll puff and I'll puff till I blow the place down!'

'As I said, a mad man,' she giggled. 'I think all you Irishmen are mad.'

'Are we now?' Jack wrapped his arm around her neck and she wriggled so unexpectedly they both fell off the sofa.

'Oh, you are a bully, Jack.' Chantelle gave an exaggerated groan. 'You have bruised me.'

'Really? Where? Show me.'

'I will not! You are a very rude man.'

'Show me. I want to rub it better.'

She pretended to beat his hands away and now they were wrestling, rolling around the floor with false anger and pretend aggression. Chantelle gave little yelps of laughter as he tried to pin her down by the arms.

Jack laughed too as she wriggled out from under him and launched herself on top of him.

'Surrender,' she demanded, pressing his shoulders into the carpet. She grabbed his face and pursed his lips.

The wind blew down the chimney and fluttered the flames making the shadows dance wildly around the room. Chantelle leant down and kissed him on the mouth, gentle at first then a lot harder. And it unleashed an unexpected surge of passion.

Sunday afternoon they took the train to Dublin where they were met by a surprised Uncle Colm. And they moved into the apartment a few streets away from the Foreign Office.

Jack's mother wasn't happy about it, though. It was all too soon, she insisted. She was a very moral lady. She believed what they were doing was wrong. He understood when she didn't come to the station to wave them off.

Three months later Chantelle bounced in the door and her face beamed as she threw her handbag on the kitchen table. She sat Jack down and poured him a large glass of Paddy whiskey.

'You are going to need this,' she panted. 'I have just been to the doctor. You are going to be a daddy.'

Jack explode with delight. He wrapped himself around her and hugged her.

Then a totally unexpected image of Kathleen filled his mind and the stab of guilt made him gasp out loud. In another life this baby would have been hers. He closed his eyes and squeezed Chantelle even tighter. And he forced himself to bury the thought.

They married in the local church when spring came and the sun shimmered on the medley of colours thrown up by the flowers. Few people attended the church this time. But one thing did touch Jack's heart. Seeing his mother step off the bus at the last minute and slip quietly into the back row. No fuss, no words, just a forgiving smile. Then she got back on the bus and went home.

This time there was no elaborate honeymoon either. Just a few days in a small guesthouse by the coast. Their room looked out over an old fortress wall and gave them a delightful view of the ocean. And they sat for ages watching the enormous ships gliding in and out of the harbour.

And at night they drank in the Red Rose Cafe with the sailors whose young faces were lined with an awesome weariness. The boyish glow they had just a few months ago was gone. The horror of war at sea had changed their lives forever.

The wedding photos arrived and when Jack saw the tiny face of his mother at the back of the church he had a sudden urge to go home for a few days to visit her.

Lying in bed in his old room he noticed a cardboard box on top of the wardrobe. He couldn't remember what was in it so he decided to lift it down and take a look. What he found was a small bundle of photographs and some sketches that he'd made of Kathleen.

He picked them out and spread them on the bed. And his hands were shaking as he touched them one by one. Because the awful realisation that he was already forgetting her hit him so hard he couldn't breathe. He could barely remember her face, her voice, her smile. His recollection of her was like a shadow behind a grey veil. And it was fading more with every passing day. A dark curtain of despair wrapped around him again and bathed him in the familiar, depressing cloud of anger and guilt.

He sat on the edge of the bed in bitter silence. After

all they'd been through, he was actually forgetting her. How was that possible?

He knew the only way to prevent that happening was to keep something to remind him of her. He put the photos and sketches in his suitcase and took them back to the flat with him. And he lined them up along the mantelpiece.

When Chantelle came home from the shops she looked at them in silence. Her eyes were like sharp flints, unusually cold and bitter. She'd already sensed the change in Jack the moment she walked through the door. The darkness in his mood frightened her.

It reminded her of a time that was horrible for the both of them. When she eventually spoke her voice was heavy and sad.

'Jack, you cannot sacrifice the living for the dead.' She took him by the arm and led him to the sofa where he sat down quietly. 'Kathleen is the past. She is gone now. You have your whole future in front of you. You have me. And soon you will have our baby. Nothing else must ever matter. Kathleen is dead. She is dead and she is gone. And it is important that you never let her come between us. We talked about her for a long, long time, Jack. We are not going to talk about her ever again.'

With that she took the drawings and the photos and spread them on the fire. And the flames reflected in Jack's tears as he watched them curl and blacken and finally crumble.

The day was bright and warm. A gentle breeze nursed small clouds across the sky and shadows rolled after them along the street. Jack lay back in the armchair in front of the open window and let the warmth of the sun

110

and the hum from the street lull him into a comfortable daze.

Chantelle had gone down to the shops and left the baby asleep in the cot. So Jack settled down to a quiet and peaceful few hours.

The baby was a beautiful little girl whose head was already a mass of tiny black curls. They'd bought her a cradle and a pink pillow to match the eiderdown that was embroidered with little Beatrix Potter rabbits, a surprise present from Jack's mother.

But Jack's peace didn't last for long. A loud knock on the door made him jump. He got up slowly and rubbed his face with his hands. It was probably Chantelle. She'd be carrying a pile of groceries, which was probably why she couldn't use her key.

He pulled the door open. And he hesitated as a beam of sunlight fell on the blond hair of the beautiful girl in the yellow cotton dress.

'Jack?'

His mind spun in a wave of bewilderment as he looked into her deep brown eyes that were already filling with tears of joy.

'Kathleen?' The word dried in his throat and came out as a croak.

Before he could say another word she grabbed him in a frenzied embrace, squeezing him so tight he groaned.

She kissed his neck and then his cheek. He stepped back and took her by the shoulders, and gently moved her away. She smiled up at him and her face was streaked with the tears.

'Kathleen?' he stuttered. 'How ... I don't understand. You went back to the church! I saw you go back to the church. How on God's earth could you ...'

She put her finger to his lips.

'Someone was watching over me.' She wiped her eyes with the back of her hand. 'I think it was my mother. All I remember is a huge explosion and a flash of light. The next thing people in white coats are looking down at me. I was in a hospital. People were lying all over the place, some with terrible injuries. Dying people. I was there for an awfully long time. No one knew what I was saying. Not that they had the time to care anyway. Eventually I manager to contact the Red Cross. They were wonderful. Once the Germans realised I was an Irish citizen they sent me home.' She gave a beaming smile. 'To you!'

Jack had to lean back against the doorframe. His head was reeling. Kathleen walked past him into the room.

'Oh, Jack. Do you know how long it took me to find you again?' She gave a wave of her hand as she walked over to the window. When she turned back to him her hair bounced. 'You should have seen the look on your mother's face when I turned up at the house. She was speechless. Like she was after seeing a ghost.'

Sweat streaked Jack's forehead and dripped onto his cheek. He ran his fingers through his hair as he followed her into the room, flicking the door shut behind him.

'Kathleen, I …'

'Is this your own flat or do you rent it?' She took a handkerchief from her handbag and dabbed at her eyes.

'We … I rent it.'

'Isn't it a lovely place, though? Is it very expensive? I expect it costs …'

She stopped and her face went deathly white. Her hand went to her throat as she looked down at the cot in the corner with the tiny bundle sleeping peacefully in it.

When she looked up at Jack again her eyes were wide and questioning.

Jack bowed his head.

'I'm so sorry,' he whispered. 'I thought you were - you know ...'

'*Dead*?' Kathleen finished for him. 'You thought I was *dead?*'

Her eyes grew wet again and she gave a shudder.

'Oh, Jack! All this time ...' she made a frantic gesture with her hand that embraced the whole room. The baby in the cot. The flowers in the jar by the door. 'All this time when I was desperately trying to get back to you, longing to see you again, praying day after day that you were safe and ... and you thought I was *dead?*'

'I'm so sorry, Kathleen. I ...'

She looked around again, desperation in her eyes. And Jack knew what she was searching for. Something familiar. Something that had been theirs. Hers.

'All this in such a short time,' she was saying, almost to herself. 'It isn't even a year yet.'

'Look, Kathleen, I ...'

'Do I know her?'

'No,' he answered quickly. 'You wouldn't know her.'

She reached down and touched the baby's face. Then she ran her fingers through the fine hair.

'And do you love her?'

Jack looked down at his hands. He couldn't answer her.

'Do you love her like you loved me?' He felt her eyes watching him, waiting for the answer.

He turned away. His ears were straining, listening for the footsteps on the stairs. Chantelle would be back any minute now. She would come staggering in with her bags of shopping and he could already see the look on her face when she saw Kathleen. She would crumble with the shock.

Kathleen was crumbling too. She wanted an answer too. He could see the fear in her eyes.

'I do love her,' he said eventually. And Kathleen's eyes flashed. 'But I love her in a different way from how I loved you. What we … it's different. What you and I had was so different from what I feel about Chantelle. Ours was special. You were the first person I ever loved. My first, special love. I could never, ever feel love like that again.'

He reached out to her but she backed away.

'Kathleen, I really thought I'd lost you. I was so desperate. I'd never felt pain like that before. Such terrible hopelessness. I felt so alone and empty. I really thought I couldn't go on living.' He gave a little wave of his hand. 'Chantelle helped me through it. She talked to me. She understood. She was a shoulder to cry on.'

'What about all *our* promises?' Kathleen snapped. 'All those dreams, those … things we said. What about them?'

She glared at him, searching for something she could cling to. Anything to ease the surge of disappointment that was drowning her.

Jack's head was shaking, his face contorted in a mask of despair. Kathleen hesitated, seeing him through different eyes now. She'd always carried an image of him as a strong, dependable kind of person. Not a man to cry easily. He was crying now, though.

'I should have known something was wrong when I saw your mother.' Kathleen gave a long shiver and wiped her nose with her handkerchief. 'I sensed something was not quite right with her. She seemed reluctant to tell me where you were, *how* you were. I thought it was because she was worried about the shock it would give you. I should have known, though. I should have known.'

The creak of footsteps on the stairs outside made Jack spin around. He rushed to the door, reaching it as the key clicked in the lock. He pulled it open and held it.

'Chantelle.' He gave a feeble smile.

'Jack,' she yelped. 'You fool. You nearly pulled me off my feet. You heard me coming up the stairs, did you? These shoes do make an awful noise.'

'Yes!'

'Come on,' she frowned at him as he held onto the door. 'Let me in. What's the matter with you?'

Jack stepped back and let the door swing open, and Chantelle stepped around him into the room. He closed his eyes, listening to her cross the room and putting the groceries on the table. Then patter back across to the cot.

'Hello, my beautiful little baby girl,' she sang. 'Did my darling Rosebud miss her Mammy, then?'

The baby gave a shriek of delight and Jack opened his eyes again.

'Have you been a good little lady for your daddy while I was out?'

Jack looked around the room. And a frown made deep lines on his forehead.

Then out through the kitchen he caught a brief movement as the door to the fire escape swung shut and cut off a strand of sunlight.

His heart exploded. He almost called after her. He wanted to run after her, bring her back and explain it all to her. She *deserved* an explanation.

'What's that smell, darling?' Chantelle was saying. 'It smells like cheap perfume. Have you had a visitor while I was out?'

Jack staggered over to the window and looked up and down the street. But it was too late. The beautiful girl in the yellow cotton dress was nowhere to be seen. She'd disappeared into the pulsating bosom of the chaotic wall of humanity.

He buried his face in his hands and his whole body shook as the pain and the grief tore at him.

'Jack? What's the matter?' Chantelle's voice, high and anxious, calling him from somewhere in the distance. He felt her arm around his shoulder and she drew his head to her breast.

'Darling, what is it? What's the matter?'

'Nothing,' he said as he struggled to compose himself. 'Nothing at all. I just had a dream, that's all. It was just a dream.'

'Dad?'

Jack Cassidy turned sharply and looked into Rose's soft smiling eyes. Sometimes it startled him how much like her mother she was, her hair as black as a raven's wing and shining in the weak afternoon light. 'We're here.'

Rose was pointing through the car window. Jack frowned and followed her finger. In front of them was a massive old mansion, surrounded by a beautiful landscaped garden. A polished brass plate beside the elegant oak doors told him this was the St Brendan's Retirement Complex.

He shook his head, struggling to drag himself out of the haze. *God, he hated this*. How was it he could

116

remember people and places, even conversations, from years ago but now he couldn't remember why he was sitting in a car on a bitter cold day like this?

His heart was racing, he knew that. But he couldn't remember why. That dreadful fog had descended on him again, clouding his mind so much he couldn't think outside it.

He felt strange, as if he'd been in a deep sleep. And dreaming of something intensely emotional. Something so deeply passionate it was almost making him weep. But he'd been woken too soon and the dream evaporated in the blink of an eye. It fragmented into thin wisps and floated away, and took everything with them. He felt totally exasperated.

'Dad, you're going to be fine,' his daughter was telling him as she walked around to his side of the car, opened the door and took the box from his lap. 'Come on.'

She helped him out of the car and up the steps to a wide hallway. Two winding staircases went up to another floor. Mrs Parry, the deputy Manager, shook his hand and made a great fuss of him.

'First, I'll show you to your room,' she panted, leading him along a shiny corridor and through the fire doors. 'Then, when you're ready, come down to the lounge and we'll have a nice cup of tea. I'll introduce you to the others residents.'

A shriek of laughter and three elderly ladies came rolling around the corner in a flurry of excitement. Mrs Parry stepped aside to let them pass. All of them were talking together and no one drew breath long enough to listen.

'We're off to the Bingo, are we, girls?' Mrs Parry

beamed. The bunch of keys in her hand rattled as she spoke.

'We are,' they all agreed, nodding in unison. 'We wouldn't miss Bingo for the world.'

'You have to get there early, you know,' one of them insisted, catching Jack's eye and giving him a quick smile. She went to walk on but something made her hesitated. She looked back at him, her gentle brown eyes flicking as if something had triggered a spark of recognition. Her hand went to the thin chain around her neck and she touched the little cross that hung on it.

Jack gave a quick smile back and turned away to follow Mrs Parry and Rose, who were already walking on down the corridor.

'Will you come on, Kathleen,' the other ladies chided as they walked back and took her arm. Kathleen sighed and shook her head. She dismissed the incident with an irritated frown. And they all chuckled together as they pulled each other along.

'We'll be seeing you later, so,' Mrs Parry called after them.

'Yes,' they chorused together. 'We'll be seeing you later.'

Jack's room was neat and cosy, decorated in soft pastel shades with matching curtains. A big armchair was stuffed with cushions and facing a flat screen television on a teak cabinet. An imitation iron fireplace gave a lovely impression of warm comfort. Paintings of a tranquil countryside were dotted everywhere, filling the blank spaces on the living room walls.

Rose hung her father's coat and scarf on a hook on the back of the door. Then she waved her hand around the place as if she was directing an orchestra.

'The kitchen's through here,' she announced and disappeared in through the door. 'There's a microwave, a cooker, and a ...'

Jack shuffled over to the window and pulled back the curtain, and he nodded at what he saw outside.

'It's very nice. What's it called again?'

Rose frowned and came back into the living room.

'What's what called, Dad?'

'This hotel,' he answered, giving her a look that said *pay attention*. 'I can't remember what it's called.'

Rose looked into the watery old eyes and she felt her heart sink down into her boots. These lapses were becoming too frequent now. The doctors put it down to old age; a natural degeneration. She could accept that, of course. And she'd resigned herself to the fact that it would gradually get worse too. But sometimes - when a sudden dark hole appeared out of the blue, a rip in the fabric that was her father's mind - it threw a blanket of hopelessness over her.

To safeguard her sanity - and deflect the frightening realisation that she was sometimes talking to a complete stranger – she'd learnt how to distract him. If she could get him to focus on something trivial, like the football score or the weather, it would flick him back to the present.

Looking around for inspiration she spotted the box on the coffee table. 'So, tell me about that lady in the photograph.'

'What lady?'

Rose reached into the box and rummaged through the items until she found what she wanted.

'This lady.' Rose held it out so her father could see it. 'Who is she?'

119

Jack leant closer and screwed up his face as he studied it.

'Who is she?' His expression was blank, no trace of recognition.

'I'm asking *you*.' Rose answered more abruptly than she intended. 'It's *your* photo. *You* tell me who she is.'

Jack shrugged.

'She does look vaguely familiar,' he muttered, taking it from Rose and going over to the window to see it more clearly. 'I just can't ...'

There *was* something about the way she held her head, though. And the way the beautiful dark eyes smiled back at the person behind the camera. *And that yellow dress...*

He blinked and scratched his nose. *How did he know the dress was yellow?*

He just sensed it, that's all.

But no, he couldn't remember that girl at all.

Dreamin' Dreams

Last Train to Cork City

Richard Mann braced himself against the blustery wet night as he darted across the road to the letterbox set in the old brick wall of the Post Office. The trees rocked and the rain blew in waves across the solitary streetlight as he checked the two letters for the very last time.

He sighed and dropped them through the slot.

It had to be done - he knew that! Sooner or later it had to be sorted. And it might as well be now. H timed the letters to arrive by the first post on Friday.

Back in the car he wiped the wet from his face, annoyed that he couldn't stop the guilt from tugging at his heart.

Because the first letter was to Bridget, his wife of twenty years.

With her flame red hair and slate-grey eyes he once thought she was the most beautiful woman in the world. She loved him too, of course. But somewhere along the way the light began to fade until eventually those same eyes looked back at him with total indifference. So now they just drifted along from day to day. Tolerating each other. Going out to work in the morning and coming home again at night.

Richard Mann knew tonight wouldn't be any different. By the time he got home she'd have already eaten. She'd ask about his day as she put his meal on the table. But she'd turn away and carry on doing something else as his answer drifted past her. He'd go for a shower, read the paper, and she'd watch television late into the night.

Maybe if the children were still at home, maybe if … Well, it was too late now, anyway.

Dreamin' Dreams

The letter simply said;
'*Bridget,*

You knew in your heart this day would come, and I only hope we can part with dignity. By the time you get this letter I'll be far away, starting a new life somewhere else. I want nothing from you, so you'll never hear from me again. And you'll never find me anyway, even if you wanted to.

Richard.'

The second letter was also to a girl who called Bridget. Everyone called her Bridie. She was very special to Richard Mann.

Richard Mann remembered how, years ago when they'd first met, he called his wife Bridie. But as their lives became more formal it began to sound hollow. So she became Bridget again.

The long sigh he gave caused a patch of the windscreen to steam up. As he wiped it away he wondered how different things would have been if the factory hadn't hit the buffers when it did. A crucial order was cancelled and it threw the whole operation into turmoil. It was touch and go as to whether the factory could survive such a serious downturn.

Everyone braced themselves for the worst. But at the last minute another company took over and their jobs were safe again - for the moment. The new management wanted far more stock than the workforce was used to producing so their working routines were changed. Grateful to still have a job the workers agreed to twelve-hour shifts, seven days a week until the re-structuring was bedded down.

People were shifted around, moved to different machines, sometimes even to different departments. And they often worked in pairs. Bridie Cox and Richard Mann slotted in so well together the supervisor was impressed enough to keep them on the same rota throughout the emergency.

What amazed Richard Mann was that both he and Bridie Cox had worked in the factory for years. But it was only when they were thrown together under such enormous pressure that he really noticed her. And for the first time in years he looked forward to going to work again.

The work was hard and the hours were long so everyone felt they deserved a quick drink on the way home. And Richard Mann and Bridie Cox seemed to gravitate naturally towards each other at every opportunity.

When the crisis ended things began to return to normal. But they both knew they couldn't just slip back into the old routine of eight hour shifts and not seeing each other every day. The feelings they had for each other were only a few weeks old but they'd already burrowed deep into their lives. It was not so easy to let them go.

So what used to be snatched tea breaks behind the sheds became a whole lunch hour together in the canteen. And the quick drink in the pub after work turned into a drive in the country. They looked for reasons to work late. Or to go away on training courses together.

Eventually it consumed them to the point where they flip-flopped between two intense emotions. Guilt about the way they were betraying their partners. And the need to be together.

One minute they'd agree to finish the affair and never

see each other again. But the next they'd realise they couldn't and they'd discuss making the break from their partners.

A friend even offered to rent them a room in her house.

But for Bridie it would mean taking a huge risk. Her husband Tom was a good man and a loving father. And he worshipped Bridie.

He would be desperately hurt so she had no way of knowing how he'd react. He certainly wouldn't let her take the children from him. Not without a fight.

Bridie often wondered if Tom already knew something was going on. She'd catch him looking at her. Watching her quietly as if searching for a sign.

One day he tried to ask her outright, fumbling over his words and stuttering nervously. She couldn't bear to tell him the truth. She hugged him and promised him nothing had changed. There was nothing going on.

Anyway, Friday was her day off. She should be at home when the letter arrived.

It, too, was very brief;

'Bridie Darling,

I know this will be a great shock to you but I'll be taking the six fifteen train to Cork City today, Friday the twenty first.

I've got a new job with more money, and, would you believe, a company house - with a garden! Isn't that brilliant? The kids would love it. It's big enough to play football in. I'm sorry I had to keep it a secret from you. I just couldn't tell you before now because I know it's going to be the hardest decision you'll ever have to make. And it would have been harder still if you had time to think about it. I've told no one where I'm going, especially at work. That way no one will ever find us. So if you really want to make that new start we talked about, begin the new life that we dreamed about, meet me at the Railway Station.

See you at six fifteen.

I love you so much,

Richard.'

When Friday came Richard Mann left work as soon as he possibly could and took a taxi to the station. But he still hit the rush hour traffic. As he ran onto the platform the noise from the train was drowning out the muffled announcement from the old green speakers up in the rafters.

Doors were already being slammed as he pushed through the crowd, his eyes straining for any sign of Bridie and the kids.

He scanned the windows of the train then ran across to the waiting-room. She wasn't in the cafe either. And a terrible dread filled his heart. Time was running out. Make or break, he'd said. If she wasn't there now then her answer was very clear.

He looked back at the train. And he froze when something sharp pressed into his side.

'Hello, Richard!'

He turned slowly. 'Tom?'

'Steady, now. This knife is very sharp. And we don't want any accidents now, do we?'

'I ... I don't understand. What do you want?'

'Well now, Richard, I think you already know what I want.' Sour breath tinged with alcohol. 'You see, you made one hell of a mistake.'

He manoeuvred Richard towards the car park where an old Ford Transit van was parked right over by the bushes.

'Bridie's away for the weekend, you know.' Tom had a strange sinister chuckle in his voice. 'She's at her mother's. She didn't tell you? Anyway, I opened her letter, you see ... just in case.'

He pulled open the creaking back doors of the van.

'I sealed the letter back up, of course.' He chuckled again. 'It'll be on the kitchen table for her when she gets home. I imagine she'll be very disappointed that she missed saying goodbye to you. But she'll cover it up. She's good at covering up her feelings. But she'll get over it. Especially as she'll believe you left her and you've gone   away forever.'

Now the chuckle became a deep, cruel laugh. 'But it's your own words I like the best. The ones where you said you told no one where you were going. So no one will ever find you. Well, now, isn't that the truth!'

Dreamin' Dreams

The Ghost of the Silver Screen

It was strange seeing the old Picturedrome again. After twenty-five years I really didn't know what to expect. But I never thought it would be *exactly* as I remembered it.

The big front doors were still painted the same shiny green. And the brass handles were all polished and gleaming.

A gust of wind threw a sheet of rain against me and peppered the door with tiny droplets. Thunder grumbled somewhere in the deep, dark clouds that rolled across the late summer sky.

I should have known what the Irish weather was like when I planned this holiday. They even have a name for it over there. *Summer Showers*. It's why their grass is so green.

I wiped my face with my hand and pulled my collar up as I stepped into the narrow doorway to shelter till the shower passed.

And I couldn't help taking a peek through the small glass panel near the top of the door. But the light was behind me and all I could see was my own reflection.

On impulse I gave the handle a quick tug. And to my surprise there was a click and the heavy door open outwards with a long, slow groan.

A streak of lightening lit up the foyer as I poked my head inside. And when the familiar, musty smell of the place wafted over me it was as if I was a kid again. I was transported back to a time when going to the pictures was everyone's favourite night out.

In fact going to the cinema was so popular back then we had three cinemas in our town, all within walking distance of each other. But the Picturedrome was special. It was where I had my very first summer job.

Wallowing in the sudden rush of nostalgia, I climbed the three steps to the ticket booth and across to the swing doors with the *Way In* sigh above them. I could still see Bridie Maguire standing there, taking the tickets and tearing them in half as her beautiful green eyes sparkled with the importance of it all.

I gave the door a gentle push and looked inside. Tiny strips of daylight came in the cracks in the curtains high up on the walls.

For some reason the stage curtain was pulled back now, revealing the fabulous silver screen that once attracted us like flies on a Saturday afternoon. For a brief second I actually thought I saw it flicker and I was swamped by the gush of excitement. Remember how we piled into the auditorium and flitted up and down the aisles searching for a seat? The buzz of conversation rising and ebbing around us and all the time our eyes glued to the massive stage curtain in wondrous anticipation?

My job back then was Chief Advertising Executive. Well, actually, I was still at school but it sounded good when I said it. After all, I *was* responsible for all the advertising - I had to collect the posters from the printers and stick them all over town on whatever flat surface I could find.

And I had company transport too - a bike with a big basket on the front where I carried the posters, a bucket of paste and a huge brush.

But - the most important bit - I also had to collect the films from the railway station and return them again at the end of the run. I loved that part of the job because it gave me the opportunity to help Bridie's father up in the projection room.

I spend *hours* assisting Danny up in his tiny cluttered box. I'd rewind the spools and lace up the projectors as Danny drank endless cups of tea brewed on a battered old paraffin stove. In return he let me watch the film through the tiny viewing window while standing on a chair.

'Can I help you?'

I knew I gasped as I spun around. I was so absorbed in my thoughts I hadn't heard anyone come in.

'Oh, I … I'm sorry. The door was open.'

I gave an unexpected shiver. The air seemed to turn very cold. I stepped back as the grey haired man stared at me, his heavy eyebrows low over his dark eyes. And in the faint light something about his features triggered a memory.

'Danny?' It came out before I could stop it. 'Danny Maguire?'

He blinked a few times. 'At your service, young man.' He gave a bow.

'Good grief!' I looked him up and down. 'I don't believe it. You're still here after all these - what is it, twenty-five years? That's amazing. But I don't expect you'll remember me - I was just a kid back then when I worked here.'

'Sure of course I remember you.' He gave me an enthusiastic pat on the arm. 'How could I ever forget that mop of red hair? Liam, isn't it? We called you Bill Posters - the fastest paste-brush in the West.'

'You remember me?'

'Of course I do.' He rolled his eyes. 'Didn't you have tiny little legs back in them days? They couldn't reach the ground when you got up on that big bike they made you use. You had to lean it against the railings to climb up on it.'

'That's right. I remember that. And I fell off it more times than I ever stayed on.'

'And what about the time they put up a notices saying *Bill Posters Will Be Prosecuted.*' He was chuckling happily now. 'We told you the cops thought *you* were Bill Posters. When the Sergeant came in you hid under the stool in the ticket office for an hour. He only came in to buy a ticket for Oklahoma!'

The memory made Danny throw back his head and give a huge bellow of a laugh. He patted himself on the chest.

'Good grief, I'd forgotten about that. But what about you? I never thought I'd see *you* here. Not after all this time. How've you been keeping?'

'I'm grand, sure.' He straightened his tie. 'Grand altogether.'

I glanced around at the rows of seats that swept down in front of me and I gave a wide sweep with my hand.

'Well, this place certainly doesn't look any different. I can't believe it. Even the smell of the place. But I got the impression it wasn't in use anymore. Someone told me they thought …'

'And what about yourself?' Danny interrupted, giving me a gentle poke on the chest. 'Where've you been all these years?'

'Well,' I sat on the arm of a nearby seat. 'When my dad lost his job on the buses we moved to America. I joined the Navy. I did twenty years. But I've resigned my commission now so I thought I'd come home and see if any of my folks were still around.'

Danny blinked a few times. 'You haven't been home for twenty years?'

'Well, I always *intended* to come home.' I tried to justify myself. 'It's just that, well you know, life got in the way.'

Danny nodded his head and gave a deep sigh. 'Look,' he pointed towards the stairs with his thumb, 'I was just going up to the box to get the film ready. Come on up and I'll make you a cup of tea.'

He stopped suddenly. 'But you don't like tea, do you?' he growled with mock annoyance. 'You always wanted that *coke* stuff. Well, I didn't have any *then*, and I haven't got any *now*.'

He chuckled again, and then took off up the stairs.

I hesitated. Something bothered me about the way he trotted up the steep winding staircase. There was something not quite right about it.

But he seemed fit enough. The same old Danny. The same old grey cardigan.

'How's your daughter these days?' I shouted after him as I took the steps two at a time. 'How's Bridie?'

'Ah, she's great, sure,' he called over his shoulder. 'Did you know she was chosen for a local ice cream advertisement? Her picture was in all the papers, smiling at the camera and holding up an ice cream cone.'

'Yes. I remember that. She was a very beautiful girl.'

'They still haven't paid her, you know,' he told me when I caught up with him. 'But I expect that's how it is in show business. They only pay up at the last possible moment.'

'What?' I knew I was frowning. His eyes twinkled. But I didn't see any humour in them.

Up in the box he rattled around, putting reels of films

back in their cases and taking others out of theirs. And he lined them up on a rack close to the projectors.

'These aren't the same old machines?' I rubbed my hand along the icy cold metal of the projector. The room was so cold my breath was coming out in little puffs.

'What do you mean are these the same old machines?' Danny gave one of them an affectionate hug. 'Now there's nothing wrong with these beauties. They're the best in the world.'

He clapped his hands suddenly. 'So will I put the kettle on? Make some tea?' He nodded towards the table in the corner.

'I wouldn't mind a coffee.'

He threw me a sour look.

'Tea it is, then,' I laughed.

He shuffled over to the small paraffin stove and moved his newspaper out of the way. Then he turned up the wick, cracked a match and held the flame to it. It gave a whoosh and he adjusted the control on the side until the flame turned an intense blue. He stood the old kettle on it.

'Yes, my Bridie is turning into a fine young lady, so she is.' Danny wiped his hands on an old tea towel.

Again I felt an odd tightening in my stomach. I wasn't quite sure what was wrong here but I was getting the most uneasy feeling about it. I blew into my freezing hands as I glancing around the small room with its grey paintwork and bank of old projectors. And I blinked several times at the names on the side of the film cases.

Dr No, The Ipcress File, Dracula, The Virgin Soldiers.

My head was starting to feel light. It was as if I'd wandered through some sort of time warp. And it was making me very, very uncomfortable.

A crack of thunder rippled through the building and threw an eerie echo back at us. Then a flash of lightening zipped past the window out on the landing.

And the sharp breeze that gusted into the room fluttered the pages of the newspaper on the table. At the same time the flame from the paraffin heater danced wildly and it seemed to snake out deliberately towards the edge of the paper. The paper touched the flame for the briefest of moments - but it was enough. The corner blackened and curled as the flame spread across it in the blink of an eye.

Danny leapt towards the table and grabbed at the newspaper. But the flame scorched his hand and he dropped it on the floor with a loud curse. The burning pages spread apart and flew off in different directions. And one of them curled around the base of a projector.

As Danny staggered back from the flames his leg clattered against the table and made the heater topple. It flipped onto its side and sent a shower of paraffin out over the fallen newspaper. By the time the fuel hit the floor it had already ignited. Flames spread with a deadly whoosh right across the floor and up the side of the projector.

'Fire,' Danny screamed. 'Fire! Help. Get some water. For God's sake get some water.'

Danny's frantic yelling snapped me into action. I grabbed him by the arm and dragged him across the room to the door. And we reached it just as the flames shot up the wall and across the dusty ceiling, sucking the air out of the room with a sinister hiss.

Danny pulled a fire bucket off the wall and threw the water into the fire but it didn't even make a splash. He threw the bucket after it with a wild yell.

'Danny, don't panic.' I tried keeping my voice panic free too. 'Let's just get downstairs and out of the front door. We can call the Fire Brigade from there.'

Gripping a fistful of his cardigan I dragged him with me. The fire had spread to the outside of the door. White-hot flames snaked across the landing towards the long curtains that hung down the wall at the back of the stairs. And with unbelievable speed it flashed up the heavy fabric and hit the ceiling before it curled back down to reach the bottom of the stairs in front of us.

I knew I was screaming as I pulled Danny through the fierce heat that was snapping at us from every angle.

Suddenly he stopped and spun around, almost knocking me off of my feet.

'Bridie!' he yelled. 'Oh my God! Bridie's still up in the office.'

'What office?' I roared at him in disbelief. I couldn't remember an office up there.

'The top office,' he roared back, spittle spraying down his chin. 'She's sorting out the money. She always banks the money on a Tuesday.'

'Don't be so bloody stupid.' I grabbed at his cardigan again and pulled him back towards me. 'You can't go back up there now. You'll never make it.'

But he fought like someone possessed, arms and legs flaying in all directions. He managed to wriggle out of his cardigan and run back up the stairs, taking the steps three at a time. His haunting voice echoed desperately as he threw himself into the thick wall of flame that was all around us now.

There was no way I could have stopped him. The flames were out of control and moving too fast and the heat was already starting to blister my face and hands. So I wrapped Danny's old cardigan around my head, threw myself down the rest of the stairs and slammed against the front doors.

The impact threw them open and I flew out into the clean damp air.

At that moment the clouds parted and the rain stopped. A beam of sunlight touched the pavement and caused little wisps of steam to rise. A young policeman standing by the kerb was waiting for a gap in the traffic so he could cross the road. He jumped out of his skin when I tapped him on the shoulder.

'Good God!' His face reddened. 'Where the hell did you come from?'

'The Picturedrome,' I panted. 'A fire ...'

He gave a relieved smile and took off his cap. 'You read about that, did you?'

'Read about what?' I put my hands on my thighs and took in long, deep gulps of air. 'The cinema?'

'Yes,' he continued without actually looking at me. 'It was in yesterday's Kerryman. There was a terrible tragedy here twenty years ago this week. Apparently that building was a cinema back in them days and it burnt down one wet afternoon for no apparent reason. They thought one of the projectors might have caught fire. Anyway, the poor old operator and his daughter were trapped in the fire.'

'What?' I stood up straight. 'What are you talking about?'

The officer looked me up and down trying to decide if I was plain stupid or just a tourist.

'The cinema.' He nodded back at the building. 'It burnt down.'

'When?' My throat had dried up completely and it came out as a croak.

'Twenty years ago!' Now he was looking at me with an annoyed flicker in his eyes. 'I'm just after telling you. You asked me about the fire in the cinema and I told you. It burnt down twenty years ago.'

I gulped and shook my head but I couldn't speak.

'Are you all right there?' the officer asked. 'You look a bit … I donno … a bit pale?'

I turned and gave the big doors a mighty tug. They were locked solid.

'You won't open them, I'm afraid.' The officer gave a nervous laugh and looked me up and down again. 'They're only there for show. There's a solid wall behind them. The place was turned into a block of flats years ago.'

He put his cap back on and looked at his watch. He had more important stuff to do than listen to the ravings of a seriously disturbed sightseer.

'Anyway,' he gave a slight wave of his hand. 'As you Yanks say, have a nice day now.'

Then he sauntered off across the road, narrowly missing an old Morris Minor being driven by a nun eating an ice cream.

I watched him walk away. Then I turned and picked up the old grey cardigan that I'd dropped just outside the big green doors.

Dreamin' Dreams

My Brother's Half-Crown

Where we got the rusty old coal shovel from I'll never know. But we had great fun out of it. The game was to throw it as high into the air as we could. We'd watch it pirouette and bank then spin dramatically back to earth and crash into the cabbage patch scattering the chickens and the dogs in all directions. The winner was the one who got the most spins out of it.

In Ireland during the summer of 1942 you made your own fun!

My turn came and I threw it the highest. But this time it came straight back down like a guillotine and took the tip off my brother's nose. We all froze in horror. Then my sister picked up the tip and stuck it back on his face a second before the scream came.

Luckily for us Nurse Nelson lived next door and she kept a whole supply of emergency equipment in a cupboard in her kitchen. She was well used to us by now. It was a regular occurrence to see our mother charging up her garden path with a towel wrapped around some child's head followed by the rest of us and the dog, and sometimes a few wayward chickens too.

Nurse Nelson found what looked like an eye patch and she slung my brother's nose in it. Then she tied it in a big bow behind his head. Of course this added enormously to the drama and it drew amazed gasps from all our pals out in the street.

Later that evening when our Da came in from work he demanded to know why one of his sons had an eye patch on his nose. Of course I got the blame and I was told to go to bed without any tea.

But just at that very moment the front door crashed

open and Uncle Dan breezed in. And he was mobbed immediately by a crowd of excited kids who piled all over him.

Uncle Dan was our favourite. He told amazing stories and he would keep us entertained for hours with the chronicles of his exciting business adventures. His latest was exporting livestock to England. The War was on and the Allied Forces were desperate for whatever food they could get. Apparently Dan went to every auction in the country and bought up all the bulls he could find. Then he had them delivered to Dublin where they were shipped over to Liverpool.

I'm sure I heard my mother say Uncle Dan was the biggest bull shipper in the whole of Ireland.

Anyway, Uncle Dan had two enormous white eyebrows that bobbed up and down when he spoke. They made his nose look like a rocket coming out of a cloud. And we loved his wonderful Kerry accent - especially when he got excited.

Then he sounded like a Gatling gun.

Now, however, he took one look at the patient with his nose in an eye patch and he was speechless.

He had half a dozen kids giving him half a dozen versions of what happened. And he managed to pull a different expression for every one of them.

Now Uncle Dan, as generous as he was with his advice and his promises, never, *ever* gave us money. He'd have to mortgage his house for that, there were so many of us. But this time, to our amazement, he took a shiny half-crown from his pocket and pressed it into my brother's hand. My brother's eyes nearly popped out of his head. In 1942 this was serious money.

'A half-crown?' he gasped. 'For me?'

Dreamin' Dreams

The rest of us glared at it, consumed as we were by a sudden overwhelming sense of jealousy.

'I never got a half-crown when the cooker fell on me and nearly broke my kneecap,' one sister said. 'I was in plaster for weeks.'

'Nor me,' another added. 'Didn't the ceiling fall on me and nearly break my head?'

'That was your own fault for swinging on the light!'

'What about me?' a brother put in. 'When the milkman's horse bolted and all those milk bottles fell on top of me?'

'That's 'cos you hit the horse with a big stick!'

'I was just sitting on the pavement minding my own business when the back doors of a van flew open and a roll of lino shot out and bounced off the road,' another sister said sorrowfully. 'Then the fella on a bike fell on top of me. I never got a half-crown for that!'

In the meantime our Da was surreptitiously trying to commandeer the half-crown.

'I think I'd better be looking after that for you, son,' he smiled, reaching for the coin. 'Otherwise you might end up losing it!'

But my brother's fist closed over it like a clam.

Our Ma was having none of it.

'The child needs new shoes!' She clutched at the clenched fist. 'The one's he's got are falling to bits.'

'Not at all!' Our Da jumped between them. 'I'll look after it for him. I'm sure it would be safer with me.'

Our Ma accidentally caught him on the chin with her elbow and he shot back on top of the range.

'Don't worry yourself. ' She gave a queer laugh. 'The money will be grand with me!'

Meanwhile Uncle Dan was elevated to sainthood by

the rest of us. We formed a circle at his feet and worshipped every movement of his hand towards his pocket. And somehow in the confusion my brother made his escape.

Now he was showing off the half-crown to his pals out in the street and he and the dog were dancing with excitement. He tested the coin by biting on it to show them it was real. Then he flipped it way up into the air, squealing with delight as the late summer sun glinted off it.

Everyone clapped and cheered and ran around in little circles. The dog yelped and took a bite at its tail.

The coin went up again, higher this time and with a lot more spins. The dog went up with it and his jaws were open wide in a strange howl.

The half-crown seemed to have a halo around it as it hung there for a precious second before descending towards the waiting hands. And the jaws snapped shut and the dog gulped.

The dog landed on all fours and just stood there looking a bit dazed. It gave a sort of hiccup.

'You've swallowed my half-crown!' my brother gasped.

Instinct made the dog realise the enormity of what he'd done and his ears picked up.

'You've swallowed my half-crown!' my brother gasped again, only this time it was louder and more hysterical.

The dog cowered.

'YOU'VE SWALLOWED MY HALF-CROWN!'

With that the dog bolted. The last thing we saw was a cloud of dust as he skidded around the corner at the end of our street and disappeared into the sunset with my brother tearing after him, his eye patch hanging loose and flapping in the wind.

It was well over an hour before my brother came sauntering back up our street with the dog panting along behind him wagging his tail. We all gathered around looking for signs of wear and tear on the dog. We were amazed that there were none.

'Where've you been?'

'How's the dog?'

'Where's the half-crown?'

My brother stopped in front of our door and turned around to face us. He took something out of his pocket with a dramatic flourish.

'The half-crown is gone.'

'Where?'

'How?'

'Well,' he put up his hand to silence the questions. 'I didn't catch up with the dog until he was outside Pa Joe's Pub in Bridge Street. And he got such a fright when I grabbed hold of him that he gave an almighty cough. The half-crown shot out of him like a bullet and hit a drunk fella on the back of the leg.'

He waited for the reaction. We all went *ooh!* He was happy with that. He continued.

'The drunk fella looks down at the half-crown for a moment and says; *'how often does he do that?'*

'Well, not very often,' says I. *'Once a day, maybe.'*

'Once a day?' says he, amazed.

'Except on St Patrick's Day,' I says quickly. *'After he's had a few pints of stout he'll sometimes spit out three or four of them.'*

'Will he now?' says the man. *'I'll give you five shillings for him, so!'*

141

'*Ah no,*' says I. '*Sure isn't he like part of the family?*'

'*Ten shillings, so!*'

'*Well ...* '

'*All right, so,*' he says, pulling out a brand new pound note and shoving it under my nose. '*Tis the best offer you'll ever get for a mangy old dog like that!*'

'Just then, as I take the pound note out of his hand, his wife comes charging around the corner looking for him. He tries to tell her about this amazing dog he's just bought when she hits him around the head with half a pound of rashers in a brown paper bag.

'*You're not bringing any manky auld dog into my house, you big eejit,*' she screeches at him. Then she turns on me.

'*And you can bugger off too,*' she growls. '*And take that stinkin' old bag of bones with you.*'

'And that's *exactly* what I did.'

With that he unfolded the pound note carefully and held it up for us to see. More gasps of approval – or was it sheer envy - then he put it back in his pocket. And he held the door open for the dog who waddled contentedly into the house.

Dreamin' Dreams

Spider's Web

His name was Dean Webb. Naturally we called him Spider.

Some people observed that with his long skinny legs and gangly arms he actually looked like a spider. But standing sideways with his tongue hanging out he looked more like a zip on a crumpled old anorak.

But that didn't mean he was soft. Far from it! When the moment came Spider could be as vicious as a marauding tarantula with migraine.

Actually he was only a Leading Steward, one step above the rest of us in the pecking order. But if Spider took exception to you he had an uncanny skill of making your life a misery. And when you're stuck on an Irish cruise ship somewhere in the Mediterranean there weren't many places you could go to avoid him. So your best bet was to just keep your head down and try not to annoy him.

Which was easier said than done, of course. Spider had skin like tissue paper. Everything annoyed him!

Anyway, one Saturday last September we were visiting Naples and it was an amazingly beautiful day. The blue-green sea shimmered in a spectacular haze and blended so delicately with the paler blue of the sky it was impossible to tell for certain where the horizon was.

Most of the passengers had gone ashore to visit the sights and the Captain was taking a group of very important Italian businessmen for a trip around the bay in his very sleek and very impressive motorboat. It was something to do with twinning Naples with Tipperary.

Of course there was no sightseeing for the crew. Work still had to be done. Stores had to be brought on board.   People had to be fed. So we were all mustered on the upper deck to help unload the pallets of stock that were hoisted up on huge cranes. The pallets were stacked along the starboard side out of sight of the jetty and the delicate eyes the passengers. Then they were stripped down and each box was passed from person to person all the way down to the stockroom five decks below.

Spider was in charge that day, even though it was such a simple task there really was no need for a supervisor at all. I mean, what could possibly go wrong? But Spider was loving it. He fluttered up and down the line trying to generate some enthusiasm in the fierce heat.

Something caught his eye and he leant over the guardrail.

'Oh, look,' he announced with a delighted yelp. 'The Captain's boat is coming alongside.'

Spider was desperate to make an impression on this tour. It was the last trip of the season and when the ship got back to Cork we were all due to be paid off. But there were some permanent jobs - like the Captain's steward. And Spider dreamed of being the Captain's steward. Consequently he took every opportunity to endear himself to the Captain.

We all stopped and looked down at the imposing machine as it glided smoothly towards the pontoon at the bottom of the starboard gangway. A young seaman waited anxiously for the boat's rope to be thrown to him. He caught it, made a loop around the stanchion and took up the slack.

The Captain stood up and with a gentlemanly wave of his hand beckoned for his guests to disembark. They in turn insisted he go first. He beamed all over his face, tugged at his immaculate white tunic and gingerly put one foot on the pontoon.

Unfortunately at that very moment a burly stoker wasn't paying attention and he heaved a case of frozen chickens to the man next to him - *me!*

Caught completely off guard I yelped like a girl as I made a wild grab for it. But I misjudged the weight of the stupid thing and it slammed into the bulkhead behind me. The box burst open and spewed out a dozen frozen chickens that careered off in all directions. I managed to wrap my arms around one of them but it was like a block of ice and it spurted away with the speed of a cannon ball. It hit the deck and hurtled towards the Captain's gangway, clattering past Spider in a blur of light.

Spider saw a glorious opportunity in this. Without a moment's hesitation he sprang at it like a Manchester United goalie in a crucial cup final. And he actually caught it!

But as his long dependable fingers wrapped around it his foot cracked against the edge of a stanchion. And he didn't land quite as gracefully as he'd intended. Instead he flipped upside down and disappeared head first down the gangway.

The young seaman at the bottom of the gangway had a look of sheer horror on his face when he saw the Leading Steward and a frozen chicken bearing down on him from a great height. He tried to dance out of the way but misjudged it by a fraction of an inch and the chicken cracked him on the shin.

His instinct was to hold onto the boat's rope. But the pain was just too much and he hopped across the pontoon clutching his leg. And the rope slid from his hands and dropped into the sea.

The boat immediately began to slip away from the pontoon and it was only held back by the Captain's legs, now stretched to capacity. His face had turned as white as his beautifully starched tunic. And he struggled to maintain a dignified composure as he snapped at the seaman to behave himself and get a grip!

Meanwhile the extra weight of Spider landing on the pontoon and the wobbling of the boat caused the strangest swell you'd ever seen. It was like a weird sort of spout. It erupted between the pontoon and the boat and it slapped the Captain on the back of the legs.

They said it was probably shock that made him use language like that. Anyway, he was quickly hauled out of the Bay of Naples. And as he staggered away supported by a cluster of anxious officers he glared furiously at the prostrate Spider.

For some reason Spider got it into his head that I'd orchestrated the entire incident just to ruin his chance of becoming the Captain's steward. He assumed his name was circled in red ink in the Personnel Office and he saw his dream evaporating like a wisp of fog when the sun came out.

He planned his revenge carefully.

He knew from the roster that I was on duty in the officer's pantry that night. I'd be going on watch just as he was coming off. So he got one of his electrician friends to fix a large battery and a switch to the shiny brass handle of the pantry door.

He was like a prancing shadow as he kept an excited and giggly lookout. And when he saw me appear around the corner he darted back inside the pantry, slid the door shut and threw the switch.

Hearing the thud of a body being struck by an enormous bolt of electricity, he switched off the battery and whipped open the door with a wild look of anticipation on his face.

The look vanished instantly, of course. Now Spider looked as if he'd been slapped in the face with a defrosted cod fillet. Because the frazzled figure stuck to the door handle was the Captain himself, his eyes unfocused and as wide as saucers.

Spider groaned like a drain in a cheap hotel. It was his own fault, though. He'd been a steward on this ship for two seasons already so he should have known the Captain always crept down to the pantry late at night to make himself a mug of cocoa before he went to bed.

Now Spider could only stand there whimpering as the Captain staggered away from him for the second time that day, muttering obscenities and trying to fit his cap back on top of his sizzled hair.

We spent the next day getting the ballroom ready for the Italian - Irish Businessmen' Convention. The Mayor of Naples was the guest of honour.

And Spider was ecstatic. The Captain's steward, Danny O'Shea, had been hit on the top lip with a bag of seedless grapes by an enraged nun who mistook him for an American preacher about to lecture her on smoking in public. His face swelled up like a balloon. Well, he shouldn't have come up on her like that in the first place. Especially with his West Belfast accent. He only wanted to say hello, but he *did* grab her arm.

Anyway, he couldn't possibly attend the top table that night. Not in his condition. So it was out of sheer desperation, and nothing to do with his ability, that Spider was pressed into taking his place.

Dreamin' Dreams

The Captain wasn't asked, of course. And no one was foolish enough to mention it to him. They were more concerned about having someone wait on the Very Important Guests than they were about the Captain's feelings.

And Spider really needed this opportunity. His golden chance to prove what a brilliant steward he was.

Meanwhile, if only he could get back into the Captain's good books. Make it up to him somehow. Keep him sweet until the moment when he could show them all what he was really made of!

By midday Spider was grovelling in earnest, bowing and scraping around the Captain and grabbing every opportunity to appease. But it was no good. Whenever he got too close the Captain bared his teeth and swiped at Spider with his cane.

Consequently by early evening Spider was pleading openly with the whole of the steward's mess. He even offering a month's pay to anyone who could come up with a solution to his predicament.

'Well, I know what you could do,' said Flynn from Tipperary. Flynn was one of Spider's least favourite people. Apart from myself.

Spider flicked him on the nose with a spoonful of cold rice pudding. 'You'd better not be taking the pi … '

'Not at all.' Flynn had a smile on his face but you never could tell what it meant. 'You have Italian blood in you, right?'

'Uh?' Sometimes it took a while for Spider to catch up.

'Your father is Italian,' Flynn insisted. 'You told us!'

'Yeah, well, on his father's side - so what?'

'Well, you know what the Captain's like, yeah? Full

of shi ... self-importance! He loves to impress.'

'Go on!'

'Well, wouldn't he be delighted if he could really show off in front of these Italians tonight, eh? Especially the women! You know how he fancies himself with the women.'

A ripple of agreement from the stewards.

Spider scratched his head with the spoon. 'What are you saying, exactly?'

'Well, imagine if you could teach him how to welcome the ladies in their own lingo.' Flynn from Tipperary moved closer in a confrontational huddle. 'They'd be really impressed. And it would be a great big feather in his cap. He might even want to keep a steward who was capable of showing such initiative.'

Spider's chest shot out. Then it dropped just as quickly.

'But I can't speak Italian. I know nothing about Italian.'

'Oh!'

'I do,' I said smugly. Then I produced my Italian Tourist Guide.

It took a lot of persuasion, though. Spider was hard to convince. But he was desperate and time was running out. So in the end he agreed to give it a go. I mean, what did he have to lose? And look at what he had to gain - his dream job! We picked a page and decided on a few short sentences. Nothing too elaborate. Just something simple and warm and inviting. And we coached Spider until he was word perfect.

Then he shot off to brief the Captain, hope written all over his face.

But the Captain was having none of it. Spider

couldn't get within ten feet of him without the words *Big Eejit* being spat at him and the Captain storming off in the opposite direction. Spider was crestfallen. But he was also determined.

The evening was perfect. A moonlit Naples, stars in their millions shimmering on the water. The lights from the city twinkling in the hills all around the bay.

The Captain stood by the forward gangway in his gleaming white uniform. He was so proud of his ship. He was proud of his crew too, and the arrangements they'd made. He really believed this was going to be a night to remember.

It would probably be in the local papers, too. There was a strong rumour that a famous photographers had been invited by the Mayor's PA to capture the event for the elections in December. The Captain would insist they only photographed his left profile. Everyone said he looked like Marlon Brando from the left side. Yes, he sighed. A night to remember!

He glanced over at Leading Steward Webb who was hovering by the main doors. He looked very smart, impeccable in full uniform and bow tie. Very smart indeed. Maybe he wasn't so dull after all. If only he'd stop grinning at the Captain like that. And fluttering his eyebrows …

A fleet of limousines swept onto the jetty and as it cruised up to the gangway the Officers Reception Party was called to attention.

The first car discharged a little round man with a huge stomach straining against his official Mayoral sash and weighed down by an enormous gold chain. A large lady followed, linked arms with him and helped him negotiate the gangway steps.

Dreamin' Dreams

They were followed by the entourage who all piled up the gangway behind them in a flurry of excitement. As the Mayor reached the top of the steps he took the huge cigar from his mouth and beamed all over his face.

The Captain smiled at the Mayor and then at the Lady.

Then he did a double take. The lady looked like Terry Wogan in a flowery dress. Her face was caked in an unusually pale, almost white makeup that gave her a surreal, comic appearance. And that lipstick? Blood red! Like a … Naw, it must be a trick of the light. But the hair - a wild mass of bright orange curls? Real hair could never be that colour.

Sod's Law - you can't drag your eyes away from the very thing you're not supposed to stare at! And the Captain was staring.

Someone gave a sharp cough and he quickly snapped out of it. He clicked his heels and gave a smart salute, bowing low by way of apology.

But before he could utter a word Spider slid between them. He gave a huge bow too. And with a beaming smile he greeted the guests with his prepared speech, enunciating each word with great deliberation.

Everyone froze.

Spider hesitated. The hint of a frown flitted across his brow. Then he smiled again at the large lady. And he continued.

The cigar was back in the Mayor's mouth where it hung for the briefest of moments before dropping onto his round belly and erupting in a shower of sparks. He gave an almighty howl of rage and swung around on his heels.

Then the whole lot of them scurried back down the

gangway, shouting and squawking as they piled back into the limousines and screeched away into the night.

The Captain's face had crumbled. His bottom lip trembled and his eyes flashed as he rounded on the stunned and horrified Spider Webb.

'*What. Did. You. Say. To. Them*?'

Spider was gone the next day. Compassionate leave, they said. Flown back to Dublin. The Captain sat on the bridge and wouldn't come down. He just stared vacantly at the front page of the local paper. His picture was in it all right.

But we never did find out exactly what Spider said to the Mayor. My Italian Tourist Guide was for Italians touring Italy, you see. There wasn't a word of English in it.

We just picked a page and told Spider what we thought it said. Maybe we shouldn't have picked the one with a picture of the carnival - all exploding colour and thrilling activity. And dominated by the white painted face of a clown with blood red lips and a wild mass of bright orange curls …

The Big White Coffin

For years we blamed Pat Hurley. He's the one who told us about cannibals.

We were sprawled out on the dusty floor of our secret hideout during the long hot summer of 1956. A fierce heat wave had developed out in the Atlantic and the first place it hit was the west coast of Ireland.

Pat said the temperature was up in the hundreds outside. I was seven going on eight and Pat was already eight which made him the oldest so we believed him.

A rare breeze filtered through the cracks in the walls and fanned us for the briefest of moments. And the flies that constantly flitted around Pat hummed contentedly.

'Isn't it strange how you don't see any cats around the town anymore?' Pat declared suddenly, his voice as drippy as a half melted ice cream. 'Now the Chinese have opened that restaurant in High Street.'

'Why's that, so?' I asked.

'Duh! Because the Chinese eat the cats, don't they?'

'They do not!' I tried to lift my head to see if he was being serious, but I was just too drained.

'They do too!' Pat insisted. 'Sure if you go there for a Chicken Chow Mien, won't you find little furry paws in it? Now how many chickens have *you* seen with little furry paws on them?'

Pat roared at his own joke.

'That's an awful thing to say, Pat Hurley.' Rita Fitzgerald had a sob in her voice. 'The poor little animals. I don't believe a word of it.'

Rita was the only girl allowed into our secret hideout. Mainly because she was the prop forward in the Kerry Junior Ladies Rugby squad. Also she could beat the

153

living daylights out of anyone who tried to stop her.

'Well, what about in the jungle, so?' Pat propped himself up on his elbow. 'They eat *people* in the jungle.'

Pat said he'd heard it on the wireless. A plane had crashed in the Borneo jungle - wherever that was - and when the rescuers got there they couldn't find a single body. A tribe called The Cannibals had eaten them!

We were stunned, shocked into a kind of stupor by the terrifying images that filled our imagination. It was like a Movietone Newsreel stuck in a loop, going round and round and getting wilder by the minute. When I looked at my little brother Joe his eyes were as wide as saucers.

The next day two men came to our house. The little fat one was sweating heavily and the tall one bent down to our level with a grin that showed a mouthful of enormous teeth.

'Hello there,' he cooed. 'Is your daddy in?'

Joe shot behind me. 'I ...'

'Who is it, Liam?' Daddy came out from the kitchen rolling up his sleeves. He beamed when he saw the two men and wiped his hands in a tea towel.

'Ah, sure tis yourselves, is it?' He greeted them with a nod. 'Have you brought it with you?'

'We have,' the little one said. The tall one grinned down at us again.

'Now will you get out of the way, boys?' Daddy waved his hands like he was conducting an orchestra. 'Or the lads will be falling over you.'

The three of them went out to a van parked in the street. A few minutes later they came back carrying a long white box between them.

'What's that?' I asked Mammy.

Mammy was sitting on the stairs. She looked dreadful. She'd been getting awfully fat lately. Now she was so big she had to sit down every now and then to rest. Her face was all red and clammy.

'Look, tis nothing for you boys to worry about.' She sounded irritable. 'Why don't you just go outside and play like all the other children?'

Later, back in the hideout, Joe looked very worried.

'I don't like that big fella. Did you see the cut of his teeth? I bet the Cannibal Tribe have teeth like that.'

'What was that big white thing they were carrying into your house?' Rita Fitzgerald rolled her eyes in wonder.

'A coffin,' Pat Hurley declared loudly. He had a strange glee on his face.

Joe groaned. 'Sure why would they be carrying a coffin into our house?'

'It's probably for your mammy.'

'What?' Joe yelped. 'Why?'

Pat sat up and scratched his head. The flies still flitted around him.

'Well, just suppose!' His eyes squinted with a sinister glint they moved slowly to each one of us in turn. 'If they *are* from the Cannibal Tribe, they'll be wanting to eat her. But not all at once, though. They'll want to be picking away at her, a little bit at a time, taking some home for their families every day. So they'll need somewhere to keep her, won't they?'

Joe's eyes were even bigger than saucers now.

'But why would they want to eat my mammy?'

'Will you look at the size of her?' Pat was warming to the theme now and he rose up onto his knees for effect. 'Sure isn't that why they chose her out of all the women in the town? There's enough meat on her to last them for a whole year.' He guffawed loudly then fell backwards in a fit of laughter.

It was late afternoon now and Pat Hurley's mammy was calling him in for his tea. Her banshee screech could be heard all over town and it was the signal for *all* the kids to go home as well.

Joe and I traipsed in through our front door and were immediately overwhelmed by a thick grey haze wafting down the hallway from the kitchen.

We peered warily around the door and the first thing we saw was the two plates of burnt toast on the table.

Daddy was standing by the old black range with his arms in full swing as he battled with some eggs in a frying pan. The kettle was bellowing steam and making the lid rattled and the fat in the frying pan was spitting out all over him.

Daddy cursed and danced out of the way. He scooped the eggs out of the pan and plopped them onto the black toast. Then he spotted us through the chaos.

'Ah, there you are. Sit down, sit down.'

We edged our way to the table and sat down, looking around anxiously for a hint of the security that was always there at teatime.

'Where's Mammy?'

'Your mammy's grand. You don't have to worry about your mammy. She's all right.'

He poured the boiling water from the kettle into the teapot.

'But where is she?'

'Now, I've told you. Your mammy is grand. Don't be worrying about her now. Just eat your supper before it gets cold.'

My eggs lay helpless on the charred bread, the yolks still raw and the edges burnt to a frazzle and curled up like an old doily. Joe prodded his and tapped at the bread. Daddy poured the tea.

Through the door to the scullery we could just see the corner of the big white box shimmering eerily behind the fog of Daddy's cooking.

That night we lay in the stillness of our darkened bedroom, staring out of the window at a sky that twinkled with a million stars.

We'd been in bed for hours but tonight there was no sleep in us. Our minds were full of thoughts that were so strange we couldn't even put words to them. All we could focus on was what Pat had said in the hideout - the men who came to our house were from the Cannibal Tribe. And the big white box was to keep our mammy in.

Down in the town the church bell gave one solitary ring.

'What are we going to do, Liam?'

'Shush, he'll hear you.'

'But I'm frightened.'

'Sure I'm frightened too. But we need to be very brave about this. We have to think about what we're going to do, how we're going to find out exactly what's going on. So tomorrow when Daddy goes out to work we'll open the box and have a look for ourselves.'

Joe groaned.

But Daddy didn't go out to work the next day. We danced around him all morning, trying to look casual and pretending to be busy. We picked up the newspaper and put it down again, flicked through the pages of a book, went out the front door and came back in again.

But it made no difference. He still didn't go to work. It was as if he had no work to go to any more!

And for dinner that day we had a very strange looking piece of gristly meat, all pink and fatty with spuds floating in a watery kind of stew.

We had the same meat for dinner the next day, too. And the day after that!

Then the next morning Daddy put on his jacket and his cap. He went out of the door and off down the street, whistling happily as if nothing had happened.

Joe and I ran to Pat Hurley's house and rapped on the door.

'You have to help us, Pat,' we pleaded in unison. 'We're going to look inside the big white box.'

'What?' Pat turned a pasty grey sort of colour and the flies disappeared.

'But you're the leader of the gang,' we persisted. ''Tis your duty …'

We had to physically drag him back to the house with us. We shuffled into the scullery in a nervous huddle, pulling and pushing each other to the front of the line.

We'd never been this close to the thing before. It was *huge*. And it had a padlock on it. We looked at it for ages.

'I know.' Pat's squeak made us jump in eerie silence. He cleared his throat. It made no difference. He still squeaked. 'I'll go and get my Da's hammer and screwdriver.'

I grabbed his arm. 'You *will* come back?'

'I will!'

It took us ages to beat the padlock off. We threw down the hammer and slowly lifted the lid. And we recoiled in horror.

It was the most disgusting thing I'd ever seen in my whole life. The pink flesh was dulled by the ice that had crystallised all over it. The distorted limbs were twisted in an obscene angle. And it had been hacked at until it was almost cut in two.

We stood rooted to the spot, unable to drag our eyes away from it.

'Where's the head?' Pat still squeaked but this time he didn't care.

Joe groaned and squeezed his eyes shut. 'Don't tell me! They're after taking her head!'

Suddenly the door crashed open behind us.

'What's going on in here?'

We jumped out of our skins, slamming the lid down as we spun around.

'Mammy,' I cried.

'Mammy,' Joe cried.

'Mammy,' Pat cried. 'I mean … er … Mrs …'

I couldn't believe my eyes. She was as thin as a brush handle and smiling sweetly at us.

'Well, never mind that now.' She held the door open and ushered us out. 'Come and say hello to your new baby sister.'

Daddy was beaming all over his face and carrying a bundle in his arms.

We were rooted to the spot.

'You know, the boys were as good as gold the whole time you were in the hospital,' Daddy was telling Mammy between emitting strange cooing noises at the bundle in his arms. 'They were absolutely no trouble at all.'

We were still rooted to the spot.

'By the way, you should see the piece of meat I got

from Liam Brosnan,' Daddy continued. 'A whole pig's carcass, would you believe. Tis huge! It took up all the room in our new freezer. We had some for dinner a couple of times. It was really lovely.'

He paused for a second, as if reflecting on something.

'Only, judging by the look on their faces, I don't think the boys actually *like* pork!'

The First Cut

Patrick Flynn lifted the ancient Samurai sword from the plaque above the fireplace and held it carefully by the thick black handle. He brushed his thumb along the razor-sharp edge and his mouth tightened into a wicked sneer.

He moved across to the patio doors and slid them open. On the other side of the garden fence he could see the tall shadowy figure with his fancy spade casually picking away at his flower patch. The straw hat was worn at an angle that allowed a sweep of thick grey hair to hang loose and caress the collar of his pink denim shirt.

Patrick Flynn hated that straw hat. He hated that grey hair. You could understand why. His eyes narrowed as they drilled into the object of his uncontrollable rage.

Still, he hesitated for a moment and angrily brushed his thin wispy hair from his sweating forehead. He didn't really understand how he'd let it get this far in the first place. He *knew* what was going on! He had actually *watched* it develop right there before his eyes. He had *watched* it grow and slowly consume everything he held so dear.

But as usual, Patrick Flynn took the easy way out. *Ignore it*! That was his philosophy. Ignore it and it will all go away.

He even tried to convince himself that his *job* was to blame. He was never at home, you see. So what could he honestly expect when Rita was left alone day after day? Sometimes for a whole week. She was a woman, after all!

And Martin, their next door neighbour for the past

fifteen years, was a strong character - bags of charm and tanned skin. And an engaging smile that showed lots of sparkling white teeth.

How could Rita *not* be susceptible to anything he might wish to do?

But today all that changed! Patrick Flynn was in the pub at lunchtime when a crowd of the lads came in. Naturally they had a few pints and a boisterous chat. And for some strange reason the conversation drifted to a similar situation involving one of their colleagues at work.

Patrick Flynn grasped the opportunity to put out a few feelers, ask a few questions - in a roundabout way, of course! What did the others feel about something like that? What would *they* do if they were in that same predicament? Not that it was happening to Patrick himself, you understand. It was just that he had this friend who wanted to know.

Anyway, the same answer came back from each and every one of them. Get a big knife and cut the flopping thing off! That would serve the bugger right. And Patrick Flynn knew deep inside they were right. The time had come to sort it out.

But just as he stepped out of the door and onto the neatly manicured lawn he heard the noise from the open bathroom window. Water thumped like a drum as it gushed into the enamel bath and Rita's voice burst into song and echoed around the pink marble tiles.

Damn! Patrick Flynn stood perfectly still. He wasn't expecting her home so early. She must have come in the front door and gone straight upstairs. She obviously wasn't expecting him home so early either.

The late afternoon sun threw down a powerful heat

and it filled every corner of the garden. And it made Patrick's hand sweat as he held the sword close to his chest.

His heart started to flutter, beating faster in his chest. Suddenly he felt the uncomfortable pangs of doubt. What the hell possessed him to even *consider* this mad course of action in the first place? It was the beer! He never should have had that last pint. They *made* him have it. It was all *their* fault! And where were they now, eh - when the dirty deed was about to be done?

He took a long, deep breath. No, he told himself. It was far too late to change his mind now. It had to be done. And it had to be done this instant!

His only concern was whether he could move fast enough, get it over with before Rita heard the commotion. Because what she'd see when she came down to investigate would leave her devastated. She'd have no choice but to admit there *was* a problem all along. But would she ever accept that it warranted such drastic action?

So Patrick Flynn braced himself and crept quickly up to the lattice fence, judging the distance to the shadowy figure bent over something with his back turned. He raised the razor sharp weapon high above his head. He knew what it was capable of. You could tell by the sheer weight of it.

Then he brought it down with a devastating crunch - on the thick stem of the enormous clematis bush.

Now the clematis bush is often considered to be an essential and colourful addition to any garden - a beautiful climbing plant of the buttercup family with wonderful purple, yellow and white flowers. But if it isn't kept in check it will quickly get out of control and invade places where it just isn't welcome.

The enormous one in Martin's garden was *totally* wild. It was sweeping over the fence and invading Patrick Flynn's side, choking everything in its path. Including his prize sunflower that he was lovingly cultivating and hoping to present at the Kingdom County Fair in Tralee.

'What the hell ...'

Martin's shadowy figure was now leaping into the air, his arms flapping in total alarm.

'It's too late!' Patrick Flynn screamed at him, his mad laugh echoing around the neat and lovingly tendered garden. 'I tried to warn you! But no, you just wouldn't listen.'

Maeve Ryan's Wicked Secret

When Edward O'Leary came home from America in the summer of 1904, Joe Coffey knew there was going to be trouble. Old flames were bound to be rekindled. And old wounds were bound to be reopened.

He just didn't expect it to happen so soon.

Edward was the only son and heir of Squire Colm O'Leary. His vast estate on the West coast of Ireland swept up from the Atlantic Ocean and touched on three counties. Joe Coffey was just one of the small army of gamekeepers that worked on the estate. And the only thing that Joe Coffee and Edward had in common was their feelings for the beautiful Maeve Ryan.

They'd all grown up on the estate. Edward lived up in the Big House and Joe Coffey lived next door to Maeve Ryan in the workers' cottages down in the village.

As children they all played together. They skipped and rolled hoops in the dusty lanes or just ran free through the woods. They swam in the lake during the long, lazy summer days and they fished in the wild River Shannon. And as the evenings drew in they sat around a campfire swapping stories and dreaming their dreams.

But then, when they grew older, Edward went off to boarding school. The only education Joe Coffey got was out in the countryside where he learnt how to be a gamekeeper.

Maeve Ryan grew older too. She changed from a scruffy tomboy who used to wrestle with the boys into a beautiful young woman. She went to work as a seamstress up in the Big House where she was coached in the finer points of decorum and etiquette as well.

As time went by Joe Coffey and Maeve grew very

close. Everyone assumed they'd get married one day, have lots of children and be together for the rest of their lives.

Edward, on the other hand, was footloose and fancy-free. He didn't need to chase the girls. He was tall and handsome with jet-black hair and eyes that smouldered wickedly. No woman could walk past Edward without giving him a second glance. All the girls in the village worshipped him. Their conversation always turned to him and his affairs.

Of course Joe Coffey was aware of all this. But it never bothered him. Because in the first flush of young love he had no reason for doubt.

Until one Sunday afternoon as they were strolling around the lake Joe Coffey noticed how Maeve became totally distracted when Edward rode by.

'Maeve!' Edward tapped his hat with his riding crop.

'Hello, Edward.' Maeve gave a courteous nod. And her beautiful grey eyes sparkled as she tossed back her hair and gave him a long and knowing smile.

Joe Coffey read all sorts of messages into that smile. And the first stab of a totally unfamiliar pain tore at his heart.

And it disturbed him so much he couldn't bring himself to even look at Maeve as they walked home in a silence that hung around them like a dark bitter cloud.

They never spoke about it, though. Joe Coffee felt it was best left alone. But that strange painful feeling never really left him until the day Edward announced that he was going to seek his fortune in the New World and he sailed away to America.

The relief was overwhelming. Joe Coffey immediately proposed to Maeve and hey got married a month later in the tiny chapel up in the Big House.

They moved into their little cottage and quickly settled into the happy routine of married life.

Now Edward was back! No warning. No notice. He just turned up out of the blue with a beautiful young American lady and announced they were getting married at the end of August.

And within a week of Edward coming home Joe Coffey began to notice a change in Maeve. And his heart sank down into his boots.

It wasn't something he could put his finger on, exactly. It was just that she seemed distant, vague, as if she had something very much on her mind. And he sensed an irritation in her too. Especially if he came home early in the evenings. Almost as if he'd interrupted something.

She'd do her best to appear normal, of course. Eagerly pouring hot water from the kettle into a basin for him to wash in before getting his meal ready.

But in the morning she'd be very anxious to get him out of the house again. She'd put his canvas sack over his shoulder, kiss him on the cheek and wave to him as he walked off up the hill to the gamekeepers hut. But before he reached the first clump of trees she'd have already vanished back inside the house.

A few days later Joe Coffey found out why.

He was out checking some snares in the woods when he lost his footing and fell into a ditch. The crusty old gamekeeper cursed him repeatedly as he struggled back out holding his aching wrist.

'Shur tis only a bit of a sprain,' he growled, ignoring Joe Coffey's yelps as he examined the damage. 'But I suppose you'd better get off home and give it a rest. But mind you're back here at the crack of dawn tomorrow or you can look out!'

So Joe Coffey came sauntering down the winding dirt track that took him out of the woods, whistling happily to himself. The sun was shining and the birds were singing. He couldn't remember the last time he'd got home so early in the day. And the pain in his wrist wasn't really that bad. Life was good after all.

But as he came over the rise in the meadow he noticed the shiny black carriage outside the front door of his cottage. He stopped dead and watched in stunned silence. Because he recognized the carriage immediately.

It belonged to Edward O'Leary.

In one split second Joe Coffey knew his worst fears had come true. Edward had been home for less than a week and already his carriage was outside Maeve's door.

Totally distraught, Joe Coffey found himself half way back up the hill to the gamekeeper's hut. He'd just turned around and run away in the confusion and the pain. Now he dropped into the long thick grass, shaking with anger and frustration.

And he knew he could never have any faith in Maeve again unless Edward was out of their lives. Forever!

Desperation welled up inside him. He *had* to get rid of Edward. He had to remove this threat to his happiness. To his very future. He had to stop Edward from taking the most precious thing in his whole life.

And the way to do it was so simple it left him breathless.

Edward was a creature of habit. All his life he'd gone riding after breakfast on a Sunday morning, arriving back at the big house in time for Mass in the tiny chapel.

Yesterday Joe Coffey overheard the groom telling the

stable lads that Edward still wanted the horse ready this weekend.

Edward always took the same route. Up over Foley's Glen to Conor Pass then back down by the River Shannon where it touched his land. It was wild and dangerous country. The scope for an accident was horrendous.

One part of Foley's Glen was just a narrow track with a high ridge on one side and a sheer drop to the valley floor on the other. Any gamekeeper would know a million ways to spring a simple - and lethal - trap.

Joe Coffey's would be the simplest of all. A thin vine stretched across the path, tied to the branch of a tree and pulled back as tight as a spring. The horse would just have to clip the vine and the branch would snap out, clearing the rider from the saddle. The only way the rider could go was down over the cliff. Nature would take care of any evidence.

So early that Sunday morning Joe Coffey went out and set the trap. And he was amazed at how calm he felt as he hurried back to meet the rest of the men. It was custom for the men to make their way to the chapel together and met their wives at the door half an hour before the O'Leary family arrived.

Joe Coffey had just reached the stables when the clatter of hoofs on the stone cobbles drew everyone's attention to the rider-less horse as it came in through the archway at a steady trot.

And it was only then that the cold reality of what he'd done hit Joe Coffey suddenly and violently like a blow to the chest. Panic took hold of him as the men rushed out to calm the sweating animal. As their worried voices echoed around the yard Joe Coffey felt a desperate need to run away again. And the only place he could think of was home.

But as he came rushing around the side of the cottage a shocked yelp stuck in his throat and he slid to an abrupt halt. There outside his front door was Edward's carriage.

His heart thumped in his ears as he sank down onto the long damp grass, and he put his head in his trembling hands.

What on earth was going on? That was definitely Edward's carriage. There was no doubt about that! But he had *seen* Edward go out riding that morning. He had seen the rider and the horse go out, and he had seen the horse come back alone.

Just then he heard the front door open. He jumped to his feet and moved quickly back into the cover of the bushes. And he frowned in confusion at the voices that floated across the small yard towards him.

Women's voices!

As they came out of the cottage the American lady had her arm around Maeve's waist.

'Finished at long last,' she was saying. 'So you'll post to today and we'll keep our fingers crossed the editor will like it.'

'Of course he'll like it. It's marvellous. And the illustrations are so beautiful. You should be so proud of yourself.'

'That's what Edward keeps telling me.'

'Then why ... '

'Not yet. Let's wait and see if it's a success first. Then I'll tell them.'

'I still don't see what you're so worried about.'

'I'm worried they're not ready for a daughter-in-law

who's a children's author. This is a different world from the one I'm used to in New York. There's so much snobbery, so much pretentiousness over here. Edward's parents are wonderful, of course. But some of their acquaintances look down their noses at me. Something to do with *working* for a living. Even some of the staff give me that look.'

Maeve patted her on the hand. 'Still, to be such a good writer, though. They should appreciate your talent.'

'I know I've said it a hundred times already, Maeve,' the American answered. 'But I have to say it again - this really is kind of you to let me sneak down here to finish my book. Edward was right when he said you were a good friend. He said you would be kind and supportive.'

When they reached the carriage Maeve stepped back and gave a little curtsy as the lady took the reins and climbed up into it.

'Thank you, Madam. I'm so proud you asked me to help you. It really is a *great* honour.'

'No. Thank *you*,' the lady continued. 'And I really want to thank you for keeping the whole thing a secret. It's very important to me. I know it seems childish but I want it to be a total secret right up to the last possible moment. No one must know what I was doing until I hear back from the publishers.'

She smoothed out her coat and straightened her hat. Then she threw back her head and laughed.

'But how on earth did you keep your husband from finding out about it?' She put her hand on Maeve's shoulder. 'It must have driven you mad, not being able to tell him about my secret visits, sneaking down here when he was out at work. It's lucky no one ever saw me!'

171

Maeve's hand went to her mouth.
'Oh dear! Just imagine …'

Dreamin' Dreams

Exorcizing Uncle Peter

I'm impatient to get going. I take a last drag on the cigarette and flick it away. It erupts in a shower of sparks on the grey stone steps before blowing away with the soft afternoon breeze.

At last the taxi cruises in through the front gate and pulls up beside us. I bend to get my suitcase but Nurse Phillips picks it up instead. She pushes past me and puts it on the back seat. Then she holds the door open for me.

Doctor Ryan holds out his hand.

'Well, Alan, this is it.' He gives a forced grin. 'Not much one can say at a moment like this, except … well take care of yourself. We don't want to see you back here again, now do we?'

His handshake is delicate, almost fragile. Nurse Phillips gives me a tender hug.

'You've always been such a good boy.' She pats me on the back. 'Always so pale, so thin. I only wish you wouldn't go back to that old house tonight. Why don't you stay in a hotel instead? Go to the house tomorrow. In the daylight. Settle back slowly, like.'

'Now, Nurse.' Doctor Ryan's voice is stern. 'We've already been over that. He's done extremely well so far. He has to pick up where he left off.'

'I know, Doctor.' Nurse Phillips sighs. ''Tis just that - well, it's been ten years since he was last in that old house. The poor boy! He'll be all alone there.'

I climb into the taxi and pull the door shut. The driver glances back at me. I nod and we move away, trailing a cloud of dust behind us. Loose chippings patter against the bottom of the car.

I'd promised myself I wouldn't look back. That I'd

just quietly slip away. But after ten years - well! The seat groans as I turn to catch a final glimpse of the huge hospital. Doctor Ryan's hand rises in a self-conscious wave that goes straight to his bow tie. Nurse Phillips has a handkerchief to her eyes.

You are now leaving Killarney. Slán Abhaile says the big sign on the side of the road as we turn out of the gate and head for Tralee.

We reach the outskirts of Tralee and take a sharp left. A few minutes later we're outside the big iron gates of the Galvin Estate.

The gates used to be green. Now they're pitted and streaked with rust. And held firmly to the ground by a carpet of weeds.

The taxi gets as close as it can and I jump out. My hands are shaking with excitement as I unlock the chain and tug the gates open. I'm home! I'm back in my own little corner of God's Earth. And I'm thrilled to bits. Somewhere up behind the thick wall of trees is the house.

And it's mine. All mine!

The driver is reluctant to take his taxi up the dark overgrown drive so I pay him. Then he's gone. I don't mind. I want to walk. I want to savour this moment.

But it never dawned on me what years of neglect would do. I remembered the driveway as a long ribbon of asphalt with borders neatly trimmed and full of colour. Now it's a wasteland. Wild nettles and giant dandelions fight for space around the roots of trees that lift big lumps out of the road.

I pass the big oak tree and I'm in the courtyard. More wilderness! Wild rose bushes strangling the forsythia hedges. Clinging clematis strangling the rose bushes!

But worst of all is the state of the house itself.

Huge patches of stucco have peeled away to expose the naked grey walls underneath. The windows are thick with dirt. Their frames are blistered and warped. The glass is cracked.

And I can't believe how small it looks. It seemed *huge* back then. Five bedrooms. Two living room. A drawing room. A kitchen. A pantry. I used to rattle around in it!

But I suppose after ten years in an enormous place like Killarney it was bound to look smaller by comparison. And of course I was smaller myself too, back then.

The big front door gives a prolonged groan as it swings open. I walk slowly into the great hall. My footsteps are muffled by a thick carpets of dust that hides the mosaic tiles. I brush away cobwebs that hang like streams of ivy from the ceiling and almost touch the floor.

The front door slams shut and causes a draught that sweeps the dust into crazy little whirlwinds. But they die again almost immediately.

Then there's silence. Not like it was when I left, all those years ago. No reporters. No flashing lights. No TV cameras. No police holding a blanket over my head.

Just the silence!

I close my eyes and breathe in the memories. I see the house exactly as it used to be all those years ago. The dark wooden panels that lined the hall. The thick blue carpet that swept up the winding stairs.

And what was that? Music?

That would be Mother playing the piano in the drawing room. Her eyes would be closed. She'd have a faint smile on her lips as her pale fingers floated over the keys. Her head would be swaying gently from side to side.

I cross the hall and open the drawing room door. There's nobody there now, of course. Just dust and cobwebs. The piano is where it's always been. The lid is open to show the strings. Rusty old strings covered in dust.

Poor Mother. She's gone now. She's been gone almost ten years. God rest her poor soul.

On the sideboard there's a picture of my father. I pick it up. I'd almost forgotten what he looked like. Small. Weak. Sunken eyes leering from under a raising hairline.

As a father he was detestable. His slightest touch made my skin crawl. Not that he touched me very often. If he did it was to hit me when he flew into one of his rages. He'd charge around the house calling *young fella!* until I came. Then he'd clout me for something stupid that he'd already forgotten about.

Not once did he call me anything other than *young fella,* and that hurt most of all.

But repulsive as he was, my mother loved him. My delicate, sophisticated mother. Her very presence made men breathless, yet she doted on a man like that! She could even say nice things about him.

But he's gone now as well, poor old sod. And may God rest his soul too.

I put the picture back on the sideboard and take a deep breath. It was *so* good to be back. In spite of my father, I really loved this place.

Up in my old room I drop the suitcase on the bed and open the wardrobe doors. I look in all of the drawers. Nothing's changed.

Dreamin' Dreams

The Estate Trustees had arranged for someone to come in and make up the bed, fill the fridge and turn on the electricity. They could have cleaned the place too. But never mind. I'm home. And I'm elated.

Wiping a hole in the dust with my sleeve, I look out of the window at the beautiful green fields rolling away into the distance. The setting sun is casting a halo of pale blue around the ridge of the impressive Slieve Mish Mountains.

And as the sun dips down behind the mountains, creeping shadows begin to appear everywhere. Growing longer and deeper by the second. For the briefest of moments the silhouette they create around the clump of trees at the bottom of the garden has a very odd and ominous shimmer about it.

Something tugs violently at the curtain of my memory.

A shock runs through me right down to my boots. I stagger back away from it and crack my leg against the bedpost. I grab my leg and flop down on the bed. What the hell was *that* all about? The only thing down there is an old quarry. Why should I suddenly be bothered by *that?* It's just a big hole in the ground.

And I'm not sure if it was even a *real* quarry - it's just what everyone called it. Maybe it's because it looks like one, as if a huge chunk had been gorged out of the side of a hill by a giant hoe. It has a semi-circular wall of rock going straight down to a bowl at the bottom. The sloping sides are rough and uneven. A forest of bushes poke out from all the cracks and hollows.

In the winter the bowl fills with water. Then in summer when the weather is dry a thick green sludge festers on the top of it.

Elm trees cling to the edge of the bowl around the stagnant water that always seems to have a strange fog hovering over it.

For generations the family used it as a dump. And over the years the rubbish built up to create a neat slope against the back wall.

And it bred rats. Some the size of a small dog wallowing in the mounds of rotting waste.

But that's all it was! A rubbish dump! I used to play there as a child, for Heaven's sake. I must have visited that quarry a million times!

So what caused this reaction now? This sudden – what? A tingle of foreboding? It didn't make any sense.

My heart batters madly in my chest as I force myself to stand up. *Go back to the window and look at it again. You're a man now - you can't be scared by a shadow!*

The creeping dusk has already shrouded the trees in a haze that distorts the shape of them and exaggerates the contour of the branches. They look as if they're actually reaching out towards the light from the bedroom window. I take another deep breath and hold my ground. The quarry is an ugly place all right!

Eventually I drag my eyes away from it and my trembling legs take me back to the bed. I drop down wearily and sigh out loud again. My first day back home and already I'm starting to wobble.

Snap out of it! You're over-tired. Make some tea and get into bed. A good night's sleep will have you feeling better in the morning.

Down in the kitchen I turn on the tap and the water bangs like a drum in the empty kettle. I put the kettle on the stove and light the gas. I'm feeling better already. The shadows in the quarry don't seem so dark anymore.

Dreamin' Dreams

I smile as a warm memory drifts into my mind. Uncle Peter! We used to go shooting down in that quarry, Uncle Peter and me. He had an old army Webley .45 that he brought home from the war. Rats, mainly, were our targets.

Uncle Peter and me! He was my best friend. He was my father's younger brother but you'd hardly notice. They were like chalk and cheese. Uncle Peter was big with deep brown eyes and dark wavy hair. The complete opposite to my father.

Uncle Peter taught me to fish, to swim, to shoot. All the things my father didn't have the time for.

The curtain twitches in the depths of my memory again. And this time a sliver of something else shimmers into view. Something to do with Uncle Peter? What? I try to focus on it but it's gone again like smoke in a sudden breeze.

Take your tea and go back to bed!

Back in the quiet of my old bedroom a wonderful sense of contentment wafts over me. I glance around at all the familiar objects that were such a big part of my life back then. The old wooden wardrobe with the big brass handles. The rickety old chair by the window. Apart from the cobwebs it's just as I'd left it.

Just as it was the day Uncle Peter went away.

Strange how he left so suddenly, all those years ago.

I sip my tea. Why has *that* suddenly popped into my head? Why, after all these years without a single recollection of that period of my life, should an image suddenly reappear now?

Anyway, what did it matter? I'm pleasantly tired and totally relaxed. This wonderful day has finally arrived. I'm home again.

179

I swallow my final couple of tablets of the day. They'll keep the chemical imbalance in my brain under control. And I allow myself to savour the comforting, familiar fragrance of my room. It wraps itself around me and makes me feel so good. So secure. So glad to be home.

Gradually I drift into a comfortable sleep. And my mind floats back to that day again. The day Uncle Peter went away.

I was lying on the sofa in the drawing room, listening to my mother playing the piano. The French windows were open. A gentle summer's breeze fluttered the net curtains and the restful music mingled with the natural buzz of the warm afternoon.

But a brooding gloom began to seep in and sour the atmosphere. *Of course!* My father was due home any minute now. It meant this glorious moment wasn't going to last for much longer. Because as soon as he arrived back in the house the friction between him and Uncle Peter would spark off another bout of moody confrontation.

They say blood is thicker than water. But in *their* case it wasn't true. There wasn't an ounce of love lost between the two of them. They were born in this house. They grew up here. They watched their parents grow old and finally die here. But they were never close.

Of course it didn't help when the estate was left to them both. Shared *equally* between them.

So they carried on living in the house and working the land in an uneasy alliance. They worked hard, which was their nature. And eventually they built it into one of the biggest estate in the West of Ireland.

But then my father got married. For obvious reasons

he tried to buy Uncle Peter's share of the house. He wanted the house for himself and his wife. He didn't want a lodger. But Uncle Peter wouldn't sell. He loved this place. This was *his* home, too. So they bickered about it for years.

Eventually the bitterness became so poisonous they couldn't bear to work together any longer. So they split the estate between them. My father took the half to the north of the river, and Uncle Peter took the rest on the south side.

But it was the house that caused the most resentment. Neither wanted to sell their share to the other. But neither could they agree which part of the house belonged to whom. It *all* belonged to them *both*! And that only exasperated the already toxic situation.

Then, for some strange reason, my father got it into his head that Uncle Peter was going to sell his share of the farm and disappear. He was slowly becoming obsessed about it. He couldn't bear the thought of some stranger suddenly laying claim to what he believed was his rightful inheritance. My poor mother couldn't convince him otherwise.

Waiting for my father to make his sullen appearance that warm, lazy afternoon - the day Uncle Peter went away - I became aware that Uncle Peter was watching me. But when I looked at him he turned away and tapped his pipe out in the ashtray. His face had a sadness to it. He put his pipe in his pocket and stood up.

'I'm going for a walk,' he called over his shoulder. 'Do you want to come with me, Alan?'

We took the path that skimmed the northern edge of the lake and when we got to the woods on the other side Uncle Peter sat on a rock and threw twigs into the water.

'Alan, I've got something I want to say to you. I'm going away. To Paris.'

'Are you? When?'

'Tomorrow. I'm leaving first thing in the morning.'

'You're going on a holiday? How long for?'

'No. It's not for a holiday. I'm going away for good.'

A stunned silence followed.

'But why?' I asked when I found the strength to speak again.

'Because I'm tired.' He threw more twigs into the water. 'I'm just so tired, you know? I'm so tired of all this - this rowing and arguing all the time. I'm sick of sharing my life with people who really don't want me here. I know what you're going to say – that I've managed to put up with it for all these year. But that was mainly because - well, I had my reasons. God knows, I had my reasons. But now I've had enough, I'm afraid. I've had enough. And I'm getting out.'

Again a long silence and my heart was down in my boots. My throat was so dry I couldn't breathe! *Uncle Peter was going away. He was leaving me - just like that!*

'But I don't want you to go, Uncle Peter.' My eyes stung and I wiped them on my sleeve. 'Can't you wait a bit longer? Have a think about it? Maybe you'll change your mind when you've thought about it?'

'No. I've thought about it every day for the past ten years. Ever since the day that brother of mine got married, I've thought about it. There's no more thinking to be done! Tis time to go.'

My eyes filled this time and the wet rolled down my face. When he saw the tears he closed his eyes and held his head in his hands.

'Alan,' he raked his fingers through his hair. 'I'm so very, very sorry. But you don't understand. You have no idea what it's like living here in the same house as him. Yes, I love this house. And I love this land. Sure haven't I spent my whole life here? I love every single thing about it. But - well, there's only so much aggravation a man can take.'

'But what will you do in Paris? How will you live?'

He glanced up sheepishly and an embarrassed grin flickered on the corner of his mouth.

'I'm after selling my half of the land.' He spoke so softly I almost didn't catch what he said.

'You sold the …'

'Lock, stock, and even the water barrel.' He glanced up again then looked back down at his hands. 'Almost a million pounds I got for it. And tis already in the bank.'

'But you promised my father you'd never sell.'

'I know.' His eyes squinted as he studied the dark water of the lake. 'But things …'

'Then how could you do it? How could you …'

'For God's sake, Alan!' He jumped to his feet and slapped his hands together. 'Don't you bloody start on me as well. I'm sick and tired of people nagging me. I'm sick of it, do you hear me? God Almighty, I'm not a child. Anyway, tis already done now. I made my decision and that's the end of it.'

My chest heaved and I wiped my eyes again. 'Are you going to …' I blinked through the tears, '… will you be taking me with you?'

He put his arm around my shoulder and pressed my head against his chest.

'Only if it's what you want.'

'It is.'

'I was hoping you'd say that.' His voice was lighter now. It had relief in it too. 'I wasn't sure how to ask you. But I was hoping you'd say yes.' He punched me playfully on the arm. 'You know you're like a son to me, Alan. And I want you to have a better life than you have here right now. But only if it's what you really want.'

'It is!' I jumped up. 'Should I go and pack my things?'

'No.' He grabbed my arm. 'We'll have to go as we are. We can buy all the new clothes we want when we get to Paris. But for the moment it has to be our secret. No one must know what we're doing. Do you understand? They'll only get upset and we don't want to upset anyone. You must promise me you'll do nothing to make them think something's going on.'

I promised. Not a word to a living soul.

Suddenly it's night. I'm lying in my bed. Outside the moon is shimmering through the ghostly trees. Everything is silent. A deep eerie silence.

Then out of the silence voices drift up from somewhere down below. Muffled. Far away. But getting louder. Voices raised in anger! I try to sit up. My eyes open but I can't move. And I'm confused.

I know one side effect of my medication is the sensation of being paralysed. An impression that you can't move your limbs. That your muscles won't respond. You feel as if the blankets are pinning you to the bed, pressing you down into the mattress.

A more disturbing side effect is hallucination. Your dreams are scrambled and it's impossible to decipher them. You can't distinguish between what is real and what is illusion.

But that's rare. And it's *extremely* rare for both side

effects to hit at the same time.

Not being able to move never really bothered me, though. After the initial, distressing few episodes I learnt how to let my mind cut away from it and flutter off to more pleasant surroundings. To places I'd read about in a magazine. Or seen on TV.

But the hallucinations are something I can *not* master. They creep up on me and hit me before I even realise they're coming. Then there's no way I can hold on to real life. Images blur, time disintegrates, reality merges with fiction.

Is this what's happening now? Has the medication caused some adverse reaction and corrupted my fragile hold on reality? I'm not sure whether I've actually woken to find I'm paralysed, or whether I'm just *dreaming* that I've woken up to find I'm paralysed.

It's impossible to decide if the voices I'm hearing are real or illusion! I try to pinch myself but I can't. I've got no feeling in my fingers.

But I'm aware enough to know I can't do anything about it anyway. It's no use fretting. I just need to lie still and let it run its course. The voices will blend in with the rest of the stuff that comes with an attack. The stream of unfocused dreams.

Then I'll wake up and it'll be morning. That's how it usually happens!

It isn't happening like that now, though. The voices continue to pierce the night. Louder. Stronger. I try to cut away from them, focus my mind on something else. But they refuse to fade away. And that's odd.

Then I sense this is not a dream. This is a *memory*! I'm revisiting something from my past. Something that actually happened. That I've erased from my mind.

Dreamin' Dreams

Something distressing? What? I don't want to cut away from it now. I feel compelled to let it roll!

I recognise them, of course, the voices. Uncle Peter and my father bellowing at each other. This time, though, the row seemed more violent. More intense.

And suddenly something else pops into the memory. I remember my father brought some friends home with him that evening! They were already in the house when Uncle Peter and I got back from our walk. They never spoke. They just sat there silently all through dinner. Scowling. Mean. It made Uncle Peter very uneasy.

Now it's all flooding back to me. Sharper. More sinister. I can't make it stop.

The shouting that night bothered me so much I'd actually got out of bed to listen to it. My father's voice was the loudest. I could hear Uncle Peter's too. And somewhere in the background the sobbing voice of my mother.

It went on and on, echoing around the drawing room. A few times I thought I heard them mention my name but why I couldn't say. I was so frightened I lay at the top of the stairs and cried.

Tomorrow, I was thinking. After tomorrow I'll never have to listen to this again.

Then a sudden crash and a desperate, agonising cry. My heart pounded in my chest. *They were fighting!*

I jumped up and ran to the banister. Voices were yelling above the sound of breaking glass. Then another pitiful cry and everything seemed to drift outside and fade into the distance.

The stairs creaked under my bare feet as I staggered down one step at a time. The drawing room door creaked too as I pushed it open. The room was wrecked.

Dreamin' Dreams

The French windows were wrenched open and most of the glass panels were broken. Shiny slivers littered the carpet. One hinge was ripped off the door taking half of the frame with it. The torn curtain was wrapped around a toppled lamp. And it dangled in a pool of blood that trailed out over the wooden doorstep.

From somewhere outside came a soft wail. My heart pounded. I crept out into the night.

They were standing around the big tree in the garden. The silver light of the moon turned them into ghostly silhouettes. The damp grass wet my feet as I walked over to them.

My mother was sobbing into her hands. Her long hair scattered around her shoulders. My father stood beside his friends with his head bowed. One of them slurped drunkenly and dribbled down his chin.

I looked up into the tree. A scream. Arms wrapped themselves around me and squeezed me.

Suddenly I'm wide awake again. The bedclothes are scattered on the floor. Sweat covers me from head to foot.

I'm no longer paralysed! I sit up and throw my legs out of the bed. This is totally weird. I still don't know if I was hallucinating. Or if I just *dreamt* I was.

My hands are trembling as I reach for a cigarette, light it and take a desperate drag on it. Then I sit on the edge of the bed and shake with rage.

Damn you, Dr Ryan! You promised me this could never happen!

After all this time, all this treatment, all this psychiatry, all this psychology, even a session of hypnotism, you *insisted* that whatever happened all those years ago was buried so deep in my mind it would stay there forever.

I could rest assured, you said. I had nothing to fear from the past, you said. It was too far down to be resurrected. In fact, it was so far down it was probably erased!

You were *emphatic*! I had nothing to worry about! And, anyway, even if it *did* start to filter back - you told me confidently - it would happen so slowly it would take years to amount to anything. And by then I'd have absorbed it, accepted it, a little bit at a time.

So why was I suddenly remembering so much of it now?

No, I'm not happy about this at all!

Then it dawns me. It was Ryan's idea that I come back here! Ryan *convinced* me I should come back home. Because he's due to retire soon – that's why! He wanted to try one last experiment.

Dr Ryan is one of the top professors in his field. He's treated - and cured - numerous people over the years. Most of them are famous and powerful people, which earned him great respect and worldwide recognition.

But his tried and tested methods didn't work on me! He couldn't breach the barrier that enveloped my memory. And it denied him the answers to what exactly happened all those years ago. What triggered the terrible events I'd instigated? He really needed to know.

So he planted the seed! He conditioned me to remember only the good times, the exciting, wonderful times I had while growing up here in this house. All the fun of living on a huge working farm, the pleasure of being part of such a loving, caring family.

He fed the desire to come back home, to re-claim my rightful place in the world.

But Dr Ryan had published numerous articles in the medical journals advocating the positive power of shock. Perhaps I should have read them in more detail instead of just skipping over them!

But I did get the gist of it. Ryan believes that under controlled supervision the shock of revisiting the scene of a traumatic event could jolt the victim into remembering exactly what happened. Once the patient remembered what caused the trauma, treatment could start in earnest.

He *believes* that! So he must have anticipated that *something* would trigger total recall as soon as I was back where it all began.

And he's right! I'm stunned by the vividness of what I'm remembering! A dark force is sliding its fingers through the gap in the curtain of my memory. And one sliver at a time it's prising it open to shine a light on the exact moment that my world began to unravel.

I've been sucking desperately on the cigarette and now it's reduced to a half-inch stub. I grab another one, light it from the butt then crush the butt out on the chair. And I continue to draw long, deep gulps of smoke that I exhale down my nose and create a grey cloud all around me.

I shiver as I recall my mother's face the next day as she tried to explain to me that Uncle Peter had gone away.

She wouldn't say where he'd gone. Or why. But I was aware of a terrible change in her. Her pretty face looked drawn and weary. And her eyes were heavy and unfocused, almost unseeing.

Something strange had happened to my father as well. His face had taken on a twisted, lopsided sneer as if he was gloating about something. And his eyes looked quiet mad. Whenever he saw me he would snigger and turn away.

My mother and I rarely spoke to each other after that.

As usual, when I was frightened or disappointed, I sat on the grass down by the lake and watched the swans gliding in and out of the reeds. I was struggling to make sense of what was happening to everyone. And why Uncle Peter had gone away and left me.

Then a breeze rustled the trees and brushed the top of the reeds. And it whispered something that I couldn't quiet hear. I looked up at the house on the other side of the lake. Its dark reflection shimmered in the rippling brown water.

How big it looked all of a sudden. Big and cold. Couched in a grey sheen. Everything about it seemed larger, darker. Intense. The big, dark windows were unblinking as they looked back at me. Were they calling me, enticing me to come home? To come closer so it could wrap itself around me, absorb me?

I jumped up and turned my back to it. I felt suffocated! My stomach was tight and my head felt light. I ran away across the fields.

Of course when I got too tired and hungry to stay out any longer, I went back. And as I went in through the side door to the kitchen it felt eerily uncomfortable. It felt as if I was sleepwalking into some deadly web. And I would never be free from it again.

I quickly got to hate that house! Especially the stairs. And the stretch of corridor that led to my bedroom!

In the darkness it seemed to grow a hundred times its size! The silence would hang around it like a fog. The shadows would shimmer as I made my way to bed. I would get the strangest feeling of being watched. As if someone was waiting in the tunnel of emptiness. Waiting for me!

With every nerve tingling I'd hurry to my room, slam the door and scramble into my bed as quickly as I could.

I spit out bits of tobacco and wipe my mouth with my hand. *For God's sake, why am I dwelling on this? Stop it! Stop it now!*

I have to shake myself out of this stupid frame of mind otherwise it'll torment me all night. I take slow, deep breaths. If I can just get through my first night without any more episodes, I'll probably have a good laugh about it in the morning.

I rummage in my bag of medicine and find a large pink pill. What's that for? Do I care? I'm sure Dr Ryan prescribed it. Probably to calm me down. I swallow it and climb back under the blankets.

But as soon as I close my eyes my mind is captured by the dark, brooding image of the quarry. *That stupid hole in the ground!* Someday I'm going to fill the bloody thing in and get rid of it altogether!

But why does it have such an odd effect on me? Fear? *Why*?

Then another flash of memory explodes through the curtain.

I was sitting on the old stone bridge not long after Uncle Peter went away when I saw my mother coming out of the house. She was walking very fast and glancing around her nervously, as if she was anxious not to be seen.

She was carrying a bunch of red roses and she held them to her chest. She didn't noticed me as she hurried by right up to the edge of the quarry.

Then she did a strange thing. She crossed herself and tossed the roses into the quarry. She bowed her head and her shoulders jerked. And the breeze caught her sobs and blew them back to me before she turned and ran away.

Curious now, I went to the edge of the quarry. The roses were scattered on the green slime that covered the water. Some petals had broken off and lay around the buds like little spots of blood.

A breeze rustled my hair and whispered something as it brushed past me.

I spun around. Thick dark clouds had swept in over the trees behind me. They dimmed the already dull light of the wet grey day.

And that awful sensation that someone – *something* - was watching me crept up my back like fingers of ice.

The clouds thickened and dropped down until they were almost creeping along the ground. Was that someone behind the trees? *Stop it!* It was only a shadow! *But it moved!*

I grabbed at the hem of my jacket as I tried to back away from the quarry. But the ground had wrapped itself around my legs and was clamping them down.

And my eyes were being dragged back into the depths of the quarry! Who the hell *was* that? And what was he *doing* in the middle of all that putrid rubbish and rats? Rats? Strange! There were no rats! Just the smell. And the grey creeping mist swirling up towards me like strips of ghostly garments.

The shadow moved again! Panic tore at my throat but no sound came out. Just a gurgle that made my eyes water.

My head was pounding. I have to move! *I have to get away from here!* I forced my eyes to close. And I used every ounce of strength to throw myself backwards.

I hit the ground with a thud that knocked the wind out of me. But it broke the spell! I sprang up onto my hands and knees and scrambled away as fast as I possibly could.

But what exactly had I seen?

Nothing, surely? Shadows, that's all! Still, it had frightened me. And it must have left a deep scar in my young mind because it's frightening me again!

The rain patters like bony fingers against the window. Through the open curtains I can see clouds rolling across the full moon. Above the gable the trees dance in the wind.

Thunder roars and the sky lights up. I pull the bedclothes tighter around me.

Dear God, what on earth am I doing here?

Nurse Phillips was right. I haven't been on my own *once* in the past ten years. There was always someone around me, someone nearby. So what was the desperate need to come back here tonight?

Breathe deeply! Let the big pink pill take effect. Relax. Let it go. This is the darkest hour. It isn't long till morning.

But the curtain of my mind has parted too much now. The slivers of light have turned into one huge beam and illuminates the memories that cascade in through the gap.

I start to remember something else!

The dreams!

They began the night I was frightened down by the quarry.

I dreamt of boots. Brown, hand stitched boots. The kind Uncle Peter wore. They were suspended in the air.

193

Level with my face. Swaying gently. As I looked up at them I heard my mother cry. And for some reason it woke me.

I sat up. Was that a movement outside my room? Someone shuffling up and down the corridor? It seemed to stop outside my door. The handle creaked as it turned a fraction then fell back into place.

Then it stopped. I remember the relief as the tension drained out of me. I stopped sweating and fell asleep.

But the next night it was back. Shuffling in a slow, dragging movement. I could hear it breathing. Heavy, uneven breathing. Like a sick person struggling for breath.

It came the next night too. And every night after that. Always at the same time.

One night the door opened.

The room turned deathly cold. And a smell of decay wafted in.

Footsteps shuffled across to the foot of my bed. I could feel the force of someone looking at me. My heart beat violently and my hands shook as I squeezed the pillow and held my eyes shut tight.

My teeth were clenched so hard I could feel them bleeding. Little spots of red and yellow spun round in my head. I held my breath until my lungs ached.

It had found me!

But just as suddenly it was gone again! In a split second it had vanished. So too had the bitter cold and the awful smell.

I opened my eyes and blinked. *Surely it was just a horrible dream!* It had to be some sort of hallucination. I sat up and looked at the door. It was open.

I desperately wanted to tell someone about this. But

in the cold light of day it seemed so childish. Anyway, who could I tell? My mother? She would have smiled vacantly and wandered off somewhere. My father? I knew what his answer would be. A snigger. And a clout of a fist across the back of the head! *If only Uncle Peter was here.*

The next night it was back again. And the next.

But one night I never heard it come in. I woke to feel the presence standing at the side of the bed.

My heart almost stopped. My brain screamed as it moved closer. The smell. The heavy breathing. And the awful cold!

It was about six inched from my face. I could feel the eyes searching for a movement. My fingers bit into my legs. A dreadful terror flooded my head.

Then it was gone. Like before, it was suddenly gone again. I dragged at the air for breath. Tears squeezed out and flowed down my face.

Strangely, it didn't come again for over a week. I began to think I'd imagined the whole thing. Was it just a fevered imagination triggered by the disappointment of Uncle Peter going away? It had to be a dream. Just an hysterical dream.

Of course it did come back.

When I least expected it, it appeared at the side of my bed. The dreadful cold flooded the room and the appalling smell wafted over me. This time it spoke. With a revolting belch, it whispered my name.

'Alan.'

God, that *voice*!

'Open your eyes.'

I couldn't. It was almost touching my face. My head thumped. I couldn't control it anymore. I screamed.

I threw myself out of the bed and fell onto the floor. Covered my face with my hands I ran to where I thought the door was. But I hit the corner of the wardrobe with a thud that flung me backwards into the room. Everything was spinning. Strong hands lifted me to my feet. Cold fingers touched my cheek.

'Alan, don't be afraid.'

I was trying to wriggle free but the grip was too strong.

'Alan, tis me. Surely you're not afraid of *me*?'

Clouds of decaying breath spread over me. I couldn't scream, it lodged in my throat.

'Open your eyes!' This time there was an annoyance in his voice. He shook me. 'Open your eyes!'

His voice was deep and hollow. I beat at him with my fists but the grip didn't ease. His hand held my face.

'Alan! Look at me!'

The icy touch numbed me and the biting radiation from his face stung like a million needles.

'Get away from me.'

'Ah, you're mad at me, is that it?'

I couldn't breathe.

He drew me closer to him. His rough lips, so cold they burnt my skin as they brushed against my cheek. 'I'm so sorry. But I did try to come back for you, you know.'

I kicked with bare feet.

'Alan, please! Don't fight with me. Not you, of all people. I've come back for you, haven't I?'

I began to vomit.

'Alan, look at me!' His voice thundered with anger now. 'All right, so I never came for you that morning, the day we were going to Paris. But do you want to

196

know why? Do you? Well, I'll tell you why. Because I was stuck down in that bloody quarry out there! And do you know why I was down there?'

His voice boomed in my head. Was he really speaking, or was I just reading his thoughts?

'I was down there because my own dear brother threw me down there, that's why! After he hanged me! My own brother hanged me. And your dear mother just stood there and let him do it. He hanged me until my neck broke and I couldn't breathe. My brain burst from lack of oxygen. How could I come back for you then, young fella? When I was dead?'

Dead? It bellowed in my ears. *Dead? Dead!*

'He was after finding out about us, you see?' The voice faded in and out through the dread and revulsion that flooded my senses. 'He found out about you and me going to Paris. He found out the council bought my piece of land and they were planning to build a huge housing estate on it. But that wasn't all he found out. Your mother had to go and get hysterical and she started telling him why I *really* wanted to take you with me!'

On and on, his voice telling me things that got jumbled up in the turmoil cascading through my petrified senses. My head was swimming and I was sick again. I would have dropped to the floor if it wasn't for the hands that held me up

'So I've come for you now, Alan. This time I've found a way to take you with me. We can spend eternity together.'

Oh, God help me. *Help me!* I don't want to spend eternity trapped down that dark, ugly quarry.

Then I heard my mother's voice outside in the hallway. She was coming up the stairs! She was on her

197

way to bed and she was mumbling to herself.

She paused outside my bedroom door. Her mumbling hesitated for less than a heartbeat before it turned into a horrified gasp.

Another flash lights up the bedroom and thunder clatters away across the sky. I kick off the bedclothes and sit up, throwing my legs over the side of the bed.

This is all too much for me now. The memories are cascading in through the curtain like a tsunami. Too fast for me to filter. Too severe for me to reason with. I'm beginning to panic. This could be enough to send me over the edge again. And all the way back to Dr Ryan.

I need a drink. I'm sure I saw a bottle of Jameson in the drawing room. *Knock yourself out! Sleep it off.* I go back downstairs.

I pause when I see my mother's photograph on the mantle above the old black range. She was so beautiful.

I remember the shock when they found her body half way down the garden path the morning after my dream. They said the look on her face was one of sheer terror. She was covered in mud. Whatever it was she was running from, she was so desperate to get away from it she fell and impaled herself on a broken fence post.

They found my father's body in the drawing room the same day. He'd put up a ferocious struggle. The police found the Webley .45 nearby. They established that it had been fired six times. But they were puzzled when they couldn't find four of the bullets.

There were powder burns on my father's hand, so it was obvious he'd fired most of them. But someone then took the gun off him and fired the last bullets into his face at close range. It threw him backwards into the bookcase.

The gun was covered in a strange, slimy mud. But they still managed to find one complete fingerprint. It was mine.

I touch my mother's photo. *God rest your poor soul!*

I lick my lips. I can taste that whisky already. *One nice big swig. Roll it around your mouth. Savour it for a moment before letting it slide down to warm the cockles of your heart! Then back to bed. Better still, take the bottle with you!*

A wind whistles through the drawing room when I open the door and a flash of lightening zips across the sky. I stop dead! The French windows are wide open and the tattered curtains are in chaos around them.

I swallow hard. I'm sure they were locked when I checked them earlier. In fact, I'm *positive* they were! Very strange! Was the wind so strong it broke the lock? I'll have to call someone in the morning to get it looked at.

I go to shut them and I notice the wooden step.

The day after Uncle Peter went away I remember a man coming to replace that step. I remember it clearly because I couldn't understand why. There was nothing wrong with it. Except maybe for an odd dark brown stain across the centre.

But he renewed it anyway. He gave us a brand new one in dark oak.

Now there was a deep groove right through the middle of it.

I know ten years of rain and neglect could corrode wood. But could the elements have worn such a neat groove in it? Like *that*?

No. This was caused by something else. By something being continuously rubbed across it. Like feet. Like dead feet being dragged over it, night after night after …

Panic rakes up my back. I push the doors shut as the next sheet of lightening lights up the night. And for a second the glass is a mirror, reflecting the room behind me.

A tall shadow moves slowly out from behind the door. A scream sticks in my throat.

I *knew* it! *He just couldn't leave me alone. All that time! He was waiting all that time. Waiting for me to come back home!*

All Uncle Peter wanted was to have his family around him again. But he couldn't have the woman he loved because she died running away from him.

But he still had someone precious. Someone he cherished just as much. Someone he knew would come back to him one day.

He was waiting for his beloved son!

He was waiting for *me* …

Who's that in the Attic?

Claire had never been in the attic in her life. She was just a baby, only a few months old, when her mother vanished off the face of the earth and her father took her to Dublin to get away from the rumours and the wagging tongues.

Now, twenty years later, she was back living with her Grandad in a small country town where she hardly knew a single soul. And with a baby too. So she didn't really give the attic any thought at all.

Yet the attic in her dream seemed *so* familiar - a long, dusty room with thick, sloping rafters and hazy beams of sunlight filtering through the small window in the roof.

And it was so vivid - one of those dreams that lingers in your mind for days afterwards. It wasn't an upsetting dream or anything like that. Probably more peculiar than distressing. So she wasn't too bothered by it. Just curious as to what it meant.

In the dream Claire was balancing on one of the beams in the middle of the attic. She was concerned that if she stepped off the beam she'd fall right through the floor into the room below. The baby was in the room below and she'd only just gone to sleep after lot of agitation and squawking. The last thing Claire wanted to do was wake her up again.

Claire had the strangest feeling someone else was in the attic too, but she couldn't see who it was. The shimmering veil of hazy sunlight obscured her vision.

For some reason, though, Claire just *knew* it was her grandmother. And her grandmother was thrilled that Claire had come to see her. Because there was something really, really important she wanted to tell her.

But when Claire went to step closer to the image she couldn't move her legs. She grabbed the rafter above her head and tried to shuffle her feet along the beam. But nothing would shift them. She was rooted to the spot.

It was only then she noticed the loud ticking sound coming from behind her.

When she turned around she was amazed to see a beautiful mahogany grandfather clock propped up against the wall and almost hidden behind the door. And as she squinted at it the light glanced off the large brass hand as it moved another notch around the ornate face.

It was approaching three o'clock. The hand seemed to quiver with a tense, muted urgency before it gave the final tick. And a deep chime vibrated through the attic.

Suddenly Claire was wide-awake. And so was the baby! Claire cursed as she mustered the energy to crawl out of bed and scoop little Zoë up in her arms.

At times like this she wished Liam was still around. At least they could take turns getting up in the night. But Liam, as Claire found out, was *not* a baby man.

Three wonderful, exciting years together. Lots of good times. Claire believed there was a beautiful future ahead of them. Then her father died and her whole world collapsed.

Her father had been her whole life, ever since her mother disappeared all those years ago. It was such a traumatic, bewildering time for them all. One night they went to bed - the next morning Claire's mother was gone.

None of her stuff was missing. All her clothes, her shoes, her bits and pieces, were still in their place. Suspicion seeped from every quarter. Which was only natural of course. But it hurt Claire's father badly when every comment from their neighbours and friends seemed to be loaded with conjecture.

There was a huge search. The Gardaí, the neighbours, all their friends turned out to look for her. But they found absolutely no trace of her.

In the initial confusion Claire's father deflected the pain by focussing all his attention on his baby girl. She was all he had left. No one was ever going to take her away from him. So he took her to Dublin and never came back.

Grandad visited a few times over the years. And it was from snippets of their conversations that Claire discovered why she didn't have a Mum like all the other kids. She got the impression Grandad thought someone else was involved, that her mother ran away with another man. It was the only reasonable explanation.

But her father never spoke about it with Claire. Whenever she tried to approach the matter his big gentle eyes would fill up and he'd quickly change the subject.

Then one day Liam appeared. At a bus stop, of all places! And everything else faded into the background. Claire's life changed gear and cruised along at a wonderful, exciting pace. Dreams were dreamed, hopes were articulated and plans were made.

Then suddenly her precious father was gone. Changing a light bulb and thinking he'd switched off the power. So simple, so unbelievably quick! Liam was the only one she had to cling to. Perhaps she clung too tightly. Perhaps she smothered him.

At first he was totally supportive. But maybe she grieved for too long, took too long let go and pull herself together. Little holes began to appear in their relationship.

But when the tests confirmed she was pregnant Claire believed this was the spark that would cement their love and bind them together forever. She couldn't have been more wrong.

Liam sulked, moaning that she'd only gone and spoilt all the plans he had for their future. All the things he'd imagined them doing together were now in shreds. He withdrew into his own world and shut her out for days on end. All the little holes were fast merging into one almighty big one.

Then the phone rang late one night and Claire got to it first. When she heard the charged silence before the other person hung up she knew instantly that she'd lost him as well.

So Claire and the baby came back to live with Grandad.

'Maybe your grandmother was trying to tell you something.'

'My *grandmother*?'

'Your grandmother! You said your grandmother was in the attic.'

Claire groaned. She knew she shouldn't have said anything to Rene about the dream.

'I did not. I said I *sensed* … I just *felt* that maybe it was her. But I couldn't really say *who* was there.'

Rene had the strangest sense of humour - as dry as a bucket of sawdust but with a keen, wicked edge. There was also a deeper, morbid aspect to it. If a house was cold she's joke that it was probably built on a graveyard. She saw humour in everything. But she'd often cloak it in a dark, sinister veil.

But you couldn't take offence because she'd dilute it

with a light-hearted, contagious giggle.

Claire met Rene at the antenatal clinic, a tiny body with a big bump and long ginger hair. She was the smallest person there but you noticed her immediately because of the dazzling smile and the intense blue eyes. And the fact that everyone around her was convulsed with laughter.

After the babies were born Rene and Claire kept in touch, meeting every Tuesday for coffee and a chat. Rene was a bundle of energy, taking everything in a good humoured stride. And her baby slept all night and most of the day as well. She was so contented she'd make you sick. Claire was tempted on several occasions to swap babies.

'Anyway, I knew you'd make fun of me if I told you.'

'But I'm not, though.' Rene moved closer. And the look she gave Claire was unusually serious. 'Maybe she was trying to tell you who murdered her.'

'*What* …?' Claire felt her heart thump in her chest and she spluttered into her coffee. 'What do you mean; *who murdered her?*'

She pushed back her chair and went to jump up. Her hand went to her mouth. 'What are you … that's a *terrible* thing to say. My grandmother wasn't … what do you mean? Are you serious? Are you saying my grandmother was murdered?'

'Oh, Claire, I'm so sorry!' Rene grabbed her hand and coaxed her to sit back down. 'I thought you knew already. Surely you must have heard about it? She was *your* grandmother! And you living in the same house as well. Surely to God someone would have mentioned it to you. Tis common knowledge around here. Everyone in town knows about it.'

'Well, *I* didn't know about it.' Claire took a long sip of her coffee, trying to clear her senses. 'When did … what happened?'

'No one knows exactly.' Rene's eyes sparkled now. 'According to my Da – you know he's an Inspector with the Gardaí? Well, when I was telling him about you the other day, the subject came up. Apparently they found your grandmother sitting in the bus shelter. The one in the street just outside your house. She'd been hit on the head with a blunt object and it seemed she died instantly.'

'In broad daylight? I can't believe … did they catch who did it?'

'Well, it wasn't exactly in broad daylight,' Rene grimaced and rubbed her nose with her finger. 'According to the report at the time it was three o'clock in the morning. The milkman found her. She was just sitting there. Apparently the poor man was never the same again. He had to give up the milk round. They say he became a bit of a recluse afterwards. *And*,' she patted Claire's hand in emphasis, 'if you were to believe the rumours, the big old clock in your grandmother's hallway stopped dead at exactly three o'clock. And there hasn't been a peep out of it ever since.'

They sat in silence for a while, both of them absorbed in their own thoughts.

'Why would my grandmother be sitting in a bus shelter at three o'clock in the morning?' Claire asked. 'Where was my Grandad?'

'Well,' Rene took a tissue from her bag and wiped the baby's nose. 'The thinking at the time was that she was meeting someone - that she had a fancy man. But she also had a baby who was only a few months old. The Gardaí believed the fancy man wanted her to go away with him but she couldn't leave the baby. When she refused to go with him, the fancy man decided if he couldn't have her then no one else would either.'

'God, that's awful.' Claire wiped her eyes again. 'Do you realise that baby would have been my mother?'

'I know.' Rene sipped her coffee. 'Didn't she disappear one day? When you were only a few months old yourself?'

'Yes,' Claire sighed as she stood up. 'And that was enough of a mystery in itself. Now this! It's all too much for me to take in, I'm afraid. I'll see you next week.'

Claire went home in a daze. *A murder?* She couldn't believe no one had ever mentioned a murder before. *Her own grandmother* – and no one told her?

Her head buzzed with a million questions to ask Grandad as she charged in through the back door. But when she saw him sitting by the window gazing out onto the garden she couldn't bring herself to say anything. He looked so thin and frail.

He was so pleased the day Claire phoned and asked if she and the baby could come to live with him. Having them around gave him a new lease of life. Now, though, as she watched the sad old face and the thinning grey hair, she realised he must have so much bottled up inside of him. She was suddenly afraid to say anything about her grandmother in case it all came pouring out.

She pushed the pram quietly into the living room and parked it in the darkest corner, hoping the baby would stay asleep for another half hour at least.

And when she noticed a large old photograph amongst the clutter on top of the piano a weird shiver ran right through her. The intense young woman's dark passionate eyes seemed to be looking directly at her. Wide and haunted as if she was trying to say something. Claire gave a startled yelp as she stepped back away from it.

'*For God's sake,*' she snapped as she rubbed her hands through her hair. '*Pull yourself together. It's just an old photo. That's what you get for listening to Rene.*'

She couldn't understand why she hadn't noticed it before, though. She sucked in a deep breath and bent closer to get a better look.

'That's Caroline, your grandmother,'

Claire jumped when Grandad spoke. She hadn't realised he was watching her.

'Has it been there all the time?'

'No, no. It was up in the attic, ever since the day …' He hesitated, as if unsure whether to go on or not.

Claire paused for a moment and rubbed her eyes. And before she could do anything about it the words came tumbling out.

'Grandad, I know all about it.'

'You do? Really?'

'Well, actually, no.' She put her hand on his shoulder. 'Not *all* about it. Only that she was killed …'

'Murdered!' Grandad snapped. 'Whatever way you look at it, she was murdered.'

'I'm sorry.' Claire took her hand away. 'I didn't mean to upset you. I shouldn't have said anything.'

'And *that's* been the hardest part of this whole sorry affair. No one *ever* wanted to talk about it. All these years, my friends, my neighbours, they all skirted around the subject in case it might upset me.' Grandad jabbed the air with his finger. 'But what upset me most was when I desperately wanted to talk about it, when I badly needed to discuss it, when I tried to ask questions and wanted some kind of an answer, they all shied away from it and changed the subject. It was as if I was some kind of a … a … delicate flower or something. That I would crumble under the pain of it all.'

He shuffled across to the piano and picked up the photograph.

'My Caroline was murdered.' His eyes glistening as he studied the beautiful face behind the glass. 'And I still don't know why. All this time I've cried bitter tears over it, not knowing why.'

The baby stirred and Claire went to the pram and gave it a gentle rock.

'Did you know the Gardaí suggested she was seeing another man?' Grandad gave a throaty growl. 'But how come I didn't know anything about that? Why couldn't I see any evidence of that? Was I so naïve? Was I so blinded by my love for her that I was oblivious to what she got up to behind my back? Was I so engrossed in my work, so busy struggling to give us all a better life that I was just too distracted to see what was happening right under my nose?'

Claire watched him with mounting sadness as she continued to give the pram slow, gentle rocks.

'Anyway, the Gardaí had a theory that she'd planned to elope with this man, whoever he was. And she went to meet him at the bus stop down by the gate.' Grandad's voice was softer now, as if he was just thinking out loud. 'I was asleep when she crept out. But for some strange reason the chimes of the clock woke me up. They seemed so much louder than normal. Almost urgent. Three loud chimes. Then I realised she was not in bed with me. You'll never know that terrible feeling. A dreadful sense of foreboding swept over me at that very moment. I just *knew* I'd lost her forever.'

The old eyes filled up and he sniffed loudly.

'Seconds later I heard the frantic hammering on the front door. And there was Larry the milkman, blood all down his overalls and the look of sheer horror on his face. The neighbours were woken by the racket, too. Some of them tried to stop me from seeing her, but they couldn't. And even in death she was so beautiful, sitting upright on the bench as if she was just asleep. I couldn't understand it. There was no sign of a struggle. Just a lot of blood from a wound on the side of her head as if she'd been struck suddenly and unexpectedly. I sat and held her until the Ambulance came and took her away.'

Claire realised her hands were shaking now and she gripped the handle of the pram. She wanted to go to her grandfather and just hold him, comfort him. But right then she didn't know how.

'What about the man who found her?' she asked awkwardly. 'I mean, didn't he see anything? Surely at that time of the morning there wouldn't have been many other people around.'

'Poor old Larry?' Grandad looked up at the ceiling, his eyes squinting as he thought about the question. 'No, he didn't see anyone. He got such a shock finding her like that, just sitting there. He never recovered from it. The Gardaí couldn't make any sense of what he was saying. He was just gibbering incoherently.'

'The poor, poor man. You said *Old* Larry. How old was he?'

'In his forties, I suppose.' Grandad nodded. 'A lovely, gentle old soul, Larry was. He knew everyone and he always had a pleasant word for you. He drove around in one of those huge American pickup trucks. A fierce big red thing with a white stripe down the side. Everyone recognized him in it, of course. But flash and all as it was, he never went very fast in it. It was all for show, you see. And it worked because everyone got their milk from him.'

Grandad rubbed his fingers softly across the glass and then put the photo back on the piano.

'But he gave up the milk round after that. It was a family business, started by his father and an uncle. And Larry worked with them all his life. But the confidence was knocked out of him. He never married, you see. He still lived with his parents. So he sort of went into semi-retirement, just doing the paperwork and stuff. I don't think I ever saw him after that.'

Claire felt her eyes being drawn to the photo again. She was mesmerized by the intense dark eyes, brown like her own but a much deeper shade. The hair was also black, but her grandmother's was cut in a typical 60's bob.

Was this who Claire sensed in the attic?

Now her head was filled with the dream again. The baby crying snapped her out of it.

Later that evening as the day cooled down they sat in the garden. Claire was still overwhelmed by everything that had been piled on her during the day. She had so many questions.

'Grandad, what do *you* think happened to my mother?'

'Your mother?' Grandad sighed deeply. 'You know, when your grandmother died the only thing that kept me going was the baby. My darling little Lizzy. I was

211

terrified they'd take her away from me. But I was determined to keep her. I devoted my whole life to her, brought her up as best I could. Eventually she met your father, a wonderful man, and they got married. And then you came along. Everything seemed so wonderful.'

Grandad shook his head slowly.

'Then, exactly twenty years to the day Caroline was killed, your mother disappeared. No explanation, no reason! You can imagine the despair, the desperation of not knowing what happened to her. Of course there were so many theories about that, too. Some were quiet ridiculous, I might add. Anyway, Lizzy just vanished off the face of the earth. Nothing was missing. Even her purse was still on the kitchen table. Your father insisted everything was fine between them at the time. He had a good job with the council. They were saving for a house of their own. Things couldn't have been better.'

Grandad took a long swig from his glass of beer.

'Anyway, according to your Dad they went to bed around ten-thirty. And he swears the next thing he remembers was hearing the grandfather clock chiming. It chimed three times, even though it had stopped working years ago and had been put up in the attic! That's when he realised your mother was not in the bed with him. She was never seen again. The Gardaí and the neighbours did a search, of course. But your Dad and I sensed everyone believed she'd just run away. Post-natal depression, they said. Or else she had a fancy man. Just like her mother! Your poor father took it very badly. He couldn't stay here any longer with all the suspicion and bogus sympathy. He got a transfer to Dublin.'

Claire poured some more beer into his glass and he took another drink from it.

'One of the things we found amongst your mother's stuff was a small pocket diary,' Grandad said after a long pause. 'She'd written lots of notes in it. Apparently she was doing some research into the original investigation of her mother's death. She was looking for anomalies, clues as to who might have been involved. She seemed determined to find out exactly what happened all those years before. Anyway, the notes were a bit scrambled, almost cryptic. But they implied she'd discovered something up in the attic. And she believed it was a clue about who the killer might actually be.'

He gave a soft cough into his fist and rested his head back. 'Of course it was suggested that perhaps she *did* find out who the killer was and went to confront him, only to end up the same way as her mother.'

They sat in silence for a while as the daylight slowly faded and the moon replace it with a soft, silver glow.

'Forty years exactly.' Grandad raised his glass.

'What is?'

'Tonight,' he nodded. 'It's exactly forty years tonight since your grandmother was murdered. And still no one knows what really happened. Except for the killer, of course.' He wiped his eyes with his fingers. 'Still, apart from myself, who else really cares? They've already forgotten about it.'

'No they haven't. Grandad - *please* don't think that.'

'Ah, take no notice of me.' He had a sob in his voice. 'Tis just how I feel right now! But I'll tell you one thing. If I could have just one wish before I die, it would be to know what really happened to them, my Caroline and Lizzy. Put an end to all this mystery - and misery.'

It was well past midnight before Grandad shuffled off to bed. Claire was relieved to climb between the cool, crisp sheets herself. It had been a long strange day. Within seconds she was sound asleep.

Then suddenly she was out on the stairs. Her heart was racing, beating in her ears. And she had the strangest flutter in her stomach.

What on earth was she doing?

Now she was creeping down the stairs and along the hallway, tiptoeing across the shiny tiles towards the front door as if pulled by some invisible force.

She jumped when she caught sight of herself in the long hall mirror, illuminated by a shaft of moonlight that came in through the little window above the door.

Why was she wearing such a gaudy pink dress? And with a hem so short she'd be way too embarrassed to be seen in? And her hair –was it cut in a bob? A 60's bob? Just like the lady in the photograph?

And those eyes! The beautiful eyes looking back at her were so dark and intense they were almost black. Claire was totally mesmerised by them. It was only the ticking of the grandfather clock that drew her attention away.

What was it doing in the hall? Shouldn't it be up in the attic? It was a moment before she realised the clock was reading ten minutes to three.

In the morning?

The flutter in her stomach intensified! Then she realised why. She was excited! It was almost time! She had to hurry. Now she was creeping out through the front door and tiptoeing down the path to the gate.

Was he there yet?

Who?

Headlights were coming up the street. Now she was breathless, unable to contain herself. The vehicle stopped about a hundred yards away. Near the bus shelter.

A tall man got out and Claire was almost overwhelmed by the awesome feeling of love she felt towards him. She ran to him. Her mind was a blur as she tried to focus on his face. Then she noticed the big red American truck. The man moved into the light from the street lamp.

Larry?

'Caroline, sweetheart.' He put his arms around her and squeezed her tight.

Caroline? He called her *Caroline*! But that was her grandmother's name. A tingle ran up Claire's spine.

What was going on?

She tried to focus, make sense of it. But Larry was moving away from her now and she detected something in the manner of his walk that caused a sudden feeling of dread to sweep over her.

'Larry,' she heard herself saying. 'What is it? What's the matter?'

'I'm so sorry, Caroline,' he said in a low, sad voice. 'I'm after giving this a lot of thought over the past few days. I really think that it would be better all-round if we were to stop seeing each other.'

'No!' Claire yelped. She reached out to touch him but he moved farther away. 'Larry! Please don't say that!'

'I'm sorry, but what we're doing is so wrong and the both of us know it.'

Larry rubbed his hands through his hair. Claire was fascinated by the incredible feeling she had for him. She'd never felt anything like this before in her whole life.

'It has to stop right now, before anyone gets hurt.'

'Larry, please … '

'What if someone finds out about us? What would happen if they told your husband? You'd lose everything. You'd even lose the baby.'

'I don't care.' Claire had a choke in her voice now. 'Please, Larry, don't do this to me. I couldn't bear it. All I want right now is to be with you. Please, just let me hold you.'

He shook his head. 'Caroline, this is hard enough already. Please don't make it any harder.'

'But why are you being like this to me?' Her head was throbbing and she had to wipe her nose on her sleeve. 'You told me you loved me! You said I was the best thing that ever happened to you in your whole life.'

'I do! You are!' He went to reach out to her but pulled away again. 'And that's why I have to let you go. Because I love you so much. I just know that if we go on like this it will only end in pain and tears. And I'd end up losing you anyway. So I'd rather end it now and remember you for the good times we've shared.'

'But what happened - what brought all *this* on? Is it because of the age difference? Are you worried about the age difference?'

'Not just that. Although that *is* important. But the fact is you're a beautiful young woman. And in spite of the way you feel right now there's bound to come a time when you'll meet someone your own age. Then you'll realize you've got more in common with him than you would with someone my age.'

'But your age doesn't matter to me. It never did. I love you for what you are.'

'As I said, it's not just that.' Larry gave a deep sigh and wiped his eyes with his fingers. 'Imagine how you'd feel if you lost the baby and we're cooped up in a tiny

216

flat somewhere on a wet and cold Sunday afternoon with no place to go. No money. And probably no job either? You'd be frantic, pining for her, terrified of missing her first step, her first words, her first day at school. No! Like I said, Caroline, I love you too much to put you through all that.'

His big hands took her by the shoulders and he kissed her on the forehead. Then he walked back to the truck.

Claire's eyes were stinging from the tears that burnt them now. The pain was horrendous, as if he'd reached inside and was pulling the heart out of her. The truck was moving away and now she was running after it, crying desperately for him to stop, to come back.

It had only gone a hundred yards when the brake lights came on and it ground to a halt. Then it began reversing back up the street towards her. Her heart leapt in her chest.

He was coming back to her.

She rushed forward and reached out to grab the door handle. She didn't see the wing mirror until it was too late. She tried to duck, but it caught her on the side of the head.

There was no pain, just a tremendous flash of light.

Larry was holding her now, his whole body shaking as he frantically tried to wake her up, crying and whimpering. He picked her up and carried her to the bus shelter, and he sat her on the bench.

It was all so warm and cosy now, making it awfully hard for Claire to open her eyes. And she felt so hungry, too. But most of all she felt relief that, at long last, she knew exactly what happened to her grandmother all those years ago.

It was just a horrible, horrible accident. Poor Larry!

Poor Grandad! How was she ever going to explain it to him? How was she going to tell him about Larry? Her heart went out to the both of them. She frowned. *How was she going to explain it to anyone?*

Who would believe a dream?

A moonbeam came in the window and fell across the cot. How big the bars looked from this side. And the colours of the mobile that dangled above her head. How wonderfully comforting they were to a baby. She was feeling so sleepy, so comfortable.

Suddenly there was a loud, urgent, chime of a clock. Then another. As the third one echoed throughout the house the bedroom door crashed open.

It was Grandad. 'Oh, no! Claire, where are you?'

For a tense moment he just stared at the empty bed. Then he shuffled over to the cot and his huge hands reached down and wrapped themselves around Claire. They lifted her gently and held her against the stubbled face. The face was wet with tears.

'Oh, Zoë, Zoë, what's happened to your mammy? Please don't say it's happened again. It can't happen again.'

Zoë? Why was he calling her *Zoë*?

Somehow, though, she didn't care. Everything was fading into a beautiful, comfortable haze now. She was still hungry, but she felt so secure in the huge arms of her grandfather who was rocking her gently …

Dressmaker

Moss Scanlon was sitting on his stool inside the window of his Harnessmaker's shop, busily repairing a donkey saddle for a local farmer, when he heard the thud from the room above. He didn't have time to react. A fraction of a second later he was slapped on the head by a lump of plaster the size of a dinner plate.

Luckily the plaster was made of soft distemper, stuff that had been applied to the ceiling over a hundred years or more. So when it landed on his head it didn't do any damage. It just exploded in a shower of tiny flakes that scattered around him like a small snowstorm.

Mick, his nephew, glanced up at the little round hole and the exposed beams.

'I told you that ceiling needed looking at,' he muttered, flicking a flake of distemper out of his mug of tea.

There was a flurry of activity in the room above - strange rattling and banging noises - and an assortment of muffled voices. Urgent footsteps moved across the floor and rumbled down the narrow stairs, crashed through the little door at the bottom and exploded right into the shop.

A flustered Aunt Fanny was the first through, followed closely by Delia and Nan. And they were all fussing around young Mrs Fitzgibbon-O'Hare who was looking distinctly agitated by this stage.

'A cup of tea, Mrs Fitzgibbon!'

'*No, I'm fine!*'

'No, no. I insist.'

'*No! Thank you. I'm grand, I tell you!*'

'But you need to sit down. Mick, a cup of tea for Mrs

Fitzgibbon-O'Hare, please!'

'*NO! I said I'm grand! Will you just ...*'

The look on Aunt Fanny's face was one of pure mortification. She could see her latest project evaporating right in front of her eyes. She gave a desperate groan as Mrs Fitzgibbon-O'Hare reached the front door and practically threw herself out into the safety of the street.

'About the dress, Mrs Fitzgibbon ...'

'*I'll be in touch*!'

'Will I bring it up to the house?'

'*No! I'll be in touch!*'

The voice was fading now as Mrs Fitzgibbon-O'Hare scurried across the street and disappeared through the archway into the cattle market.

The three women huddled for several minutes in a gloomy silence by the door, looking forlornly after their lost client. Delia sighed, turned around and shuffled towards the tiny kitchen at the back of the shop.

'I'll make the tea, so!'

'Right you are,' Aunt Fanny agreed. And she and Nan traipsed along behind her.

Moss Scanlon rolled his eyes.

'Women!' he sighed. 'They should leave the work to the men.'

He nodded at the wisdom of his observation. But in his heart he knew he was talking tripe. He was well aware that it was the *lack* of work that forced the women to take this course of action in the first place.

Times were changing, you see. And not necessarily for the better. And because of those changes the Harnessmaker's trade, handed down from generation to generation, from father to son, was slowly shrivelling on the vine. In the relentless drip, drip of progress fewer people needed him now. So in the great scheme of things he was slowly becoming redundant.

Poor Moss, how he pined for the good old days when horses were the lifeblood of the community. In his day *everyone* relied on the horse, or the pony, even the donkey.

You needed the pony and trap to get around - it took you to town, it carried you to church. Bigger horses were used for ploughing, the heavy pulling, and the dragging of the hay wagons. And even the auld donkey had his uses - it took the milk to the creamery.

And they all required the service of the Harness Maker. He made and repaired the harnesses, the blinkers, the straps, saddles of all sizes and shapes. And a whole load of other essential paraphernalia.

Then some clever dick invented the tractor!

And the combined harvester!

Of course it took a few years for these labour saving devises to filter across to the west coast of Ireland. And even when they did the cost was way beyond the means of the average farmer.

Initially!

Then Co-Operatives sprang up all over the place. The farmers were delighted. For Moss Scanlon, though, they brought with them the whisper of doom.

So he had no choice but to allow the women to assist with the finances.

Aunt Fanny was a dressmaker by trade. But she was a gentle lady and not the least bit pushy. And she didn't have the business acumen to pursue it vigorously. She did some amazing work all right, but it was usually for family and friends. They thought of it as a gift and didn't want to embarrass her by offering her any kind of payment. They thought the praise was enough!

Delia, on the other hand, worked for a wine importer. *She* could see Aunt Fanny's potential. But she wasn't sure how to market the concept.

That was until she met John Fitzgibbon-O'Hare, a brash American who had a very expensive taste in wine.

Fitzgibbon was born on the family farm just outside Listowel in West Ireland. He was taken to Arizona by his mother when he was three years old and it was there he made his fortune in cardboard packaging.

Then years later, on the very day he came back to Ireland to claim his inheritance, he met the pretty young farmer's daughter, Kitty O'Hare.

His first visit to Ireland didn't get off to a very good start, though. When he climbed into his hire car at Shannon Airport he was perplexed to find the steering wheel was on the wrong side.

He was even more alarmed to discover that, in Ireland, they actually *drove* on the wrong side as well. So, totally disorientated, he bimbled around for hours. He should have brought a map, of course. But Ireland was so *small*! His own back yard in Arizona was bigger than this.

Then, at long last, he saw the sign for Ballybunion. *Now* he knew he was close to home.

But half an hour later he was still driving around in circles. Then, during a break in the miserable rain, he spotted two men working in a field away in the distance. He decided he had no choice but to go and ask them for directions. He pulled into the only gap in the hedge that he could find, right next to a rusty old gate.

When he discovered the gate was tied up with string

he instinctively did a John Wayne leap over it. And he sank up to his knees in a mixture of soggy mud and manure.

The words he muttered as he extracted himself from the mire were both obscene and unprintable. He scurried off across the field, walking even more like John Wayne now.

When he came to a brook he decided that, as his hand made cowhide boots were already ruined, he might as well just stride right on through it. Then he stomped up the bank on the other side.

The next field was all clumps of thistles and little islands of bull-rushes. But Fitzgibbon persevered. When he eventually arrived, panting and gasping, at where the men were cutting the turf they just stood and stared at him with an amused look on their faces.

You could tell what they were thinking. What the hell was this big eejit in the expensive suit and handmade cowboy boots doing hiking across some boggy fields on a wet and cold Kerry afternoon?

Of course Fitzgibbon, the eternal optimist, believed they were thinking the complete opposite. *He* believed they were standing there staring at him like that because they were totally overwhelmed by the fact that a big American in an expensive suit and handmade cowboy boots would actually take the time to stop and talk to the likes of them.

Anyway, when he asked the older man if he knew the way to the Fitzgibbon farm in Duagh, the man lifted his cap and scratched his head.

'Nope.' He gave a casual shake of the head.

Nope? What did he mean, *nope*? Everyone knew *everyone* in Ireland! Everyone knew *about* everyone in

Ireland.

Maybe Fitzgibbon hadn't pronounced the name correctly! Maybe he was missing the slant of the Kerry accent. So he repeated the question, changing the inflection of the words. But the man shook his head again.

'Well, I've lived here all my life.' The man spat a lump of tobacco onto the grass. 'And I've never heard of that place, and that's a fact.'

Fitzgibbon sighed deeply. He didn't have time for this! It would be dark soon and he wasn't sure if the cars in Ireland had headlights.

He spun on his heels and set off back down the fields to his car with an irritated suck of his gums.

This time he manoeuvred around the mud patch and climbed the gate very carefully. With a frustrated grunt he glanced back at the men. And he was surprised to see the older one waving frantically at him, beckoning for him to come back up the fields.

Fitzgibbon was back over the gate like a shot. And knee deep in trouble again. But he shrugged it off. Because with any luck he would be home soon.

This time the man was beaming all over his face and he put his arm around the shoulder of the younger man.

'This here is Tom Brennan,' he nodded in emphasis. 'Now, Tom's lived here all his life too, in that little cottage over yonder. And *he's* never heard of a Fitzgibbon farm around here either, I'm afraid.'

It took a moment for what the man said to register with Fitzgibbon. *Was the crazy old guy trying to be funny?* Fitzgibbon just stood there like a dummy, struggling to decipher the blank expressions behind the big grin on the faces of the two men.

Then a red mist of rage exploded in his head and he flew back down the fields in a blur of motion, and he scrambled over the gate with a furious flourish.

And he almost collided with the pretty girl with the basket who was walking by the gap.

'Gee, I'm so sorry!' Fitzgibbon gave a partial bow and touched the rim of his hat.

'Not at all,' the girl smiled back at him. 'You're grand, shur!'

She glanced down at his mud-covered handmade cowboy boots and expensive suit and she gave a throaty chuckle. And Fitzgibbon was instantly smitten with her.

Her amazing soft green eyes bewitched him. He stood there transfixed by the way her long red hair moved in a wave around her pretty face as she gave the string on the gate a gentle tug. It disengaged itself in one long piece.

Sill smiling broadly she prised the gate open, slid in the gap and let it swing shut behind her again. The string was back on it in a second. She danced lightly around the muddy bits before walking daintily across the field to where the men were working.

When they got married a year later they decided to keep both of their names, hence Fitzgibbon-O'Hare.

Delia and Fitzgibbon-O'Hare developed a sort of rapport over the next couple of years. He came into town almost every week and called into her office to stock up on his wine cellar. And he was very impressed with her knowledge of wine. More so by the fact she knew where to get it for him.

So they had enough of a working relationship to allow her to ask him one day why he was looking so glum.

'Well, it's our wedding anniversary in one week.' Fitzgibbon had a solemn face on him. 'And we're having a special blessing in the Church. The Archbishop himself is conducting the ceremony. It's our special day, and all the family are coming over to celebrate. From the United States and England, as well as Ireland.'

'Ah, shur that's wonderful,' Delia gushed. 'Will you be wanting to order the wine from us?'

'No! Well, *yes*. But that's the least of my problems right now.'

'Oh?'

'Well, it's Kitty,' Fitzgibbon rubbed his nose with the back of his hand. 'She wants this to be a really special occasion. And as you can imagine, being a woman yourself, she wants a special dress to go with it.'

'Well, of course she would,' Delia nodded in agreement.

'And that's the problem,' Fitzgibbon sighed. 'She's seen the dress she wants in a magazine she has sent over from America every month. She likes to keep up with the current fashions, you see. Anyway, we've looked everywhere for one like it, Tralee, Cork, Dublin, but no joy. We even phoned some friends in London but again we drew a blank.'

Delia took a quick sip of her tea and put the mug back on the little table behind the counter out of sight of the customers.

'Eventually someone recommended a dressmaker in Tralee who's supposed to be marvellous,' Fitzgibbon continued. 'We contacted her and she agreed to make it for us. So we bought the material and took it in to her. But there was some sort of misunderstanding with the dates. She tells us she's going to Lisbon for three weeks on vacation. It's been booked and paid for ages ago. So now we're left with a heap of very expensive material and a very emotional Kitty who won't talk to anyone. I just don't know what to do now.'

Delia seized the moment. She persuaded him to bring the magazine picture in for her to look at, just in case she knew someone who could help. When he dropped them in the next day Delia ran all the way home in her dinner hour to show it to Aunt Fanny. Aunt Fanny was delighted. *Of course* she could make a dress like that.

I was just a child at the time but even then I sensed that pretentiousness is something you acquired. The degree of pretentiousness is determined by your perception of your own self-worth.

And I was right, of course. Kitty O'Hare had changed from the bright, bubbly farmer's daughter into the wife of a seriously rich American businessman. And she had acquired pretentiousness by the bucketful.

Needless to say she balked loudly when she was told the fitting for her splendid new dress would take place in a tiny room above the Harnessmaker's shop in William Street.

Aunt Fanny, gentle and all as she was, detested the shallowness of people like that. She would rather stick cocktail sticks in her ear than bend to their petty whims. So she flatly refused to call out to the Fitzgibbon's farm, even if they did promise to send a car for her.

No, if Mrs Fitzgibbon-O'Hare wanted the dress badly enough she would have to come to Aunt Fanny.

Anyway, Mrs Fitzgibbon-O'Hare relented. So arrangements were made for her to call in to be measured. Nan and Delia went to meet her at the front door of the shop.

In an obvious fit of pique the car mounted the pavement so Mrs Fitzgibbon-O'Hare would be as close to the shop as possible - thus avoiding any riff raff that might be loitering nearby. She slithered out, pouting and scattering her hair as she scurried into the shop.

'I'll meet you at the hotel when you've finished, Honey,' the American called after her.

Mrs Fitzgibbon-O'Hare gave a contemptuous glance around the shop as she followed Nan up the narrow stairs to the sitting room. She would probably have looked down her nose at us if she could, but being so little she would have fallen over backwards.

The first problem they encountered that evening was compatibility. Aunt Fanny was a tall, upright lady, almost six feet in her socks. Mrs Fitzgibbon-O'Hare was tiny, only four feet nine inches.

A way had to be found for them to work comfortably together. A wooden cheese box was brought in but there was no scope for manoeuvre on it. Then it was suggested that, *maybe*, the dining table might be more suitable.

Mrs Fitzgibbon-O'Hare gave a disdainful snort. But she was desperate to get it over with and get back to her socialising, so she reluctantly agreed. And before anyone could advise her to remove her shoes with their stylishly thin heels, she was scrambling up onto Nan's best velvet-covered chair.

Nan went white. The table was a solid mahogany antique that had been in the family for generations. It was lovingly handed down from mother to daughter. And kept in pristine condition. It was protected with a Maltese lace tablecloth.

And now this stuck up little bimbo was walking all over it with spikes on her feet. There was a tense few moments before Aunt Fanny suggested that if Mrs Fitzgibbon-O'Hare were to take her shoes off she would be much more comfortable. And Aunt Fanny would be better able to reach her.

Mrs Fitzgibbon-O'Hare's reaction was to grudgingly flick the shoes into the corner of the room.

Eventually everything was finalised. Aunt Fanny assured Mrs Fitzgibbon-O'Hare that she would work on it right through the night. And all the next day, if necessary. So if she would kindly come back the same time the following evening the dress would be ready for any adjustments.

Next evening the dramatic screech of brakes and theatrical opening of the car door heralded her arrival exactly on time. Nan and Delia escorted her up the stairs.

And when Mrs Fitzgibbon-O'Hare caught sight of the dress as she entered the sitting room her natural self came to the fore and her face beamed. She gave a beautiful chuckle and touched it gently. She kicked off her shoes, bounced onto the chair and up onto the table.

Then to every one's horror she shot across the table in a blur of motion. And she landed with a dull thud under the windowsill.

Now, through the kitchen door, I could hear the deep drumbeat of water being poured into the kettle. Then the kettle being slammed on to the big black range. And Aunt Fanny sighing heavily!

'What on earth possessed you to do it?' she was asking glumly.

'Well!' Nan answered defensively. 'You saw the snotty way that little madam looked at us yesterday, like we were something that dropped off a dog's bottom. She made me feel ashamed, embarrassed at the cut of the place. I thought I should make an extra effort, make the place look a bit more presentable. I gave the whole room a good clean and polish.'

'You did indeed,' Delia agreed. 'Especially that table! The top of it was like a sheet of ice. What on earth did you use on it?'

'Bees wax, of course! Tis the best thing for the wood, brings up its natural shine.'

The kettle started to whistle.

'Brought her back down to earth, though,' Delia chuckled.

'With a bump, as well!' snorted Aunt Fanny.

Ah, it was wonderful to hear such hearty peals of laughter around the auld place again.

Remember Me?

The traffic lights changed to go. As they flicked from red to amber and then to green the colours rippled across the windscreen of the solitary car waiting at the junction.

The car didn't move.

James Foley saw the lights change, of course. It just didn't register with him. His head was too full of Alexis. He gave a deep, exasperated sigh. How on earth had he become so involved with her - and in such a short time?

Rain swept down from heavy black clouds and pattered like small pebbles against the car. The wipers scooped a slice of water off the glass and threw it away somewhere but it was replaced immediately with thick, clinging dollops of rain.

The swish of the wipers beat a dull rhythm in his head and agitated the pain that was already tumbling around in there.

He felt so guilty about Sue. She'd be waiting for him at home with his supper in the oven. The children would be bathed and ready for bed, all covered in baby powder and just hanging about to kiss their daddy goodnight.

A terrible knot gripped his stomach.

What the hell had he done? What possessed him to risk everything for a few reckless moments of passion? And with a girl he'd only known for a couple of months? Now everything he had - his beautiful family, the business he worked so hard to build - was close to turning to dust and blowing away with the wind.

Yet his whole being buzzed with an intense, complicated excitement too. His emotions were spinning in a confused loop, flip-flopping between his feelings for Alexis and the brutal, cold betrayal of Sue and the children. The guilt dripped off him. He felt so bad about getting involved with Alexis. He could have stopped it happening in the first place and that squeezed his conscience even more.

The thing was, from the moment Alexis came into his office looking for a job Foley was mesmerised by her. Warning bells pinged deep in his subconscious but he chose to ignore them. She was bright, intelligent, and she was exceptionally pretty. Be careful, the bells were telling him.

But it was already too late. He justified his decision to employ her by stressing that Nanette was retiring and he needed to replace her as quickly as possible. He couldn't afford to be short staffed. It would be bad for the business.

His business. The Listowel Road Filling Station. It was the first thing you saw when you came into town, and the last as you went out again.

Foley started working there the day he left school. Back then it was just a small grocery shop perched on the side of the road with four fuel pumps lined up outside and a used-car showroom tagged onto the side of it.

Old Man Reilly was a good boss and James was very happy working for him. But Old Man Reilly preferred a long lunch in the pub to actually doing any work. He left Foley and the long serving Nanette to run the place.

So when Old Man Reilly decided to sell up some years later, James was devastated. He was married by then with a child on the way. He loved his job. He knew nothing else.

The site was on its last legs by that time and no one showed the slightest interested in buying it. The future did not look good.

Then one night in the pub James heard a rumour that a large housing estate was to be built on the land behind the petrol station. He spent a whole month putting a business plan together which he took to his bank manager. The bank manager wasn't totally convinced. But he *was* impressed by the enthusiasm and infectious energy that James displayed. He took a chance and leant James the money to buy the place.

The first thing James did was add four more pumps. Then he opened for business 24/7 to capture the commuters in the morning and evenings, and the salesmen and builder's vans during the day.

The housing estate was built and the shop now incorporated a Post Office as well. Eventually they were selling over a million litres of fuel a month. But the margin on fuel was not great. The main thrust of the business was the shop. So he had the old showroom knocked through and a seating area with a fast food counter added.

Now he had twenty-two people working for him around the clock, every day of the year.

The key to all this, of course, was Nanette. Dependable, consistent, totally loyal, he relied on her completely. So her decision to retire was a bitter blow. He hadn't planned for it - which was stupid because he should have seen it coming. Maybe he was hoping that … well, she *was* sixty. And the arthritis was giving her a lot of grief. Getting up at five o'clock every morning had taken its toll on her. Danny, her husband, was already retired so they bought a little place in Spain and hoped to spend the rest of their days in the sun - leaving James in a kind of limbo.

He wasn't sure how he was ever going to replace her - there wasn't a single member of staff capable of doing what she did. They were all part-timers with children of their own. None of them had the commitment or the ambition - no one wanted the responsibility.

Again, Nanette came to the rescue. Her final gesture before she said goodbye was to introduce a young woman her daughter met in a nightclub. She'd come to Ireland as a refugee from the war in Yugoslavia and she was looking for a job. She had experience too, having worked for a couple of years in a petrol station outside Dublin.

And the moment she walked into his office James was captured by her soft, smiling blue eyes and easy confidence. He took her on, of course.

She was good. Quick and efficient. It wasn't long before she'd convinced him she could do the book-keeping as well. Eventually she was doing all the ordering, completing the legal paperwork, even doing the weekly stocktake. James felt extremely comfortable with her.

Sue, on the other hand, was happy to let James take care of the business. She rarely visited the place. Which was just as well. She was bound to notice how distracted James became whenever he was near Alexis. And the staff might even comment on how miserable he was when she took a day off.

James would deny it, of course. But it was true - in the space of a few months he and Alexis had grown dangerously close. If she wasn't around he felt irritable, missing her smile and her cheerful banter. Even the smell of her perfume.

Then came the Christmas party. Staff only, no

partners. Lots of food and drink. Not a good combination. It ended with a lingering kiss under the mistletoe.

They both pretended it was nothing more than a comfortable friendship, a working relationship. Nobody was fooled by that. The signs were written everywhere.

Then suddenly, earlier this evening, everything stepped up a gear.

Alexis usually walked home from work. But tonight the dismal evening had clouds that were so low you could reach up and touch them. They caused a heavy drizzle that stuck to everything and would soak you to the bone in minutes. James couldn't let her walk home in that!

Naturally she asked him in for a cup of coffee. Then she went straight to the bedroom to change into something more comfortable. What she came back in was a short, pink bath towel.

As she shook her long blond hair around her shoulders the towel accidentally slipped to the floor. She didn't react. She just stood there posing in front of a full-length mirror. Then she gave James the most amazing smile and beckoned him with her eyes.

Did he regret it? He couldn't honestly say.

An angry toot from a car snapped James out of his daze. The old Ford Fiesta behind him revved its engine aggressively and made the doctored exhaust roar. Then it skimmed out around James in a flurry of spray. Four faces scowled from dark hoodies as they zoomed past.

James forced a smile and shuffled the gears. But before he could move the Fiesta's brake lights came on. It slid to a halt in a glare of red then came hurtling back towards him.

Dreamin' Dreams

James instinctively went for the mobile phone in his shirt pocket. It was a chunky model, not slim and sleek like the modern ones. You'd have to study it hard to find the two secret chambers - one on either side with a .22 bullet in them.

His friend Mick Griffin had been on a tour of duty with the UN in Bosnia. He picked it up for the price of a packet of fags and a cup of real coffee. And he gave it to James the day after some local eejits high on crack and carrying a shotgun tried to rob the petrol station.

Mick Griffin had it adapted to make the loudest bang possible. In his experience, a pack of clowns like that lot in the Fiesta was usually made up of spineless nerds who attach themselves to someone with a big mouth. Hit the one with the big mouth with a lot of noise and smoke. When they see the main man go down they'll be off like rats up a mouldy old drainpipe.

But right now James was too emotional about what happened with Alexis to get involved in a stupid confrontation. He slammed the car into reverse and raced back down the road before doing a neat handbrake turn. He spun around in a cloud of mud and spray and cruised away from the scene.

He glanced in the rear-view mirror. The Fiesta had copied him and was racing after him.

James knew he could easily out-run the little Fiesta in his Lexus but he was just too tired. He didn't want to waste any more time playing games with a load of morons.

He knew this part of town. There was a road branching off to the left. He spun into it and flicked off his lights.

Seconds later he watched the Fiesta shoot past in his

rear view mirror.

Grinning broadly, he flicked the lights back on and headed back towards the town.

Then something hit the front of the car, crashed against the windscreen and rolled off the bonnet onto the grass verge.

James yelped as he slammed on the brakes, slid sideways across the road and smashed into a tree. The door flew open with the impact and now he was hanging upside down, held in place by the seatbelt and almost suffocated by the exploding airbag.

His head throbbed violently as he untangled himself, slid onto the ground and scrambled back to see what he'd collided with. And in the dim light from a nearby streetlamp he was horrified to discover it was a man.

He dropped on his knees and turned the body over. The man groaned as James wiped the mud off his face.

'Where the hell did you come from?' James heard himself shout, his voice high and frantic. 'You're dressed all in black. In this weather! I'm sorry, I just didn't see you.'

The man's breathing was erratic and when James tried to lift him up something made him hesitate. There was something familiar about this man. James looked closer, but the light was too weak. But there was definitely something. Did James know him? He shook his head.

'First things first.' James pulled out his phone and waved it in the air. 'Call an ambulance!'

But it was no use - he couldn't get a signal. He was in some sort of blind spot.

The man opened his eyes and gave a soft cough. James leant closer. And when the man saw his face lit up by the glow from the phone he gave a strangled cry.

'*You*?' he gasped. 'How the hell can it be you? For God's sake, how can it … what the hell's going on?'

His hand shot out and grabbed James by the throat with fingers that felt like steel clamps.

'This can't be happening!' The man's face was contorted in horror.

In sheer panic James threw himself backwards and the fingers lost their grip. The man gave a desperate sob and he too fell back onto the grass.

James jumped to his feet and staggered back away from the man, rubbing his bruised neck. Who the hell was this guy? He obviously knew James. But not in a good way, apparently. And the voice! James Foley knew that voice! He was sure he knew that voice.

A movement behind him made James spin around and he got the impression someone had darted through a gap in the hedge.

'Hey!' He jumped up and sprinted after the shadow. 'We need some help over here.'

The gap in the hedge had a small gate and a path that tapered up to a large old house. James was amazed. He thought he knew every house in the town. He'd cycled through these lanes a million times as a child. How could he have misses one this big?

The front door of the house was open and there was a light on in the porch. As James approached he could hear faint voices. And soft laughter. He tapped on the glass and went straight in. The voices led down the hall to another open door leading to a large wood panelled drawing room.

A man and woman were leaning over a huge desk studying photos that were tumbling out of a printer.

They seemed pleased with the photos because they chuckled as they passed them to each other. It took a few moments for James to register what he was seeing. Then his heart gave a violent thump in his chest.

The man was older, with a mop of white hair and an expensive suit. Alexis looked small and fragile beside him. They were both quite animated, all waving arms and flicking heads. And speaking in a foreign language. When Alexis reached up and kissed the man lightly on the lips, James groaned out loud.

Alexis spun around. And she hesitated for the briefest of moments before she gave him a huge, disarming smile.

'James!' she beamed.

'Alexis,' was all James could say. His mind was racing, thudding with confusion. He'd left her apartment just a short time ago. How could she have …?

Of course! He'd been so befuddled by his wild moment with her that he couldn't risk going straight home. He needed time to think. He went back to the shop and had a wash in the toilet, trying to erase her scent from his hands and soul. How long did that take?

'What are you doing here, James?' Alexis smiled again, arching her eyebrows in mock accusation. 'Have you been following me?'

'*What*?' James swallowed hard to sooth the bitter dryness in his throat. 'Why the hell would I be following you? I didn't even know this place existed.'

Alexis and the man glanced at each other and a conspiratorial smirk passed between them. James couldn't read anything in their faces.

'Look, I've had an accident.' He couldn't hide the anger in his voice. 'Right outside your gate. A man's been hurt. I couldn't get a signal on my phone so I came in here to use yours.'

Alexis took the photos out of the man's hand, shuffled them and put them on the desk.

'The phone's in the hall,' the man said without looking at James. He disconnected a digital camera from the printer and dropped it into a drawer. Then he put his arm around Alexis's shoulder and drew her closer to him.

'And who the hell are you?' James glared at the two of them, fuming at their apparent affection. He was even more confused when Alexis laughed back at him.

'His name is Stefan,' a voice behind him said. James spun around. A young man was leaning against the door and he had a sly smirk on his face. His arms were folded loosely across his chest. James could see a Walter .22 tucked in his belt. 'He's her husband.'

James could feel his heart pounding even harder now. This was so unreal! He only came in to use the bloody phone. Now a spotty yob with a gun was telling him the love of his life was already married. And to a man who was old enough to be her - what - grandfather?

He had to take a slow, deep breath to regain his composure.

'What's going on, Alexis?' It came out as a croak.

'James, my dear, dear friend,' She gave him another beautiful smile. 'You really shouldn't have followed me here.'

'I've told you already. I didn't follow you. I had an accident. I knocked down some poor eejit right outside your front door. He needs an ambulance! That's why I ...'

'You could have spoilt everything.' She pouted and

gave a wave of her hand.

'Spoilt what, exactly?'

'Well, maybe it wasn't such a bad thing after all, you coming here.' The older man slid his arm from around Alexis and tapped the photos with his finger. 'You weren't supposed to see these, of course. Well, not yet, anyway. But now that you're here, please come and take a look!'

James didn't have to get too close to see the photos. They were of himself and Alexis in some seriously intimate poses. The groan he gave was deep and bitter.

How on earth did she do that? Surely he would have noticed a camera. *But of course!* The big mirror by the bedroom door! His face burnt red at the thought of someone standing there watching them, filming them. It was unbelievable. Alexis was performing for the camera all the time. And he'd assumed her enthusiastic display was a spontaneous act of genuine love.

'What's this all about, Alexis?' He gave a soft cough to clear his throat. 'Are you blackmailing me? Is it money you want from me?'

All three of them laughed out loud.

'Actually, no.' Stephan gave a patronising shake of his head. 'The fact is we want to give you money. Lots of it.'

'I'm sorry?' James felt himself sway and he rubbed his hand through his hair. 'You've lost me there, I'm afraid.'

Stephan took a glass off the sideboard. 'Can I offer you a drink, James?'

James waved it away. 'Just tell me what's going on, will you?'

'Well, it's very simple, really.' Stephan sloshed some

whisky from a decanter into the glass. 'You have a nice, solid little business here in this quiet town of yours. The tax inspectors looked you over and found everything to be in order. Trading Standards, Environment Health - in fact everyone who's likely to show any interest in you has been, had a look around and went away satisfied.'

He raised the glass in salute.

'So, the situation is this - our company, which is an invisible asset company and not listed anywhere, currently has a surplus of funds. We need - how do you say? - a nice discreet home for these funds.'

'Are you talking about money laundering?' James spluttered. 'Are you … what are you implying? Are you saying you want to use my company to launder your dodgy money? Not a chance. There's no way on God's earth I'm going to get involved in that. Do you know what would happen to me if I got caught? Do you really expect me to get involved in something like that and risk spending years in jail?'

'But you're already involved, I'm afraid,' Alexis interrupted with a throaty chuckle.

James took a step backwards. His eyes were suddenly blurred with anxiety. 'What do you mean?'

Stephan smiled down at Alexis again and put his arm around her shoulder.

'When was the last time you actually looked at your books, James? How many suppliers do you actually pay on a weekly basis? Do you actually know how many people you employ? Have you ever seen them all, put faces to the names on your payroll?'

James couldn't think straight. He tried to shake the mist from his eyes. When he did he was startled by the expression on Alexis' face. She was looking at him but her eyes were so empty it frightened him.

Earlier that evening, such a short time ago, he would have sworn she had feelings for him. *Seriou*s feelings! Otherwise how could she have shown such passion, such raw emotion? It stunned him to think someone could actually be acting that. He felt sick. She had him hooked and now she was reeling him in like a stupid little lovesick fish.

The thumping of his heart was making the blood pulsate in his ears and he had to swallow hard again. He was struggling to think clearly. All he could think about was what this was going to do to Sue and the children.

Suddenly his whole world had turned to sand. It was filtering through his fingers at a ferocious speed, squandered in a matter of seconds because he'd become infatuated by a beautiful face.

'If that's the case, what do you need those photos for?' he heard himself asking.

'Oh, they're just for insurance.' Stephan gave Alexis a gentle kiss on the forehead. 'You see, now your business has become so successful we've decided the workload is really too much for one person. We believe what you need is a partner to share the burden with. We also believe it's in your interest to make Alexis that partner. So you can spread the load and ease the pressure on your good self.'

He took some papers from his inside pocket.

'Of course you'll need to sign the relevant paperwork,' he chuckled. 'And, amazingly, we happen to have that paperwork right here.'

'But why me? Why my business? Surely my little shop isn't that good a proposition?'

'Oh, don't underestimate that little gold mine of

yours,' Stephan pushed the typewritten forms across the desk. 'Of course on its own it would not be so attractive. But as part of a bigger picture it becomes very significant indeed.'

'What bigger picture?' James' hands felt lifeless, dangling loosely by his side. And his feet were stuck to the floor.

It was never like this in the movies. If John Wayne was here right now he'd formulate a plan in the blink of an eye. But James wasn't John Wayne. His mind was a blur. All he could think about was Sue and the kids. She'd be devastated if she finds out about this, the photos, the betrayal. It would destroy her.

'The bigger picture is a beautiful thing,' Stephan was telling him from somewhere in the fog of his panic. 'All over this beautiful green island there are hundreds of small, relatively quiet little businesses just like yours. They were just ticking over, quietly plodding along from day to day. Then with a little help from us they become moderately successful. Slowly, of course, so as not to arouse attention, you understand. As I said, the big picture is … '

'The petrol station outside Dublin,' James spluttered, glaring at Alexis. 'I presume that was one of your … whatever you call it.'

'Oh, yes!' Alexis gave another disarming smile and shook her hair in a wave around her shoulders. 'One of the easiest too, I must say! The owner jumped at the wonderful proposition we presented to him. And he never even saw the photos. He'd already left his wife and seven children after our first night together. He signed the partnership the very next day. Unfortunately he died not long afterwards.'

'*What*?'

'Oh, it was natural, James,' Alexis laughed out loud. 'Nothing sinister, I promise you. He was an older man. He liked his beer and his food. And he certainly liked his … anyway, his heart couldn't take all the excitement.'

Stephan gave an impatient rap on the desk. 'It's getting late. Your wife will be waiting for you. Just sign this and you can go on home to her. And the children. All right?'

James looked at Alexis. She looked away. A terrible dread flooded through his whole body. What happens if he signs? Was he really going to just walk away? Alexis would own the lot if he just vanished off the face of the earth. He closed his eyes. Where was John Wayne now?

He jumped when the phone in his hand rang. It was Sue.

'Give me that!' The young man behind him snapped his fingers. 'Don't answer it. Give!'

James studied the phone. 'That's odd,' he mumbled, turning to face the young man. 'I couldn't get a signal outside. Now I can. Isn't that weird?'

A sudden, strangely unreal force seemed to possess James. He calmly flipped back the cover of the phone and gave the little handle a soft tug.

The young man snarled as James raised the phone and pointed it at his face. And an ice cool calmness surged through his veins as he pressed the red button. And through the thick explosion of smoke and the shattering bang he saw a tiny red dot appeared in the middle of the young man's forehead.

That's another thing that's different from the movies. There was no dramatic, slow motion spinning backwards with flying arms and legs. The young man just dropped straight down like a sack of spuds off the back of a truck.

Everything froze. James was stunned. How could he have done that? He'd actually shot someone. It was unbelievable! He'd actually fired a gun and shot someone!

Stephan was the first to move. James turned just in time to see him reach into the drawer of the desk. When his hand came back out it was holding a small handgun.

But he fired too soon. The explosion took a chunk out of the corner of the desk. The phone in James' hand gave another shattering bang and Stephan dropped back into the big leather chair. His limp hand dropped the gun with a clatter onto the wooden floor.

James was mesmerised. He'd done it again! He'd shot another person. But there seemed to be no apparent damage to Stephan, no spatter of blood. James couldn't even see where Stephan was hit. Then a tiny trickle of blood appeared on the front of his shirt, right in the middle of his chest.

James felt oddly detached, as if he was looking at all this through someone else's eyes. Everything was so sharp and clear now. Was this how John Wayne felt in the shootout with the Commancheros?

He turned to Alexis. She was slumped in the corner by the fireplace, the flames glistening on her face. Her eyes were looking in his direction but they were totally unfocused.

He rushed across to her and dropped to his knees. And only then did he see the thin stream of blood oozing through her fingers that were clamped tightly against her side. The wild shot Stephan had taken ricocheted off the marble fireplace and killed her.

James stood up slowly. He was amazed that the

feelings he had for her had already evaporated like the smoke from the gun. He didn't even feel pity for her. Maybe relief, but he didn't have time to dwell on that right now.

Right, he said out loud, *think*!

Fingerprints. The only thing he'd touched was his own phone. He put it back in his shirt pocket. Using a handkerchief he picked up all the papers and photographs on the desk and put them in a pile on the fire.

He watched the flames lick the edges before devouring them totally and leaving just a lump of grey ash. Next he looked in all of the drawers on the desk. Apart from the camera there was nothing in them except a stapler and a roll of sticky tape.

All Stephan had in his pockets was a wallet and some loose change. The wallet went on the fire. James threw the camera against the marble fireplace then picked out the bits that looked like electronic memory components. He knew you never totally erased anything from a memory chip - everything left a ghost that was easily recovered by an expert. It all went on the fire. The printer followed, the relevant bits separated and smashed to a pulp.

He took one last look around and headed for the door.

The cold rain slapped his face as he ran out into the dark wet night. He'd forgotten about the injured man! He checked his phone. Still no signal! His best bet was to try and get the car started and take him to hospital himself.

He sprinted out of the gate and into the road where the car should have been. He hesitated. Where had it gone? He ran over to the tree.

This had to be a trick! This was the tree he skidded into - but there was no mark on it, no sign of an impact. There weren't any tracks across the wet grass either.

He stood there for a moment, totally confused. What was going on? He turned and ran back in through the gate. Perhaps there was another way out of the house. But there wasn't! This was the way he'd gone into the garden. This was the only way in from this street, and this was the only way out.

He staggered back out to the road and walked along to where he was sure the man would be lying injured. His heart was thumping again. The ice cold John Wayne feeling was gone. Confusion filled his head now. What was going on here? Was this some kind of a dream, an hallucination?

He wiped his face with his shaking hands and took a deep breath. Right, walk along to the corner of the road and look again. He must have come back out on a different side of the house. There was no other explanation!

Suddenly a car came screeching around the corner, its lights sweeping the street. But they flicked off immediately and James was immersed in a black empty void. Another car raced past along the road behind them and disappeared.

James froze in the middle of the road, his frazzled mind unable to react. Then the lights came on again, exploding in his eyes and totally blinding him.

Instinctively his hand went up to shield his eyes and the basic need to survive made him spin around and try to run - but it was too late. The car was already on top of him.

The impact threw him into the air. Then the thump of

the wet grass threw a blanket of darkness over him.

Now someone was turning him onto his back. He groaned in agony as they wiped the mud off his face.

'Where the hell did you come from?' he heard a man saying, his voice high and anxious. 'You're dressed all in black. In this weather! I'm sorry, I just didn't see you.'

The man breathing was erratic, his words frantic. And there was something very familiar about his voice. James tried to lift his head and look at him, but the light was too weak to see his face properly. But there was definitely something about him. Did James know him?

'First things first.' The man pulled out his mobile phone and waved it in the air. 'Call an ambulance.'

James gave a soft cough and the man leant closer. And when James saw the face lit up in the glow from the phone he gave a strangled cry.

'*You*?' he gasped. 'How the hell can it be you? For God's sake, how can it … what the hell's going on?'

His hand shot out and grabbed the man by the throat.

'This can't be happening!' he cried, his face contorted in horror.

In sheer panic the man threw himself backwards and the fingers lost their grip. James gave a desperate sob as he too fell back onto the grass. The man jumped to his feet and staggered back away from him, rubbing his bruised neck.

A movement behind the man made him spin around and James got the impression someone had darted through a gap in the hedge.

'Hey!' the man jumped up and sprinted after the shadow. 'We need some help over here.'

Then he disappeared into the night and James sensed

everything around him dissipating. And a dark cold mist started to envelope his feet, then his ankles, then his …

Dreamin' Dreams

Going Through Changes

A sheet of rain blew across the street and slapped against the bus shelter. A wave of water spattered the plastic windows that were already distorted by the graffiti scratched all over them. Some of the scribbles you could almost read but most were just a jumble of crude obscenities and scratched-out phone numbers.

The wind gusted again and rattled the trees. A spray of wet leaves blew in the hole where one of the panels was missing. Katie pulled her collar up tighter around her neck and shrank back into the corner as far away from it as she possibly could.

She groaned out loud. She was already soaked to the skin and half an hour late for football practice. The only sensible thing to do now was skip football and go straight home. Given the circumstances her mum was bound to understand. She'd send Katie for a nice hot bath and make her a mug of hot chocolate when she came back down.

But as Katie trudged up the path towards the welcoming light of her house her mother whipped the door open.

'Katie!' Her hands were clamped angrily on her hips. 'Why aren't you at football practice?'

Stunned at the sharp tone of her mother's voice, Katie could only stand there and blink the rain out of her eyes.

'Mom!' she managed to splutter eventually. 'It's like, *raining*! I'm wet and I'm cold. It's gone right through to my skin. I thought you'd understand.'

'I don't believe this!' Katie's mother had a throaty sob in her voice. 'Are you telling me you're afraid of a little bit of rain? For heaven's sake, Katie! Do you think any of those famous footballers you're always going on about would stop playing football because of a little drop of rain? Do you realise how hard I have to work to pay for your football practice? I can't afford to just throw my money away like that! There's very little of it coming into the house as it is! I have to struggle for every penny I've got. Ever since your father died I ... '

Tears sparkled in her eyes and she wiped them away with the back of her hand. Then she took a sharp gulp of air in through her nose as she stepped back into the hall and held the door open for Katie.

'Get upstairs.' Her voice was still heavy with annoyance. 'Get out of those wet clothes before you catch your death of cold.'

Upstairs in her room Katie flicked on the bedside lamp and flung her sports bag down on the bed so hard the pillows went flying onto the floor. She was visibly shaking as she scooped the stool out from under the dressing table with her foot and plonked down on it.

But it wasn't just because of the wet clothes that were tight and cold around her shoulders. There was also a sharp angry pain wedged like a heavy ball in the pit of her stomach. She couldn't put it into words exactly. It was like a solid lump of sheer frustration and it was getting worse and worse with each passing day.

She was fourteen years old, for heaven's sake. Yet she was made to feel like she was still a little child and not capable of doing anything right.

Of course it didn't help being piggy in the middle either, forced to share a house with a younger brother and a stroppy older sister. *They* certainly didn't help the situation with their flippant attitude towards her and the constant ridiculing of her passion for football.

Dreamin' Dreams

At moments like this she hated them all!

Her eyes glistened in the weak light as she glared at herself in the mirror. They were tight with anger and ringed with dark red shadows. She grabbed her hairbrush and started tugging furiously at the knots in her sodden hair. And she gave a long rippling shudder that made the stool shake under her.

All of a sudden she had a strange impression that she wasn't alone. There was someone else in the room! Thin fingers of alarm brushed the hairs on the back of her neck and made them stand on end. The very notion that she was being watched made her skin crawl!

And there was something else!

She scanned the room through the mirror, moving only her eyes. Something was missing from her room! Right at that moment she couldn't think what it was. But something definitely wasn't where it should have been.

She turned her head slowly. And the scream she gave exploded like a gunshot when the wardrobe door burst open and her brother James flew out with a wild shriek.

Katie's hands jerked so wildly they knocked all her stuff off the dressing table and sent them crashing across the bedroom floor.

Hysterical bursts of laughter rippled around the room as James struggled to catch his breath.

'That was awesome,' he gasped. 'I really scared the life out of you! You must have jumped six feet in the air. I nearly made you jump out of your skin! That was wicked!'

'You stupid fool.' Katie flew off the stool and grabbed at him, missing him by a fraction of an inch as he dodged around her. 'Look at what you've made me do. Look at my stuff! It's all ruined - my ornaments, my makeup! They're a mess. What did you think you were doing?'

Then she yelped even louder when she noticed what her brother was wearing. *That's* what was missing from her room! The life-size Amazonian mask she'd spent ages making in art class!

James had it strapped to his head and now it was ruined, the coloured string broken and dangling from the end of a torn strip of parchment.

'You stupid lump!' Katie danced in frustration and ran at him again, crying hysterically and grabbing at the mask. 'Look what you've done to my art project! You've wrecked it! It took me ages to make that! You *knew* it was my best work. You *knew* it wasn't a toy. Now you've ruined it. It's useless. This isn't funny, James. I hate you. Get out of my room. *Get out*!'

As Katie grabbed a handful of her brother's shirt and dragged him towards the door her sister Clara came charging into the room.

'What's on earth is going on in here?' she yelled. 'Katie, let him go!'

'Look what he did to my art project,' Katie yelled back. 'He's ruined it. It was my favourite piece. It isn't funny …'

'Oh c'mon!' Clara pulled a dismissive face. 'He didn't mean to damage your stupid mask. He was only playing with it, that's all. And it's only a bit of old cardboard, anyway. What's it for? Aren't you *supposed* to wear it? Well, he *is* wearing it! He was only having a bit of fun with it.'

'Well he shouldn't have been in my room in the first place …'

'It's isn't *your* room.' Clara pulled James away from

her. 'It's *our* room. And I'm the oldest, so if I say he can come in *our* room, he can come in *our* room. *All right*?'

'That doesn't give him the right …'

'What *is* the matter with you, Katie?' James shook himself free, pushed his way between the two of them and ran out of the room. 'You're no fun anymore,' he called back. 'You've turned into a right old moody cow. I'm going back to my own room.'

After a second a door slammed down the hall.

'He's right, you know!' Clara curled her nose up in agreement. She flicked her hair from her face as she swung around on her heels and strutted over to the door. 'There was no need to yell at him like that. You have to realise that he's only a child!'

With a loud huff Clara pulled the door behind her and Katie flinched as it slammed shut with the force of a hard slap. She sagged down onto the edge of the bed and burst into tears.

If only her dad was here. *He* would listen to her. *He* would understand how she was feeling, how she'd been treated by the rest of the family over the last few months. *Everyone* was so horrible to her. *No one* ever took her seriously.

As she moved her foot it brushed against something on the floor. She bent down and picked it up. It was the picture from her bedside table, a photograph her father had taken during their last holiday in Ireland.

They were on the cliff above the Ladies' Beach in Ballybunion looking down at the Castle Green. He'd zoomed in on the castle with his new digital camera just as a shaft of sunlight popped out from behind the rolling bundle of clouds that had been hugging the horizon all evening. For the briefest of moments the castle was wrapped in a soft golden halo making it appeared to shimmer. Then in a heartbeat the clouds folded over again and the sunbeam was gone. And a dull curtain of fading daylight came back down around them.

But Katie's father had captured a rare, precious image. He was so proud of it he had it framed. And it took pride of place by Katie's bed where she could look at it every night before she went to sleep.

Her dad once told her that the photo encapsulated the very essence of his own childhood in Ireland, growing up on a small farm in County Kerry. The farm was on the outskirts of Listowel, just a short bike ride from Ballybunion and the miles of sandy beaches. And even though everyone knew dear old Dad was prone to generous helpings of selective memory, he still insisted his school holidays were just one long, happy round of swimming in the sea and playing football on the sand.

One day when they were sitting on the rocks watching the rolling waves crashing against the bottom of the high black cliff, Katie asked him why, if he loved the place so much, he didn't just stay here and not go back to London.

He took a long, slow drag on his pipe as he reflected on the answer. Then he took a deep breath and started to sing a verse from his favourite song:

To the fields and the farmyards
Where I ran as a lad
Came the stories of London
And the times to be had
So I saved all my money
Came as fast as I could
And the stories were true one

Dreamin' Dreams

And the times they were good
Ah, but now and then I miss North Kerry
And I dream of the auld days
And I swear to go home
But the work and the money
Make a man play a part
And in the clay and the concrete
He can bury his heart ...

His eyes sparkled and his voice broke with a soft sob.
And Katie understood the confusion of feelings that
danced in his heart. London was a great place to live and
he was very happy there. But it was natural that
sometimes the pull of the green, green grass of home
could be almost overwhelming.

However, he made up for it by taking the family back
to Kerry for a holiday every summer, come rain or shine.
It was almost like a pilgrimage.

The farm was long gone now and his relatives were
scattered to the four winds, so they usually rented a
caravan on the edge of the town overlooking the beach.
And they spent the two weeks re-visiting the same old
haunts while Dad bored everyone within earshot with the
same old stories about the wild and wonderful
adventures he and his pals were always getting involved
in.

Katie wiped the tears from her eyes as she held the
photo to her chest and reflected on how different
everything had been back then when their life was so
normal, so very ordinary. They were just a typical,
contented family, doing things together, going places
together. Nothing special.

How could it have changed so suddenly, so

unbelievably quickly?

A stupid woman nattering on a mobile phone while doing 52mph in a 30mph zone! She didn't see the lights had changed. Katie's dad was on his way to work. He didn't survive the impact. The woman escaped with a broken wrist.

They knew he wanted his ashes scattered on the beach at Ballybunion. He'd said it often enough. But now, in the terrible surge of grief that was overwhelming the family, they just couldn't do it. Not yet. They needed him near, close enough for them to visit, safe in a place where they could stills spend some precious time with him.

Maybe later, when the pain had eased a bit. But not now. So the ashes were placed in a garden of remembrance just a few miles from their home on the outskirts of London.

Sadly, in the deep, painful void that was left, the family was confused and disorientated. They just didn't know how to cope without him. And within a very short time they were fighting with each other, snapping and arguing and exploding into angry, nasty scuffles over the smallest, pettiest thing. They were all unsettled, unable to find closure.

Katie believed in her heart that if they could go back to Ballybunion just one more time and grant her father his final wish, perhaps they might *all* find some peace.

But right now, of course, it was impossible. Apart from anything else, they couldn't afford it. The insurance money barely covered the mortgage and Katie's mum could only work part time at the local supermarket because she needed to be home when the children came in from school. After everything was paid for, there wasn't much spare cash left.

Katie pulled the eiderdown tighter around her and snuggled into it as a gust of wind threw more rain against the window making it patter loudly on the glass.

Saturday was their shopping day which meant a tedious slog to the local supermarket. It was a routine that Katie absolutely hated and she would search for any excuse to avoid going.

But for some inexplicable reason she decided to tag along today. The others looked at her strangely but they said nothing as they pushed the large shopping trolley through the big front doors into the vast foyer.

After half an hour Katie had forgotten exactly why she'd come. Now she was moaning to herself as they traipsed wearily up and down the endless aisles being jostled and elbowed by the mob of disgruntled shoppers who would rather be at home with their feet up watching television than trying to manoeuvre around loads of other disgruntled people.

It didn't help that Katie's mother scrutinised every single bargain on offer, analysing them in minute detail to establish what exactly was good about them and if they were worth the price. And she squeezed the tomatoes too.

But eventually she ticked off the last item on her list and with a collective sigh they joined the end of the long queue for the checkout. As they shuffled along the line Katie spotted Mrs Kelly from the football club standing by the front door with a collection tin in her hand.

Mrs Kelly spotted Katie's mother at the same time.

'Liz,' she screeched from across the shop floor. 'How are you? I haven't seen you in ages.'

Katie's mother groaned out loud. There was no place

to hide.

Mrs Kelly's husband Declan was from Co Tipperary in Ireland and he had been a good friend of Katie's dad. His hobby was writing poetry and he regularly entered the Listowel Writers Week competition. He never actually won anything, though, and everyone had great fun teasing him about it. But it was all done in jest and he secretly loved it.

Unfortunately Mrs Kelly herself wasn't as warm or approachable as her husband. There was something oddly pretentious about her, a touch condescending in her overall manner. Also, since Katie's dad died, she'd kept her distance.

But now, of course, she was on a mission.

'You'll buy a raffle ticket, won't you?' she chirped, her ample figure rolling towards them at full speed. 'First prize is a week in Rome for a family of four.'

Katie's mother groaned even louder now. She only had enough money to pay for the groceries. She couldn't afford to buy a raffle ticket as well.

'Well, actually, I don't think I'll …'

But Mrs Kelly was already tearing off a strip. 'All the proceeds go to the club, you know,' she continued in her annoying sing-song voice.

Katie cringed and bowed her head in embarrassment. Mrs Kelly was notorious for being extremely pushy when it came to selling raffle tickets. She didn't take no for an answer. This did not look good for Katie's poor mother.

'Well, that *is* a good cause,' Katie's mother smiled reluctantly. 'But as I said, I'm afraid I …'

Something appeared to brush past Katie's ear and a soft voice seemed to whisper: 'Look down, Katie!'

Startled, Katie spun around and glared down at her brother.

'What did you say?'

'I didn't say anything'. He stepped back with an angry frown. 'What are you talking about?'

Just then Katie felt something crunch under her foot and she rolled her eyes in disgust. Reluctantly she lifted her leg to see what she'd stood in. And she gasped out loud when she saw what was sticking to the bottom of her shoe.

The five-pound note was ripped and worn, but it was *still* a five-pound note!

She stared at it in disbelief for a few seconds before quickly picking it off and unfolding it as best she could. Then she stepped between her red faced mother and Mrs Kelly.

'We'll have five pounds worth, please, Mrs Kelly,' she beamed, wagging the battered and wrinkled note at Mrs Kelly. Mrs Kelly hesitated. Her eyes scanned the offending object. Then she took it between two quivering fingers and held it at arm's length as if it was about to explode in her face.

'The draw will be at six o'clock tonight,' she mumbled, cringing as she tried to coax it through the slot in the top of the tin.

Katie folded her legs under her as she squatted in the corner of the settee, and she ripped open a bag of crisps as the theme tune for EastEnders blared out of the television in the corner of the living room. Clara was curled on the armchair in the other corner of the room and she fiddled with the earpiece of her iPad and frowned at whatever she was listening to. James was sprawled on the carpet playing with his collection of football cards he'd spread out in front of him in the shape of a big fan.

They didn't hear the doorbell ring and they all looked up in surprise when their mother flew into the room, snatched the remote control and flicked off the sound.

'Mom!'

'Turn it down,' their mother yelped. 'I can't hear myself think with all that racket going on!'

Behind her the ample figure of Mrs Kelly filled the door space and Katie jumped up immediately, her heart skipping a beat.

'Mrs Kelly?' she croaked, her mouth dry. 'What are … is it about the …have you come about the raffle?'

Clara jumped up as well and gave an expectant gasp as Mrs Kelly cast a casual eye around the room, her nose high and inquisitive.

'Yes,' she purred vaguely, patting her mop of ginger hair with the palm of her hand. 'Well, sort of.' She cleared her throat. 'Well, actually, no.'

Four faces studied her with growing intensity.

'Well, what I mean is, the draw *has* taken place. But I'm afraid your ticket wasn't the winner, if that's what you're asking. Sorry.'

There was a collective sigh of disappointment. Clara frowned even more angrily. Katie felt an odd sensation in her stomach, almost like disbelief. She hadn't forgotten how she'd found the five pound note, the strange whisper that told her to look down. She could have sworn it was an omen, that she was bound to win the raffle. She felt her eyes smart as she turned away and sat back down on the settee.

'Well, never mind,' Katie's mum said after a moment, trying to sound more cheerful than she actually felt. 'I'm not sure I'd like Rome anyway.'

No one agreed with her. She turned around to face her visitor

'So what can we do for you, Mrs Kelly?' she asked with forced politeness.

Mrs Kelly looked like she was going to sit down on the arm of the settee but decided against it, considering the dark looks she was getting from the two girls.

'Well,' she cleared her throat again. 'You know my Declan is the Secretary of the local Writers Circle and that we go to the Listowel Writers Week every year?' She waited for a response. She didn't get one. 'Anyway, due to unforeseen circumstances, we won't be able to go this year, so we were wondering if you'd like to go in our place.'

They all blinked together.

'Eh …'

'The coach and the hotel have already been paid for,' Mrs Kelly continued quickly, unsure of the reaction she was getting. 'So everything's been taken care of. You shouldn't have to pay for a thing.'

There was another awkward silence as Katie and the others studied Mrs Kelly with wide open mouths.

'Look, I know it's short notice.' Mrs Kelly's hand went nervously to her throat. 'The coach will be leaving tomorrow morning in time to catch the three o'clock ferry from Fishguard. But it really would be a shame to waste the tickets. I'd rather someone else had the benefit of the occasion, someone who would appreciate the chance of a free holiday.'

'Gosh,' Katie's mother managed to say after taking a long deep breath. 'That's really kind of you to think of us like this, Mrs Kelly. I don't know what to say. But, unfortunately, there are four of us, as you know.' She waved her hand around the room in emphasis. 'So I'm afraid we'll, er, have to give it a miss this time. Sorry.'

'No, no,' Mrs Kelly laughed, her voice croaking as if dust had got into the hinges. 'I haven't made myself clear, have I? I should have said that *two* rooms have been booked. Two couples have backed out, you see. So it'll be up to yourselves to decide who sleeps in which room. But there will be two rooms.'

'Wow!' Katie's mother rubbed her mouth and gave another little chuckle. 'I don't know what to say. This really is very kind of you, Mrs Kelly. But I'm afraid you've caught us on the hop. I'll need time to think about this. We …'

'Well, that's up to you.' Mrs Kelly had a slight hint of impatience in her voice. She handed an envelope with the tickets to Katie's mother. 'But the coach will leave at nine o'clock sharp. So if you do go, have a wonderful time, won't you?'

She was already waddling back down the hallway towards the front door.

'How come you can't go yourself?' Katie's mother was asking as she followed along behind her. 'Declan loves going to Listowel. He must be really disappointed that he can't go this year. What happened?'

Mrs Kelly turned and for a second a shadow of embarrassment flickered in her eyes. 'Well, actually, we'll be going to Rome.' She coughed into her fist and cleared her throat yet again. 'With Barry and Jo Delaney, you know. They - ah - they were the ones who won the raffle.'

She opened the door and practically threw herself out onto the path, pausing briefly to look back at Katie's mum. 'It was all above board, I assure you,' she insisted. 'A member of the public drew the tickets in front of loads of independent witnesses.' She waved goodbye as she reached the gate. 'Anyway, they wanted to share the trip with their best friends, me and Declan. And of course Declan thought of you immediately. He thought you'd appreciate another visit to good auld Ireland.'

James threw the crust from his sandwich high into the air and there was an immediately explosion of chaos as a mob of seagulls launched themselves after it. One seagull slapped is wings back and turned itself into a missile, snatching the crust out of the air and spinning away in a blur of motion. James whooped in delight as the gull disappeared over the edge of the cliff followed closely by the rest of the flock, all screeching and flapping like frantic banshees.

'You should eat your crusts,' his mother chided, thumping him playfully on the arm. 'They'll put hairs on your chest.'

'What chest?' Katie spluttered. 'Look at him! If he turned sideways and put out his tongue he's look like a zip.'

'Hey!' James snorted and threw another crust at her. 'You can talk, skinny legs!'

'Skinny legs?' Clara joined in the banter, shoving James along the bench with her hip. 'We had a girl at school with legs like that. We called her Wednesday Legs'

'Wednesday Legs?'

'Yeah. We used to wonder 'when's they' going to break. Especially when she played volleyball.'

This time even their mother laughed out loud. Katie

felt a wonderful, warm sensation wrap itself around her, soft and comforting and soothing. It was such a beautiful thing seeing the family all laughing and joking together again.

They were sitting on a bench looking down over the Ladies' Beach towards the Castle Green. The very same spot from where their father had taken his wonderful photograph.

Only this time there wasn't any golden glow from a beautiful clear sky. Instead the afternoon was enveloped in a dull colourless haze, courtesy of a continuous ceiling of grey cloud that hung so low you could almost reach up and touch it.

Of course that was nothing new. In Ireland the weather was as contrary as a nest of farmers at a horse fair in Tralee. But it wasn't going to blight their special *Scattering of the Ashes* celebrations. Katie and her family were determined that *nothing* was going to spoil that!

Because of the threatening weather there were very few people around when Katie's mother opened the small silver urn and let the ashes float away. They were carried by the breeze out over the Ladies' Beach in a fine cloud, wide and light and as free as the breeze itself.

Katie's mother said a special prayer she'd written herself, a joyful little poem that spoke of hope and remembrance, and promises that they were determined to keep.

They bowed their heads in respectful silence for a minute, lost in their own thoughts. Each of them sensed an odd kind of relief, a comfort in knowing they were finally able to let go of all the anger and frustration they were carrying around in their hearts. And which had created an invisible but tangible barrier between them that their father would have hated.

Katie couldn't put it into words but she felt by letting her father go she was somehow bringing him closer.

'Rest in peace, Dad,' she whispered as they parked themselves on the bench and opened the brown paper bag with the string handles.

'The wettest country on the whole planet and they give you a paper bag to carry your stuff in,' Katie's mum laughed as she scooped out the packages that were wrapped in grease proof paper. 'In this weather you lose half of it before you get to where you're going.'

They each took a package and unwrapped it.

'These look delicious.' Clara took a huge bite out of her sandwich.

'They should be.' James also took a mouthful of his. 'You made them.'

'We *all* made them,' Katie corrected him. 'Just like Dad would have made them.'

Katie's dad had told them often enough about the fantastic picnics he'd take with him to the beach when he was a kid. A couple of leaves of home grown lettuce stuck between two thick slices of homemade bread. And cold tea in a bottle with a wedge of tightly rolled newspaper jammed into the top as a stopper.

So first thing this morning they called into the local baker and bought a crusty loaf that was freshly baked on the premises. Obviously the lettuce from the Spar wasn't home grown but they didn't think it really mattered that much. They also bought a large bottle of lemonade which they poured down the sink before filling it with tea they brewed in their hotel room.

Katie's dad would have been thrilled by such a

considerate and thoughtful gesture.

He would have been even more amused by where they scattered his ashes.

The Ladies' Beach originated in a time when the Catholic Church held a lot of influence in Ireland. The very idea that a man should have access to a beach where ladies were bathing was scandalous.

Never mind the fact the ladies were wrapped up in costumes that were bigger and thicker than the average overcoat. Still, there was a chance some young lady might inadvertently expose a naked ankle and subject some innocent male hovering nearby to serious corruption of thought.

The little cove between the cliff and the Castle Green was an ideal spot to contain the situation. Surrounded on three sides, when the tide was in you could only get down to the beach along a steep path or a narrow road. So the men were confined to the stretch of beach on the other side of the Castle Green. Rumour had it the priests patrolled the area to ensure no man accidently wandered onto the wrong zone. Or no woman either, for that matter.

'I hope Thandie Newton doesn't turn up here to sun bathe,' Katie's mum laughed. 'I don't think your father's heart could take it.'

'Who's Thandie Newton?'

'Dad's favourite actress,' Clara told him between loud chortles.

'I never heard him mention Thandie wot's her name.'

'He didn't have to!' Katie's mum had to put her hand over her mouth to stop herself from spraying sandwich all over her dress. 'You only had to look at his face whenever he was watching Mission Impossible II.

Which was at least once a month!'

'Yeah,' Katie hooted and Clara gave her a conspiratorial pat on the arm. 'Did you notice every time she appeared he'd lean forward and pretend to be getting another crisp from the coffee table?'

Then all rocked together as they laughed out loud again, and Katie took a long swig of the tea from the plastic cup. She felt so happy now. It had been such a wonderful, glorious week. At long last everything seemed to be slipping back into the way it was before.

A soft breeze fluttered through the grass behind them and as it passed by her Katie swore she heard a whisper with a laugh in it; 'Thanks, Guys ...'

Katie spun around. She didn't see anyone, of course. But she knew who it was.

After all, her father had made all this happen. Hadn't he?

Leg O'Lamb: Village Butcher

Everyone in the village of Ballycumscut thought Leg O'Lamb was a little bit - you know - *strange?* It wasn't something you could actually put your finger on, though.

And if you heard people talking about him they'd probably say he was nice enough, *really!* They'd probably add he was quite friendly too - in his own sort of way. Because he'd always greet you with a cheery hello whenever you went into his butcher shop.

He'd smile, too, of course. But it was always just the mouth. The eyes didn't smile. They were expressionless. Shiny, slate grey pebbles in a big round face. They would scan you from the top of your head right down to your toes every time they looked at you.

And you could never tell what he was thinking. He had that kind of vacant expression on him.

Someone once joked that he was probably analysing your body mass - comparing it to the animal carcasses that hung on steel hooks all along the wall in the stockroom. You could just glimpse them through the open door behind the counter.

And he knew everyone and their dog! Everyone knew him too, of course. Because Liam Edward Gerard O'Lamb had been our local butcher here in Ballycumscut - a tiny village tucked away in the McGillycuddy Reeks near Killarney - for almost thirty years now.

But did anyone really *know* him? Did they know what he got up to when the shop was shut? Where did he go? What did he do in his spare time? What deep, dark secret was he hiding in the gloomy recess of his massive walk-in freezer tucked away in that dusty stockroom at the back of his shop? The freezer that no one ever saw him open?

And would they believe him anyway, even if he told them himself?

Because they didn't believe him when he called into Leary's pub a few years ago and told Paddy the Pipe he was only having one quick drink because he was on his way over to Lisa Lavender's place. He was taking her out on a date!

There was a shocked silence for the briefest of moments - then an almighty spluttering into beer glasses and sniggering into the palm of hands.

'What's happening?' Mo Quinn bowed her head towards Leo Fanning.

'Lego's going on a date,' Leo told her to another round of spluttering from the regulars strung out along the bar. '*With Lisa Lavender*!'

'What?' Mo's eyes bulged. 'I don't believe him!'

Actually, *no* one believed him. And they had great fun out of not believing him.

The thing is, Lisa Lavender was a very pretty young woman. Leg O'Lamb is - well, you couldn't call him pretty in any shape or form. OK, he's supposed to be very rich according to spotty Kieran Mulcahy who works part time at the Post Office and claims to have seen Lego's account. But still!

And Lisa Lavender wasn't just pretty. She was also very bright. She could have her pick of men. Would she really want to be seen out and about with a man like Leg O'Lamb just because of the size of his wallet?

Anyway, we never found out if it was true or not because no one ever saw Lisa Lavender after that. She took off for Australia, according to rumour. Just packed up and went without as much as a goodbye.

And Leg O'Lamb never mentioned her again.

He didn't mention Kitty O'Hare either, for that matter. She also left the parish rather suddenly after Lego dated her - *allegedly* - on Christmas Eve the following year.

Then there was supposed to be an Eleanor Flaherty, though no one could remember what she looked like. Whatever happened to her? She also took off.

There was a lot of speculation about those dates, of course. Was it something Leg O'Lamb did? Or was it just the after-shock of spending so much time in his company, listening to his obsessive rambling about meat?

Leg O'Lamb loved his meat. He talked endlessly about it, how to hang it, how to cut it, how to age it, how to cook it. If worshiping meat ever became a religion Leg O'Lamb would be their high priest.

He couldn't understand why no one else felt the same way. He was totally oblivious to how people's eyes would glaze over whenever he started drooling over the finer points of a lamb cutlet. You'd think he'd cop on when they said they were just nipping out to the toilet - and never, ever came back.

Anyway, one dull evening back in February Leg O'Lamb was about to shut the shop and go home when he glanced out of the rain-spattered window at the receding daylight. And he groaned out loud.

The Widow Mariah was lumbering along the pavement towards him.

Bugger, he muttered loudly. But still, a customer *is* a customer!

His heart sank all the same because he knew *exactly*

what she was going to ask for. She'd gone through the same old routine every time she came into his shop for the last thirty years!

'Can I have a pig's head please, Lego,' she would screech from the pavement before she even reached the shop door. 'And could you leave the eyes in to see us through the week?'

Gaaaaad!

Or else she would ask for pig's trotters and would he be so kind as to leave the head on, please!

Of course he'd laugh as if it was the first time he'd ever heard her say it. Because, you see, the Widow Mariah was the mother of the beautiful Eileen Grey.

And Eileen Grey was the love of Lego's life, ever since that beautiful sunny day when she called in for some lamb chops on her way home from work.

It was the tattoos that did it for him! Eileen wasn't quiet as big as her mother but she still had a nice round shape to her hips. And she showed an ample amount of bare skin between the waistband of her low cut jeans and the tiny pink t-shirt. When she bent to put her purse back in her bag, there they were. A beautiful vibrant butterfly on one cheek and a dark green shamrock on the other.

Lego was besotted. But he was much too afraid to tell her. Or anyone else for that matter. He just *knew* what the reaction would be - Lego and Eileen? Are you serious? No, you can't disguise the look of horror on a person's face, no matter how fleeting it might be. So he kept his feelings to himself and dreamed that one day maybe …

But this evening the Widow Mariah didn't go through her usual routine. Instead she waddled right up to the counter with a strange look on her face.

'I have a message for you,' she told him in a gruff voice.

Lego had already started the obligatory laugh right on cue and it took a few seconds to register what she'd actually said.

What confused him even more was the strange way she'd said it. Her voice was usually - he couldn't quite think of the right words to describe it but it always reminded him of the day he was strolling through the churchyard when one of the battered old slates on the ancient church roof came loose and slithered down, rattling and clattering in the quiet of the afternoon.

And she always ended her sentence with an odd sort of screech, which made him think of the slate flying out over the moss covered gable and shattering into bits against the two-hundred-year old gravestone of the Reverend Pat Curran.

Father Pat was a bit of a local hero back in the dark old days of Irish history. He'd been the local priest but he also administered to another kind of spirit - *poteen*. According to legend he kept the whisky still under the altar where the marauding Brits wouldn't look for fear of being struck down with the religion.

He made quite a bit of money out of it as well - for the Church, of course - by supplying it to his parishioners. But only for medicinal purposes, you understand!

Anyway, his demise was a very strange affair to say the least. Apparently his cat discovered the vat of poteen in the vestry and had a really good slurp out of it. Then in its intoxicated state it mistook Father Pat's flowing ginger beard for a foxy feline. It came at him like an Exocet missile and attached itself to his face with needle sharp claws.

Unfortunately Father Pat was riding into town at the time on a seventeen hands high grey mare. Being only five-foot-two himself it was a long way down to the ground.

Anyway, that's a different story.

Right now Lego was so dismayed by the change of routine that all he could say was: *'What?'*

'I said I have a message for you.' The Widow Mariah drew the words out as if she was unwrapping a precious gift. 'From my Eileen. You *do* know my Eileen, don't you?'

Lego thought a moment.

'I do.' There was hesitation in his voice.

'Well, she wants to ask you over for dinner,' Mariah continued. 'What she'd really like is for you to bring the meat and she'll arrange the vegetables. This Friday night, if that's all right?'

'Oh,' Lego replied in a totally unmanly soprano croak. 'Yes, of course. Yes. I'd be … yes … well, I mean …'

The Widow Mariah nodded gravely then turned and floated out of the shop.

Lego was stunned. Could this be true? Was this really happening to him? Had Eileen guesses how he felt about her?

Then the cynicism kicked in. What were they up to? The Widow Mariah had been married - and widowed - three times already. She had acquired a reputation as a bit of a gold digger.

Apparently her first two husbands died after accidentally eating poison mushrooms. The third one died of a broken neck after falling down the stairs. Cruel gossip at the time hinted that he fell down the stairs because he refused to eat the mushrooms!

But she was supposed to have inherited a load of money from them. So why would she be after Lego's? He decided it didn't matter anyway. If Eileen Grey wanted his money she was welcome to it.

Well, not *all* of it! But he wouldn't mind sharing some of it with her. Well, maybe *share* was a bit too extreme. All right, she could have a look at it, if she wanted. As for *giving* her some, well, he'd have to wait and see.

In the meantime he was so elated by this sudden request that he danced on tiptoe right around the counter and across to the door. Actually, being twenty-two stone it was more of an awkward lumber. But it did show the excitement that welled up inside him. He locked the door with a flourish of the wrist. *Eileen Grey!* His dreams were coming true!

On the Friday afternoon Lego carefully selected his choice of meat - two generous steaks from a bull that had been lovingly hand-reared on a farm near Aberdeen by a man called Angus. And they were enveloped in all the adjectives that Lego could possibly think of - succulent, juicy, rare, tender. The vision went on and on to the point where Lego couldn't even think about them without dribbling.

Even as he bathed and powdered himself - applying obscene amounts of deodorant - he could only dream of the copious amounts of tender vegetables the beautiful Eileen was preparing for him. Yes indeed, this was going to be a night to remember!

Then suddenly he was there, standing outside the Widow Mariah's chocolate-box thatched cottage. His fists were clenched in an effort to control the mounting excitement in his heart. And his nostrils savoured the aroma of the raw steaks he'd wrapped up in a brown paper bag.

But before he could announce himself in the manner someone as beautiful as Eileen deserved, the bright yellow door flew open. Lego jumped back and clutched the brown paper bag to his chest.

'Lego,' the Widow Mariah cooed. '*Helloooo* there.'

Lego gulped. 'Er - hello there yourself, Mrs - er - Mariah.'

Mariah beamed.

'Ah now, don't be looking so worried, Lego dear,' she purred in a loud stage whisper. 'Shur I won't be staying in tonight. I'm actually on my way out this very minute. I have an appointment, don't you know. So I'll leave you and my Eileen all alone, all by yourselves. Now be good, won't you. But if you can't be good, don't get caught!'

Maybe she laughed but Lego certainly didn't hear it. In the hallway mirror he caught a fleeting glimpse of a beautiful woman as she fluttered down the stairs. Her hair was flowing like wisps of gold behind her and his knees began to tremble. Eileen was *so* beautiful! And to this day he couldn't remember actually crossing the hall to the kitchen. He wouldn't normally be so presumptuous!

But he *did* remember the moment the horrible truth hit him like a slap in the face from a de-frosted cod fillet - the moment he looked at the spotless pots and pans standing in a neat row behind the sanitised worktop.

The shock of what Eileen was serving up as veg with his lovingly chosen meat made him gasp.

A wet and dull Saturday morning a week later and Danno Connolly was pointing at the tray of thick juicy steaks on the cold slab of Lego's counter.

'I'll have another one of those for my tea,' he slurped, giving Lego a lopsided grin.

Lego didn't smile back. He had a face on him like a robber's dog. And a moody cloud around him too. But Danno didn't notice. His mind was on his stomach.

'The one I had yesterday was absolutely delicious,' he was saying. And he was still slurping. 'And I'll have a pound of mince, too, if you have any left. That'll do for the missus.'

'I'll get some from out the back, so.' Lego gave a vague nod towards the stockroom.

Out in the stockroom Leg O'Lamb patted the cold white door of the freezer and gave a long, distressed sigh. He couldn't shake himself out of the dismal mood that had gripped him all week after his - well, he didn't want to dwell on that! But it wasn't the first time something like this happened - a strange blackout that hit him whenever something went drastically wrong.

It was usually after he'd become infatuated with some beautiful young woman and he'd put her up on a pedestal and worshipped her unreservedly.

But they always let him down. *God*, how they always let him down!

Surely Eileen Grey *knew* that next to a beautiful woman Lego's passion was for perfectly cooked food - *properly* cooked food. His heart had fallen down into his boots that evening when he turned around in Eileen's kitchen and asked her outright - *where was the veg?*

Eileen just laughed - *big mistake!*

'Veg?' she giggled. 'I don't cook vegetables! I don't cook *anything – ever*! That's what the chippy's for. If I want veg I have chips. Chips are veg. I have chips with everything!'

A strange black cloud descended on Leg O'Lamb that evening and it brought a terrible retribution. He couldn't remember exactly what happened but he did recover enough to realise that the Widow Mariah would be home shortly. He knew he had to deal with her as well.

The local paper ran a story a few days later about how the Widow Mariah and her daughter, the beautiful Eileen Grey, had suddenly and unexpectedly disappeared off the face of the earth.

Rumours were rife, ranging from the sheer ridiculous to the weirdly strange. The local Garda spokesman Detective Inspector Pat Cassidy insinuated there was a huge debt left behind and the two of them were well dodgy anyway. It was good enough for them if no one bothered looking for them.

Lego wrapped the mince in brown paper and flopped the steak onto a sheet of greaseproof paper just as Danno's missus clattered in the door and poked Danno with her walking stick.

'I don't know why you're buying that rubbish!' she griped. 'Tell him about that other one you bought. Tell him about the funny bit on the skin. It looked like mould - a funny bit of mouldy auld skin. I wouldn't eat it if I was you.'

'Shur isn't that why you're having the mince, my little bag of rusty spanners,' Danno beamed. 'You'll be having the mince, and I'll be having the steak - if that's all right with you?'

'Well, it'll serve you right if you pop your clogs after

eating it!' She pushed her glasses higher up her nose. 'Just don't expect me to clean up the mess after you. And what's that? Look, right there! That piece has a mouldy bit on it as well. See? Right there. You said you thought the other mouldy piece looked a bit like a butterfly. Well, this one looks almost like a - well, it could be a shamrock!'

Dreamin' Dreams

Thank you for taking the time to read ***Dreamin'
Dreams***. I hope you enjoyed reading it as much as I
enjoyed writing it.

I would be delighted if you were to visit my web site
at ***bgobrien.net*** and let me know what you thought of it
by leaving your views on my guestbook page.

Printed in Great Britain
by Amazon